To Ta —
Enjoy the mayhem!"

Pretty WICKED

KELLY CHARRON

all the best!

Kelly Charron

Pretty Wicked
Copyright © 2016 Kelly Charron
ISBN: 978-0-9952765-2-9

This edition first published in Canada in 2016 by Dark Arts
Publishing.

Library and Archives Canada Cataloguing in Publication

Charron, Kelly, 1979-, author
    Pretty wicked / Kelly Charron.

(Pretty wicked series ; 1)
Issued in print and electronic formats.
ISBN 978-0-9952765-2-9 (paperback).--
ISBN 978-0-9952765-0-5 (kindle).--
ISBN 978-0-9952765-1-2 (epub)

    I. Title.

PS8605.H3727P74 2016   C813'.6
C2016-905824-7   C2016-905825-5

*This is a work of fiction. Names, characters, businesses, places,
events and incidents are either the products of the author's imagination or used in a fictitious manner. Any resemblance to actual
persons, living or dead, or actual events is purely coincidental.*

Book design by CCS-Crystal Clear Solutions.
Book cover design by Kellie Dennis, of Book Cover by Design.

For more information, visit www.kellycharron.com

For Mom and Dad,
and Jason, for believing.

Chapter **ONE**

*S*ome people are called to certain things in their life. That's what hunting is for me. An urge. A desire. The closest thing I have to a calling.

My name is Ryann Wilkanson. I'm fifteen years old.

And I'm a killer.

❖   ❖   ❖   ❖

It was hard to pick my first.

Call me sentimental, but it had to be just right. I knew what I wanted. What I needed. Someone worth the risk, the challenge. Somebody who deserved it. Now, I'm not talking about the horrible, abusive assholes you see on TV. I wanted someone who I thought deserved it…

And to be honest, that could've been just about anybody.

Some people might think it's odd to contemplate killing someone, but it was the most natural thing in the world to me. I didn't dare talk about it—I somehow knew that much—but my thoughts raced with vivid, red-tinted images.

While my fantasies were fun, I had to wait. I still lacked the skill and organization to actually go through with it.

And, as I matured, I realized part of me was still hesitant. A piece of the puzzle was missing. It was as though I was waiting for *permission*. Something to give me the final push into action.

Funnily enough, I got that that clarity six years ago, when I was nine. My dad thought he was simply giving me a ride to school, but he initiated the defining moment of my life.

I remember it like it was yesterday. He'd just come off nights and wasn't in the best of moods when my mom asked him to drive me and Bri. I'd raced to the car first, winning shotgun, leaving Brianna to storm behind me. She was a sore loser, and it only made my grin bigger.

We were just a few blocks from the house when Dad started with one of his commentaries on all that was wrong with society.

"Jesus. People like that make me sick."

We had stopped at a red light, and I spotted a guy standing on the corner with a sign that read *Please Help*.

At first I felt kind of bad for him, and I didn't understand why Dad was upset. "At least he's not dealing drugs," I suggested.

"Brilliant observation. Maybe we could put that on a T-shirt for him," Bri said. My father laughed and my stomach dropped. She never wasted an opportunity to make me look stupid.

Dad grunted. "Don't be naïve, Ry. He's probably scraping enough together to get his fix. People like that are after one thing—and it's not a job." He rolled his eyes, disgusted. Not a minute later, while we were still waiting at the light, a kid in a fancy sports car passed us. "See, look at that. Punk probably had it handed to him from Mommy and Daddy. He's what—seventeen? Probably hasn't worked a day in his whole goddamn life. Entitled brat. This is the problem with the world. You got two lazy bums on opposite ends of the spectrum, and neither are worth their salt."

My father didn't have a whole lot of empathy for anybody, and he certainly didn't entertain excuses. I had to be the best if I wanted him to love me. "People need to either lead, follow—"

"Or get out of the way," I finished. He patted me on the head. I knew this rant well and kind of understood my father's reasoning. The homeless guy couldn't even be bothered to walk up and down the rows of stopped cars to beg. He just stood there with an empty cup. He really was a waste.

I fought the urge to point out to my dad that I was

nothing like those people—and never would be—but I knew he wouldn't care. He loved me, but nothing I did seemed to impress him, especially since my older sister Brianna, the golden child, had perfected everything before I even had a chance to try.

I had to do something really big to make an impression.

I had to be a leader.

In the car, all those years ago, I realized that my desires could turn into something much more. Those entitled, useless people my dad despised were taking our hard-earned money, space, and air. And I was someone with deadly urges who wasn't afraid to do something about it. Not everyone could say that.

But unfortunately, I would have to wait. I was much too young to execute my plans in the way I wanted.

My thoughts, however, were uninhibited, and I became enamored with the power and control that selecting the right kill could bring. The foreplay was intoxicating. I daydreamed about the countless ways I could do it. About all the places I could sneak up and strike. About the legacy I would leave behind.

For years I researched and studied serial killers—or as I liked to call them, *The Greats*. Most of The Greats hadn't started until well into their adulthood. Call me an overachiever, but I wanted more kills in less time. I had all the qualities required: above-average intelligence, inside information (Dad was a cop), and a sweet cherub face.

But I also had something more. Tenacity. I knew what I wanted, and come hell or high water, I was going to get it. By fifteen, the thirst inside me could finally be quenched.

Cue my first *planned* victim—a snotty little brat who lived only a few streets away from me. Olivia McMann. *Ugh.* She was exhausting. Spoiled. Whiny. Brianna used to babysit her. I'd be dragged along because my parents usually worked overtime at their respective jobs. I was twelve and old enough to stay home alone, but they insisted. Like I had nothing better to do.

Brianna would be online with her friends or texting her boyfriend, and she'd stick Livy with me. Olivia wouldn't leave me alone. One night she pestered me for hours on end until I lost it on her. Then she got the quivering lip and teary eyes and went crying to Bri.

Bri's voice ripped across the room. "Ryann, what did you do now?"

"Nothing! Why do you always assume it was me? Maybe *Livy* is being a little crybaby over absolutely nothing," I said, arms crossed tightly across my chest.

The brat came running up behind me. "You're mean, Ryann. I hate you!"

I swept my hair into a ponytail and turned my back to her.

Death glare in full force, Brianna dug into me. "Why are you being such a pest? Leave Olivia alone already. Go find something to do, and don't think for one second I'm giving you any of the money."

She proceeded to get Olivia some licorice. A reward for her evilness. Maybe they were in on it together and shared private laughs while discussing different ways to torture me.

Brianna was seventeen at the time, and she hated me. No matter how hard I tried, she always dismissed me like I was an annoying pain in her ass.

"Not everything is my fault, you know," I said, determined to stand my ground.

"Well, she's not the one in my face right now. Go play with her for an hour until her bedtime, and maybe I won't tell Mom." Smiling smugly, Bri tilted her head. I wanted to punch her. As soon as we were out of her sight, Olivia stuck her tongue out at me and danced around, joyous in her victory.

"See, I told you I'd get you in trouble. I always get my way. You have to do what I say." She laughed.

I promised myself I'd never forget.

Back then, I'd imagined choking her or holding one of her mom's embroidered pillows over her face until her squirming stopped. I knew her parents were well-off. Only the best for their princess. Olivia was the type of kid who tantrumed, tattled, and fake-cried to get what she wanted, no matter the cost to anyone who got in her way.

Olivia was going to turn into the same kind of spoiled, manipulative bitch I'd seen time and again at school.

I knew how to deal with someone like her.

After all, I *had* killed.

Once.

Chapter
TWO

It wasn't a conventional murder, if there is such a thing. It wasn't calculated. It was more of a...*mercy.*

I was twelve. My elementary school, Deer Lake, was situated on an enormous property of woods with little streams that would flow after too much rain or melting snow.

It was a January afternoon and I was playing with my classmate, Veronica Sanders, out at the edge of the field. Most of the kids stayed closer to the school; I preferred to explore a bit, not that there was anything much to find.

"Ryann, you know we're not allowed to go past the fence. We're going to get in trouble." Veronica seemed a touch frantic about the crime we were about to commit.

"Relax. We're going to have a look in the forest.

It's not like I'm asking you to rob someone."

"But what if we get caught?" Her eyes widened as she bit her bottom lip.

I stepped forward to put a reassuring hand on her arm. "We won't get caught. And if we do, we'll say that we saw a puppy running in the woods, and we just wanted to make sure it was okay." I smiled confidently and saw Veronica's forehead smoothen. It was obvious she was dying to do something bad, but she needed a push. I was happy to help.

She looked around; no one was paying any attention to us all the way out there. "Okay, but only for a few minutes," she said with a gleam in her eyes.

I was already opening the gate. "Follow me. I've been out here a ton of times before." I led her onto the snow-covered path and into the dense forest.

"Wow, that's really cool."

I was showing Veronica the tiny waterfall a short walk away from the main path. She bent down and picked up a few pebbles to toss in.

I joined her, wiping the snow off some stones with my gloves. We had a competition to see whose rock would create the biggest splash. But after a few minutes she stood. "We'd better go back now. The bell's going to ring any second, and I don't want to get caught."

Ugh. She was such a goody-goody. "You're scared of everything." I sat down on one of the small boulders that surrounded the water.

"I came out here, didn't I?" She crossed her arms and shot me a dirty look.

I laughed at her attempt at boldness. "Go if you want to. I'm staying. It's boring over there, and *I'm* not a chicken."

"Screw you." She whirled around to storm off, but her boot got caught in a small crevice between the rocks. She went down. I heard a crack as her head smashed off a jutting rock.

I froze. My breath caught as I screamed out to her. "Veronica! Are you okay?" She didn't answer. Or move. I rushed over and knelt beside her. Her eyes were open as blood trickled down the side of her head and pooled under her cheek.

Leaning closer, I watched her eyes flutter, her body quiver. She was like a baby bird that had fallen out of the nest and hit the ground. "Can you hear me?" I whispered. This time my voice was steady.

She tried to answer, but her speech was muffled. She was probably asking for help.

I stared at the dripping blood. It contrasted so vividly against her pale skin. Her light hair soaked it up like a sponge and lay limp across her cheek. I pulled a glove off and ran my bare fingers over a drenched strand, moving it out of her eye. It was warm and sticky. Repulsed, I cleaned my bloody fingers in the stream.

Veronica seemed serene and terrified at the same time. "You're scared, aren't you?" I asked. Again she didn't answer. She didn't look good.

A twinge crept into my bones. What if she told a teacher that going out there had been all my idea?

I could get into trouble—my dad would kill me for deliberately breaking a school rule. I'd be grounded for a month, but that wouldn't be as bad as the look he'd give me, or the speech he'd recite about how much I'd disappointed him and how Brianna never did anything like that.

I did the only thing I could.

I took my glove and shoved it into Veronica's mouth. She made a low, muffled, grunting sound. Her eyes rolled and darted wildly. "Shh. It will be over in a minute," I said. Leaning closer still, I pinched her nose between my thumb and index finger, watched, and waited for her blue eyes to become vacant, the way they were supposed to with death.

I'd finally get to see it for myself.

My pulse quickened as my hands worked, steady and sure. My peripheral vision narrowed, until all I could see was Veronica's face and the blood dripping down her plump cheek in the most beautiful shade of red.

It surprised me when she squirmed a little. Perhaps there was more of a spark in her than I'd believed, though she was too badly hurt to fight it. *To fight me.*

I squeezed her nose tighter and thrust my glove farther into her mouth, pushing harder and harder. I gasped for breath. The intense pulsing in my ears drowned out the sounds of the water falling around us. My arms and legs tingled, goose bumps running the lengths of them.

After a minute she stopped moving altogether, and her eyes closed. I released her nose and yanked the glove from her slack mouth. I'd noticed that on TV people leaned down to check for breathing, so I did too.

She was dead.

I'd put her out of her misery. She probably would've ended up on life support—brain-dead, paralyzed or something. It was the only thing I could've done.

I heard the bell ring in the distance. Lunch was over. I leapt up to go when I was struck with panic. What if someone had seen me walk out there with Veronica? No one could know what I'd done. My breath hitched.

I ran as fast as I could back to the yard and to the first teacher I saw.

"Mrs. Hopkins! Come quick, Veronica's really hurt!" I pretended to be hysterical so effectively that she couldn't understand me the first few times.

She bent down so we were at eye level. "Where?"

"We went into the woods at the far end of the property. I'm sorry. I know we're not allowed, but she fell and she's not moving! You have to hurry!" I sobbed, shoulders shaking, snotty nose. I don't know how I'd managed to look so distraught, but I nearly convinced myself.

Mrs. Hopkins turned to a kid named Austin, who was in the grade ahead of me. "Go get Mr. Chute. Tell him to call 911 and to come out and meet me in the woods."

Austin, who was paper white, nodded and took off like his ass was on fire.

I ran back with Mrs. Hopkins to the rocks where I'd left Veronica. She was in the exact position. Thankfully there was no miraculous recovery waiting for us.

After she was taken away in an ambulance, Mrs. Hopkins and Mr. Chute walked me back and called my parents.

My dad showed up to the school, hugged me, and told me how brave I was.

After my mother had finally stopped fussing and checking on me every twenty minutes, I sat on my bed and thought about Veronica. It would be weird not to see her in class every day or hang out with her at lunch, not that we hung out that much. I was usually with Bao-yu anyway, but sometimes she came along. Maybe now B and I would be better friends. She wouldn't have to share me anymore.

I wondered what I was feeling—if I was missing Veronica. But I didn't think that's what it was. The twinge in the bottom of my stomach didn't have the achy hollowness that people refer to as a *pit*. It was more like butterflies.

❖   ❖   ❖   ❖

It was arduous to wait three more years, but it was necessary. I still had a lot to learn. There's a distinct difference between a kill of opportunity and a planned murder. Trust me, I was looking for more opportunities, but none had presented themselves.

Until the day one did.

The second time I got the butterflies, I was riding my bike home, basking in the memory of what I'd just done to Olivia.

It wasn't the most comfortable bike ride with the heat wave. Colorado didn't normally reach the nineties at the end of May, but there I was, sweating, dripping, and disgusting, though the adrenaline helped me pedal.

I replayed every moment of it in my mind. It was the best Sunday night I'd ever had.

I'd left my house at 8:30 p.m. to go for a walk, or so I'd told my mom.

I'd snuck around back to get my bike. I didn't normally go for bike rides, but tonight it was a crucial part of my plan. It was still early, so I wasted some time riding around, thinking. I knew where I'd end up and couldn't wait to see little Livy again.

This time it would be by choice.

I had faith in myself. I was ready.

I'd researched and planned, learning from The Greats—Gacy, Rader, Kemper, and even little Mary Bell. How they hunted, manipulated their victims and the cops, erased the evidence, and celebrated their kills. I could do that. Steady and strong. Nervous people made mistakes, and I wouldn't make a mistake. I'd even bought multiples of the same shirt and hoodie in case I got blood on mine.

I'd need to replace any that got ruined, since my mom took stock of my clothes and would notice if something went missing. She'd obviously think it was weird if I had too many of the same, so I kept my spares down in our unfinished basement, in old board game boxes that Bri and I hadn't opened in years.

My bag, or 'tool kit,' was packed, including a knife I'd stolen on a trip with my dad to Dick's Sporting Goods, an hour outside of Dungrave.

The plan was to lure Olivia away from her home, then surprise her so she wouldn't have time to run, or scream. No witnesses—that was an obvious one—and no evidence pointing to me, which meant I needed to be extremely careful about cleaning up after. I'd learned everything I could about DNA and trace evidence from my dad, though I'm sure he never thought I'd use the information.

An hour later I arrived in the McManns' backyard. They had a fence with a gate off the back alley that was never locked. Olivia's room was on the ground floor, at the back of the house, making it even easier for me to access.

I peered inside her window. She was still awake, sitting on the floor in her neon pink beanbag chair and reading a book with a flashlight. It was clearly past her bedtime, but the brat always did like breaking the rules.

I tapped softly on the glass, my smile ready.

She turned around, and I put my finger to my

lips before waving her over. Dropping her book, she headed toward me, pointing her flashlight directly in my face. I squinted, trying to look through the sudden glare. She dropped the light. It took a second for my vision to settle, and when it did, I found her standing, arms crossed, her lips in a scowl. I'd expected this, since we hadn't exactly been besties.

I motioned for her to slide the window open. As she struggled to move it, I managed to get a few fingers in the crack and pulled.

"What are you doing here, Ryann?"

Her sour look told me she remembered our time together accurately. "I was out for a walk and thought I'd come by." I gave her my sweetest smile.

"Why? You hate me. Besides, we have a front door."

Sassy little thing. If she was this grating at twelve, what would she be like as a teenager? "Duh, I thought it would be fun to surprise you. And you know what would be even more fun? Sneaking out to come on a little girls' night with me." I batted my eyelashes at her and even reached in through the window to lightly stroke her sand-colored hair.

She took a small step back, eyeing me. "To go where?"

"I'll take you to Maggie's to get some frozen yogurt. My treat." *Just take the bait. Don't make this harder.*

"But it's late and I've got school tomorrow. And what about my mom?"

My heart beat faster, and I grabbed her shoulder before I knew what I was doing. "No. She already tucked you in, right? As far as she knows, you're already asleep."

"I don't know..."

I had to hold back a sigh. "We're just going for a treat. You'll be back by ten thirty. Your parents won't even know you were gone."

Olivia's eyes narrowed and she put a hand on her skinny hip. "Why would you wanna take me anywhere? You hate me."

"I was going to tell you when we started walking, but I can see you're not going to make this easy. The reason I want to take you out is to apologize. I know I was a jerk. I've thought a lot about it and realize that the way I treated you was a lot like the way Brianna treated me, which sucks. So I'm sorry. Do you want to come or not? If you're scared about getting in trouble with your mommy, we can forget it." I knew her arrogance was her downfall.

She inched closer. I was winning. "Okay, but I'd better be home soon before my mom or dad check on me. If I get in trouble, I'm telling them you *made* me go."

I bit the inside of my mouth hard enough to taste blood. Anything to keep me from throttling her right there. "Fine. We'll be back in a half hour."

"I need to change out of my pj's first."

"Hurry, before we get caught." I feigned another

smile. She changed quickly and threw her sneakers on, while I stood lookout.

The window had no screen, which worked beautifully in my favor. I simply put my hand out to grab her, then eased her down to the grass below. Her parents really should have considered better security.

"There. Now, be quiet. We don't want your parents to hear us." I motioned for her to follow me around the fence line and out the back gate. She was so hot on my heels that she literally stomped on them. I stopped and she crashed into me. "Do you mind?" I said, trying not to roll my eyes.

"Sorry."

We kept going through the back alley. It was dark. Under the cover of night was always a safer bet—or so I'd read.

"This way. We'll go to the end of the alley and down Manchester Road." I took a breath before beginning the monotonous, small-talk portion of the evening, all the while going over the attack in my mind. Would it better to strike from behind, when she least expected it, or did I want to see her eyes when I lunged toward her? I wanted my first planned kill to be memorable. Perfect. The kind of kill that, if The Greats knew about it, would make them proud to call me one of their own.

I needed to keep her guard down. "What kind are you gonna get? I love chocolate ripple with coconut, chocolate sauce, and those little chunks of cheesecake."

Her eyes widened. "That sounds good, but I like chocolate everything. Oh, and strawberry and hot fudge and…"

I blocked her out. My plan was working. She was at ease, and the last thing she'd ever expect was an ambush. I could hardly wait.

I know what you're thinking. What kind of fifteen-year-old plots to kill a young, helpless girl? My answer's simple:

This one.

Chapter
THREE

$\mathcal{O}$livia and I had almost reached the dimmest, most secluded part of the alleyway. As we walked, I scanned the area for anyone who might later identify me or remember the two of us. So far we were alone. Not many people strolled the back alleys at night, which was exactly why I'd chosen this particular backdrop on a surveillance trip a few weeks before. Huge trees shielded us from the light of the few street lamps. Long wooden fences separated the houses from us by a good twenty feet. We were sheltered.

"Are we there yet? This is taking too long. I'm going to get caught." Olivia peered down the lane. "Maybe we should go back?"

Her whining pleased me. Mostly because in a matter of minutes I'd never have to hear it again. No one would. I was doing people a service. I smiled, tilting my head empathetically. "It's just two more blocks. I told you, the alley is a shortcut. Just think, it'll be worth the wait when you taste it." I patted her gently on the back, shooing her forward, the edges of my mouth turned up at the corners.

Like a good little lamb, Olivia plodded on. I was definitely the shepherd this time. If only my dad could've seen me.

"It's really dark, Ryann," she said with a quiver, still walking a few feet ahead.

"There's nothing to be afraid of. Only a little farther."

Quietly, I fished in my pocket for my nitrile gloves. I wasn't stupid. I'd taken them out of my father's office weeks before. They were a bit big, but they'd do the job. Slipping them on, I reached into the side pocket of my bag, where I'd *stowed* it.

The long, shiny blade captivated me. I must have held it hundreds of times. I'd practiced on an old pillow, a variety of melons, a water balloon, and even a grassy field—driving the blade into various surfaces to experience the thrusting pressure running through my hands and up my arms. To feel the pull and, finally, release of the blade as it left whatever item I'd chosen. But nothing would come close to the satisfaction of doing it for real.

A few more steps and we would be at my preplanned spot. I took a few deep breaths, noting the smell of freshly cut grass as I attempted to shake the nerves bustling inside me.

Stupid first-time jitters.

This wasn't the time to second-guess myself.

I'm not your average killer. It's not like I'm depraved or anything. I've never killed or tortured an animal. I help the occasional old person cross the street or carry their bags from the grocery store to their car. Selecting a kill isn't frivolous but a means to an end. I have to do it—it's like the urge is encoded somewhere inside me—so I chose wisely.

Being with Olivia was different. It was something just for me. It wasn't connected to the rest of the world I'd built—to my family, my friends, or the Ryann they knew. I tried to be the girl they all wanted, but no matter how hard I struggled to play my part, I was never quite good enough. Always compared to Bri. Always coming up short.

Well, I was about to prove them wrong. I'd worked for this moment, and I'd chosen wisely. It wasn't like little Livy was innocent simply because she was a kid.

Everyone is guilty of something.

Olivia was still in front of me, shadowed by the dark, without the slightest clue about what was going to happen next. A giddy feeling enveloped me.

I felt for the blade in my pocket and stroked the edge with my index finger.

But then something happened that I hadn't anticipated. A rush of anxiety flooded through my blood.

I wasn't sure if I could do it.

At least not *that* way, and I had no idea why. I'd dreamed about it for so long, but my hand could not free the knife from my pocket. My heart raced; sweat dripped down my face. It wasn't like she was the first. I hadn't hesitated with Veronica.

Olivia was practically skipping in front of me when everything stilled. I couldn't leave without doing it. What would that say about me and everything I'd worked so hard for? I couldn't be a failure. I could do this—the very thing no one else I knew could ever even dream of doing. Small shudders tingled up and down my arms and legs.

My eyes traced every inch of the alleyway around us. I had to do something. I couldn't have lived with myself if she'd walked away. Not after everything.

I spotted a small stack of bricks next to a row of garbage bins. My stomach released the twisted knot it had been housing. Yes. It was the perfect way to end her.

I ran over, crouched, and picked up a brick. The red clay was heavy, with small grooves that bit into my gloved fingertips.

Olivia turned around and stalked toward me. "What are you doing over there?"

Straightening, I set my eyes on her. "Thought I saw something, but it was nothing." I kept the brick behind my back and closed the gap between us, my breathing hastening with each step closer.

Chapter
FOUR

Three hours later

The body was small. Female. Bloody.

It was just after one in the morning on Monday, the twenty-eighth of May, and Sergeant Roberto Estevez could see it, illuminated by his cruiser's headlights, just beyond the yellow police tape. A swarm of uniformed officers and two CSIs handled plastic evidence bags. Having been tied up on another case, he'd arrived about an hour after everyone else.

His shirt and pants stuck to him. The thick humidity left an uncomfortable, greasy layer on his skin. As he got out of his car, he pulled his dress shirt away from his chest and stomach, trying to look presentable and not like the soaking mess he was.

While his colleagues searched the area, taking photographs to log into evidence later, he knelt beside the body. With fourteen years on the job and eight at the Dungrave County Police Office, he'd seen his fair share. He'd hoped to never see this.

A pool of darkened blood seeped into the surrounding pavement, highlighted slightly by the distant streetlamp. Her body was slumped on her right side, her face obscured by a mess of hair. He could tell by her size and clothes—shiny sneakers and light pink shirt—that she couldn't have been more than eleven or twelve years old.

"Estimated time of death?" Estevez asked Warren, the medical examiner.

"Little over three hours ago, around ten."

"What the hell was a kid doing out here at night on her own? Especially in a darkened back alley?" the sergeant asked, wiping his brow with the back of his hand. He motioned to Warren for a pair of medical gloves and yanked them on. He hated the way the powder coated his skin. He hated wearing the gloves in the first place. They made his hands sweat. He knelt and traced one finger along the side of her face, moving a chunk of blonde, blood-soaked hair out of her eyes. Estevez's body tensed.

She was only a baby.

Nausea fluttered in his stomach at the sight of the body—the sandwich and coffee his wife had made him take for the drive over wasn't sitting well.

He shook his head, trying to compose himself. "ID of any kind?"

Warren continued to inspect her body. "Nada."

"There wouldn't likely be any," a woman said. "She's too young, unless you see something like a student ID or name sewn into her clothes somewhere."

Estevez didn't need to look up to know who it was. "Hi, Amelia."

"It's Detective Marcus," she said in a flat tone.

He smiled. "My apologies. Good evening, Detective Marcus. Do you have anything on this kid, like who she is or where her parents are?" He gazed up at her shadowed silhouette.

She stepped forward. Her black hair was pulled tightly back in its customary bun. Minimal makeup, except for dark-rimmed eyes. "That guy over there, he's a neighbor, said she lives over on Chesterfield. Knows the family. He was taking a shortcut through the alley when he spotted her just after midnight."

Estevez exhaled and stood in a swift movement. "Shit. Has anyone notified the family yet?"

"Ikonov was just about to head over. The parents called her in missing around 11:30 p.m. The victim matches their description," Marcus said.

"Ikonov is as gentle as a bag of hammers. I'll do it." Estevez returned his attention to the ME. "Cause of death?"

Warren pulled off his gloves at the wrist and balled them up, shoving them into the pocket of his white medical jacket. "Multiple blows to the head with a blunt object. I'll need the autopsy for definitive answers." He pointed to the ground about five feet from the girl. "I'm guessing that's your murder weapon, seeing that it's covered in blood and there's a small piece of red clay in the wound."

Estevez bent to take a better look at the blood-covered brick.

With approximately thirty thousand people in Dungrave County, Colorado, Estevez had thought coming to work here from Chicago would quiet things down. It was a sleepy town that revolved around high school football and sitting on the front porch with your neighbors and a couple of beers. It was what drew him here. The last thing he needed was a child killer on the loose. He shuddered. He had three kids; he wanted to believe they were safe here. He'd thought they were. There had only been three murders in Dungrave over the past ten years. But they were drug related.

This…this was malicious. Evil.

He took in the surrounding area. Tall wooden fences lined the alley, bordering the backyards of homes and a few stores. Garbage cans and dumpsters had been placed along the fences for early morning pick-up. The smell was overwhelming on a muggy summer night. Like rotting meat and produce mixed with a healthy dose of dirty diaper.

"We're going to flip her now," Warren called out.

Estevez turned his attention back to his friend and forced himself to watch while Warren's assistant, Frank, grabbed her legs. Warren placed his hands around the girl's shoulders and together they straightened her slumped body, laying her on her back.

The girl's eyes were open. A vacant, staring blue that made a shiver run the length of Estevez's spine. Blood splattered her cheek and forehead.

"There looks to be at least a dozen blows to the side of her head." Warren took the silver spectacles off his nose. "The blows escalated in violence. This was a brutal attack."

The officer who had been taking the pictures came and snapped a few more, now that she was face up.

"Whoever did this was not much taller than the vic, actually. You can tell by the angle of the wounds. I'll know more when I get her on the table. Strange though…the killer used a brick, probably from that pile over there."

Estevez knew where he was going with this. "You're thinking crime of passion or opportunity? Not preplanned obviously."

Warren pursed his lips. "I'm glad I don't have your job."

Estevez backed up to make room for the body bag, which was laid open beside her. Warren's words repeated in his head: *not much taller than the vic.* Did that mean they were similar in age? Not many adults hovered around five feet.

Warren ran a hand over the girl's colorless face, closing her eyes, before he and Frank lifted her down into the black, nylon bag. She could have been asleep. But she wasn't. He watched as the zipper closed, starting at her legs until it covered her head. A breath caught in Estevez's chest, and he thought of all the other murder cases he'd worked on in Chicago. Somehow this one seemed more tragic. More vicious.

"Up." Warren and Frank carefully lifted the now-full bag onto a gurney and into the back of the body removal van.

The poor thing would have to undergo an autopsy. As if she hadn't been butchered enough.

The immediate scene was cleared now, except for Estevez and Detective Marcus. He crouched down one more time to study the pool of blood.

A hand rested on his shoulder. "You okay?" Amelia asked.

"Not really. You?"

"Are we ever?"

"Nope."

"Come on, I'll go with you to the house for questioning. It's not something to do alone if you can help it."

He nodded, about to stand, when something caught his eye. There was a small, slender object near the dark pool. Taking his pen out, he hooked the item on one end and pulled it closer to get a better look.

Amelia crouched next to him. "What's that?"

"Not sure."

"Hey, wait. I know what that is. It's a friendship bracelet."

His eyebrows lifted. "A what?"

She smiled. "Little girls make bracelets out of beads or colored string and give them to one another as a symbol of friendship."

Estevez had his phone out by now and took a few photos of the item. "Really? She must have been wearing it at the time of the attack."

"But it's still knotted at the ends. It's too tiny to have fallen off, even in a struggle." Amelia grabbed the pen, the string bracelet dangling off the end. "We should bag it. Got any—"

Before she could finish her question, Estevez had a small evidence bag open. She dropped it inside and he closed it.

"So how would it have come off our victim?" he asked.

Amelia bit her lip and shrugged. "Maybe the girl took it off before the attack."

What kind of killer, he wondered, would choose such a trophy?

"Or maybe our killer was going to take a memento—"

"Then thought better of it?"

"Exactly."

Chapter
FIVE

The next morning

𝒥 woke up beaming. Thoughts of Olivia's wide, panicked eyes, and the way her mouth formed an 'o' when she gasped, made my heart beat in its cage. The sounds still rang deliciously in my ears.

Practically springing up from my warm bed, I stood in front of my full-length mirror to take inventory. I was certain I'd look different somehow. And I did. I stood taller. My eyes were brighter, more focused. I carried a newfound responsibility: the power to stop a beating heart. To stop lungs from taking in air.

To decide who got to live and who didn't.

My father wasn't the only one who decided people's futures.

Perhaps kids at school would notice. They'd

ask what was different about me, not knowing the magnitude of the shift. I'd smile and thank them, feel the warm glow of recognition, and claim I didn't know what they were seeing.

It was different than it had been with Veronica. This had been a choice. It took a lot of intelligence and determination to pull off a kill and not get caught. Olivia's murder wasn't me simply taking advantage of a situation that presented itself—someone helpless in the woods. Olivia was the execution of years of work and skill.

I felt tingly on the inside, gratified that I had done what I was meant to in this world. Somewhere in the back of my mind, I'd worried that Veronica had been a fluke, and that the only reason I didn't feel guilty was because she would have died or been crippled anyway. But it wasn't that. Olivia proved it. She solidified how extraordinary I was.

I made it to school a few minutes earlier than normal, too excited to wait. What if news was already out about Olivia's death? I scanned the halls for my friends, but saw no one particularly interesting.

I wondered how everyone would react. The anticipation of her discovery made me want to run laps around the building, shouting that I'd finally done it, and that it was more glorious than I'd ever predicted.

So far everyone I observed was acting the same boring way they did any other Monday morning. Knowing that the news could spread any minute motivated me.

After loitering around the cafeteria with none of my friends in sight, the first period warning bell rang. I made my way to my locker, shoved my bag in, and gathered my socials books. When I got to class, a few of my friends were huddled together looking giddy. So that's where they'd been.

I strode over, butterflies fluttering carelessly away in my stomach. "What are we discussing?" I could only hope it was rumors of Olivia.

Lucas and Bao-yu parted, revealing our other friend, Asad.

"We were discussing Jane and Evan. They were caught cheating on the math test. Word is they might be expelled," Lucas said.

My stomach dropped when I realized the murder hadn't gone public yet. If it had, they would have been talking about Olivia and not some stupid test. But that wouldn't ruin my amazing mood. Good things come to those who wait.

"No way, not for a regular test. Maybe if it was our final exam. This will get them suspended. Tops." Asad was always so confident. He was kind of a know-it-all, but I appreciated him for it. At least he didn't apologize for who he was, like so many of the pathetic losers here.

"Everyone, take your seats. We need to get started right away." Mr. Jonas was nice, but he always had a stick up his ass, nagging at us to "stop talking" and "get back on track." He never played a movie like the other teachers, not even the day before Christmas break.

I took my seat at the back; my legs were already sticking to the chair. The oppressive heat left the hair on my temples and the back of my neck damp.

His chattering was my cue to mentally fade away. I was back in the darkened alleyway with Olivia.

Her light eyes, clear and trusting, changed when she registered my hand grasping the brick. Her arms flailed out protectively. But my swing continued and I struck her in the temple. The way her body gave beneath my weight only invigorated me. My hands were working, but it was almost like I was watching myself do it from afar. I was a movie in slow motion. My arm raising and coming down. The terrified look on her face.

Olivia must have let out a muffled scream, though I could barely hear past the pounding of my heart. I needed to silence her before someone heard and came out to check. She stumbled forward, gasping, and collapsed—

"Ryann, I assume you have finished page 91 and are moving to the next part like the rest of us?"

"Yes, Mr. Jonas." I hoped my face didn't appear as flushed as it felt. My vision was disoriented and fuzzy, like when you're awakened from a dream.

I glanced at the time. I needed to focus for twenty more minutes.

And it dragged.

Class was finally dismissed. There was a rush of kids to the door and down the hallway—no one wanted to spend a single second more than necessary in a classroom, including me.

I was pushed and jostled. A hand messed up my hair. I smacked Lucas away, knowing instinctively it would be him. It was always him. "If you wish to keep your hand, I suggest you remove your greasy fingers from my head."

He laughed. "What was with you in class? You're usually so attentive, my little brownnoser."

"Yeah, you looked right out of it. You didn't even hear Mr. Jonas call you," Asad said.

I held my books closer to my chest and pushed back the memory of forcing Olivia's face into the ground and holding it there until she went still on the gritty concrete, the small pool of crimson flowing around pebbles and broken glass.

"I'm just really tired today. I had kind of a long night." I smiled.

"Ohhh, what does that mean? Is there someone we don't know about?"

"Maybe." I shrugged playfully. "I was up late watching an eighties horror movie marathon, complete with *Halloween*, *A Nightmare on Elm Street*, and *Sleepaway Camp*. It was awesome."

Bao-yu made a face. "I don't understand how you can watch that crap."

"If you tried to watch one, you might realize you like being scared," I said.

We all went our separate ways for second period. I dreaded gym. I hated getting sweaty. None of the girls ever wanted to use the communal shower, myself included. I couldn't find anything less appealing than stripping down to be further judged in front of people I saw every day. Not to mention the inconvenience of drying off, getting changed, and redoing my hair and makeup in the fifteen minutes before the next period. So I usually gave an excuse about having my period, complete with bending-over-in-agony cramps.

It didn't always work. Sometimes Coach would tell me to walk it off. Today was unfortunately one of those days. We were going outside to do laps for track practice. We had a meet coming up, and even if you weren't on the team, you were made to suffer along.

At least it was a solitary sport. I could just run and think.

The track was rubberized and never-ending. It bordered the football field, which forced us girls to ignore the perverted stares of some of the guys playing during their phys ed class.

The sun was relentless. Beads of gross sweat trailed under my boobs and down my back. My lungs burned. Trying to catch my breath, I stopped and bent over, hands on my thighs, to steady myself. It was just like the night before, when I'd bent over Olivia's body. My arms and legs had tingled then, too. I inhaled and made myself go around for another lap, enjoying my memories.

The kill had been everything I wanted. I heard every bird in the trees and smelled every far-off flower. My senses were heightened. I imagined the feeling was similar to a lion's after hunting and seizing its prey in the wild.

Despite the thrill, I kept a clear head and checked myself over. Blood moved from my gloves up my bare arm. I figured I could easily wipe it off my skin, but it begun to smear. There were red splatters across my torso, and a twisting erupted in my gut. I hated feeling dirty. I needed to get it off—but I didn't have time. The only thing I could do was strip the shirt and thrust it into a plastic bag, then into my backpack. I threw on the hoodie since it was the only clean thing with me. It was hard to tell in the dim light if any blood had speckled my sneakers. I hoped not. I didn't want to get rid of them.

Olivia lay there, beautifully decorated with sprays of red, her blue eyes open. She reminded me of Veronica.

I wanted to watch her, motionless, where I put her, but I'd already been there too long. I had to go. But then something caught my eye. I leaned closer. It was a knit bracelet, made of green, purple, and blue yarn, the kind I'd made for my friends dozens of times. I reached down and lightly fingered the band. I wanted it. It would have kept me anchored to the moment. It was stuck at Olivia's wrist, so I pinched her skin and yanked until it finally slid off. I held it in my hands and felt the tightly woven pattern through my gloves. The prize I'd finally won.

I sighed, knowing better.

There could be no evidence connecting me to Olivia.

I carefully rolled the gloves off my hands wrist first, just as I'd watched my dad do when he was handling evidence at the station, and placed them in a small plastic bag and into the pocket of my backpack.

I blinked away the thoughts. My lungs were on fire. I had to stop running. I'd been going faster than usual, the adrenaline egging me on.

Moving over to the grass bordering the track, I flopped down. It wouldn't be long before Coach spotted me and demanded I get back up, so I cherished my few minutes.

Gazing up at the blue sky, I couldn't help but wonder how long Olivia had lain on the ground before someone found her. What had been their reaction? Were they picturing her right now, like I was—haunted by the same image that I savored?

The knowledge that Olivia's last glimpse had been of me sent shivers down my spine.

Perhaps wherever Olivia was, she was haunted too.

Chapter
SIX

$\mathcal{I}$f I wasn't exhausted and sweaty enough from running in gym, I had cheer practice after school. It was the last thing I felt like doing, but since Coach Warilee was both my gym teacher and cheerleading coach, I couldn't feign illness. I just had to get through an hour of practice, and then I could go home and find out if any details regarding Olivia had made it into the news yet. They must have. Something this big would have people in my small town clamoring for every ounce of information they could get their bored little hands on.

No one had been home when I'd gotten back from the alley the night before. My mom, a waitress at The Sizzling Griddle, worked the night shift, and my father, detective extraordinaire, was on duty. He'd likely been tied to the hip of his partner, Sergeant

Estevez, who'd always rubbed me the wrong way. Would it kill the guy to smile once in a while? I'd see him at the station when I visited my dad. Sometimes he came over to the house for beers. He was the kind of guy who liked to be the smartest person in the room and made sure you knew it.

Had my dad been called to the crime scene? My crime scene? A shiver swept through me as I meticulously considered what I'd done.

I straightened my burgundy cheerleading skirt and bent over to lace my shoe. Was there any way I could be connected to *Olivia?*

No. I'd done everything right. Why did I doubt myself? It was stupid.

Coach called for everyone to set up. We were going through the top five cheers we did at every football game for the Dungrave Duggars, our lame-ass high school team. My friends Mackenzie, Katie, and Lucas were also on squad, which made it a bit more bearable. Lucas thought it was an amazing way to meet girls. He could hold them up in the air and look up their skirts without getting in trouble. It was his dream. I, of course, refused to partner with him, because that was just gross.

I knew it was stereotyping to assume that every female phys ed teacher and coach was gay, but I was pretty sure Coach Warilee was a big lesbian, which was cool with me. I didn't care, as long as I continued to be the main focus in the routines. I wasn't the captain, but I was the best on the squad.

As a flyer, they had to put me in the center of things or the whole routine would fall apart.

I fell into the flow of the routines. We'd practiced them so often I could do them in my sleep—which was all I wanted to do, since I'd had less than three hours the night before.

It had been nearly one in the morning by the time I sat on my bed and tuned into the local stations for any mention of Olivia. It was too soon for any details, but I was compelled to listen, just in case.

I yanked my shoes off to check them for blood. It was difficult to see since the material was black canvas, but a few splatters were definitely visible. Saving them wasn't going to happen, but I could soak them in bleach and hopefully get my DNA off before throwing them in a random dumpster. How many people owned black Converse sneakers? Good luck tracing them back to me. I'd tell my mom I accidentally left them behind after an away game. No biggie.

My hair was sopping wet from my evidence-cleaning shower. I combed it through while debating my next move. I was desperate for information. Any crumb would do. I just needed something. I promised myself that I wouldn't contact my father, since I didn't often call him at work. But I couldn't stop myself.

Grabbing my cell, I hit his number. It rang a few times, but I knew he'd pick up for me. He'd be nervous as to why I was calling so late, especially when I had school the next day. Before the fourth ring, I'd heard his gravelly voice. "Ryann? What's wrong?"

"Nothing's wrong. I'm just bored. I can't sleep. Mom's at the diner, so I thought I'd call and say hi."

He exhaled loudly. "You know I'm busy at work. Remember what we said? You'd only call if it was really important, right?"

"I know." I decided to make it worth his while. Depending on his reaction, I'd be able to tell if he knew about the little twit yet. "Truth is, I was a little scared. I thought I heard something outside my bedroom window. I can't sleep knowing I'm alone."

"Where's Brianna?"

"At Morgan's house for the night."

"What kind of sound? Did you put the alarm on?" He sounded strained.

"Of course I did…as soon as I heard it."

"Heard what? Is someone trying to get in?"

Oh, he knew, all right. All it would take was a little prodding and—

"Ryann, push yourself through the boost. It's too slow. Do it again." Coach's orders jerked me out of my daydream.

I nodded and forced myself to focus, which was proving more difficult than I'd anticipated. I had to match my lift to the timing of the three other flyers: Melanie, Ling, and Katie. This time I launched into the jump on cue with the music. Truth was, I didn't like Melanie. She was a bitch. Always thinking she was a better athlete and gymnast than me. Her mother had been a Dallas Cowboys cheerleader, as if wearing tacky mini-shorts and a sparkly bra top was something to be proud of. She'd always try and take over our routines or play secondary coach, when in truth she relied on her mother's reputation instead of working for anything. I wanted to shove her maroon plastic pom-poms down her throat. Now there was an idea.

"Better. Let's run through the last two. Everyone on their marks." Coach blew her whistle. I winced. My head pounded, partially from the heat and partially from last night's vodka—the celebratory drinks I'd indulged in didn't feel so celebratory today.

A few more jumps and handsprings and I feared my lunch might return. If it went all over Melanie, it might not be so bad.

We were all on the ground for this one. Melanie was on my left. Last night's success had upped my courage… As I bent and popped, I flung my arms out a little too far and felt my hand connect with what I knew was Melanie's face.

I dropped my arms, backed up, and stared at her like I wasn't sure what could have gotten in my way. "Oh my God, Melanie! I'm so sorry. Are you okay?"

Her hands covered her face. Tears streamed from her eyes. I'd gotten her good. A few of the others, including Katie, went into Girl Scout mode, sitting her down, running inside for ice, and falling all over each other to help. I hovered too. I had to if I didn't want to be suspected of doing it on purpose.

"Seriously, Mel, I'm really sorry. I didn't think you were that close to me." I crouched in front of her. "Move your hands and let me see." She pulled her hands away tentatively. A drizzle of blood came out of each nostril, sending me right back to Livy and the spray that had been all over my arms.

The uncertainty of what the cops had uncovered tightened my throat. I'd gotten rid of all the evidence that could tie it to me. I was sure.

I didn't let my dad get off the phone last night until I heard some sort of confirmation that Olivia had been found. It was a stupid move, but the urge to know had been eating at me.

"Why so busy?" *I asked innocently.*

He sighed. "I didn't want to tell you this over the phone. Olivia McMann was found dead a little while ago. Murdered. I know you and your sister used to watch her. I'm sorry, honey."

Pure satisfaction smoothed the fluttering of my insides. I inhaled deeply, savoring the moment. I wondered if I'd feel remorse or guilt when my dad said the words—if fear, shame, or regret would rear their ugly heads. But I felt...complete. Just as The Greats had.

"Oh my God, Daddy! What happened?" *I added a quiver for good measure.*

"We're not sure yet. We've got our best people looking into it. I don't want you to be afraid. We're going to catch the guy who did this. Stay inside with the alarm on until your mom gets home. Don't open the door for anyone, you hear me?"

"Of course." *I pretended to sniffle.* "I can't believe

it. How? Are you with her?" I smiled, anticipating his answer. It had been riskier to execute my first kill on a night my father was working, but it was necessary if I wanted precise, firsthand knowledge about my crime. The newspaper always missed things or misreported information. Whenever my dad was on a case, he'd tell me how wrong the reporters got it. I knew if I wanted accuracy, it would have to come from my father or another cop.

He huffed. "No, some of our other people are there. And the how isn't important. You don't need pictures of it floating around your head. Try and settle down. Go to bed, okay?" The line went dead.

He managed me like I was some witness on the street. Grabbing my ancient clock radio, I'd hurled it against my bedroom wall. It shattered into shards of plastic and loose wires. I yelled out.

This was my kill. I was entitled to know whatever I wanted and not be shut down.

Shaking, I paced my room, trying to relax, taking deep breaths. Damn my bad temper. It sucked forever monitoring myself. It would be nice to rage openly when the occasion called for it. But it was not part of the perfect Ryann profile. I wasn't going to throw away years of doing exactly what I was told for the momentary satisfaction of a temper tantrum that would place me in the spotlight.

Downing the last of my cocktail, I tossed the empty glass onto my bed. I grabbed my iPod, put my earbuds in, cranked the volume to one of my favorite metal bands, and began dancing around my room.

Unaware of the time, I startled when a hand touched my shoulder. I shouted and turned, fists up, to find my mother's worried face. I yanked my earbuds out.

"Shit, Mom, you scared me." I'd put a hand to my chest.

"Ryann, it's nearly 3 a.m. Why are you awake? You have school in the morning." Her narrowed eyes were bloodshot.

"Did Dad call you?"

"Yes, he told me you were worried about being home alone. He also said you were about to go to sleep, so what's this?" She pointed around my room, namely at the empty chip bags and candy bar wrappers. Thank God I finished the vodka.

"I was wired. You know how I get when I'm freaked out." I bit my lip and held my breath, waiting for her to tell me about Olivia.

My mother led me by the arm to the bed, sat me down and brushed my hair off my face. "Yes, he called, and I'm very sorry. I know it must be quite a shock." She tilted her head, as if looking at me from a slightly different angle was going to somehow soothe me.

I adopted my most grief-stricken expression. "I just can't believe it." I shook my head as if trying to grasp the heaviness of the situation. "Who would do such a thing?"

Melanie's cries yanked me back to reality.

Coach was inspecting her nose. "Well, it could be broken. Go to the office and call your parents to come pick you up. You should see a doctor." I appreciated Coach. She was a no-bullshit kind of woman.

Which meant she also had no sympathy. As soon as Ling had walked Melanie to the office, Coach had the rest of us back at it.

I couldn't keep this up.

Flipping and aerials were too much right now. My mouth was cotton, not to mention that the ground didn't stop spinning when I did. "Coach, can we take five, please? I'm not feeling well." I aimed my best, big-eyed pleading face at her.

"Five minutes and we go over the pyramid routine."

I nodded, plopped down on the lawn, and downed half a Gatorade, praying it remained in my stomach. Closing my eyes, I inhaled a slow, deep breath and thought about my mom.

I didn't often care about what people thought of me, especially when they were weak-willed. They could never understand the way I saw the world.

Sitting beside me on my cheery, pink-flowered bedspread, my mom took my hand, looked me in the eye, and said, "I don't know what kind of person could do such a disgusting, horrible thing. A monster."

My mom thought I was a monster. I supposed deep down I knew the day would come.

I stared blankly at the poster of two kittens in a

basket that she'd given me a few Christmases before. My gut felt hollowed out. And my buzz was definitely gone.

What had I thought her reaction would be? Not that it mattered. It wasn't as though her opinion counted. She didn't understand who I was or what it was like to push and strive to be the best at something. She was mediocre and okay with it.

That would never be me.

I always did everything I could to please her. I studied hard, became a cheerleader, joined school clubs, and made friends. And now she was disappointed in me? I knew she wouldn't be proud of me for killing someone—but it would be nice if she'd been impressed by how well I'd done it, if she'd recognized the skill and sacrifice involved.

Katie ran back over, stopping in front of me and panting. "Are you okay, Ry?"

I gave her a questioning glare. "Sure, why wouldn't I be?" I retied my shoes so I wouldn't have to look at her.

"I know you feel bad for breaking Melanie's nose, but she's okay. Her dad came to get her. The nurse said it wasn't as bad as it looked. She doesn't think Mel will need surgery." Katie grabbed a seat next to me on the grass.

Right, that. "Of course I feel bad. I feel horrible. I'm so glad she's going to be okay, but what does that mean for squad? Can she still cheer?" I squeezed my eyebrows together.

Katie put a consoling arm on my shoulder—which I only tolerated because it was expected. Touching was one thing if I instigated it. But I resented it when people thought it was appropriate to inflict themselves on my body. "Probably not for a bit, but she'll be back," she said.

Coach called out that break was over.

We assembled into a pyramid. Joshua, my partner, launched me, and I twisted mid-air. The image of my mother's disgusted face popped into my head. I missed my full rotation and landed with a heavy thud, pain searing up my leg.

"Shit, Ryann. Are you okay?" Joshua asked worriedly—as he should have. He'd dropped me, even if I hadn't exactly been paying attention.

"I think so. Sorry, Josh. I'm not feeling good. I shouldn't even be here. It's not your fault." I batted my eyelashes at him and he looked even sorrier. *Moron.*

I made a show of trying to stand, bouncing on my good foot only. I'd use any excuse to cut out of practice early. "My ankle!"

Coach Warilee came over. "Damn it, Wilkanson. Your head's not in it today. You all right?" She looked at my ankle, which was a bit tender but absolutely fine.

I touched it and winced. "Maybe a little ice would be good."

"Josh, take her to the nurse. What is wrong with everyone today? Everyone else, back on your marks."

I hobbled along, letting Josh carry the brunt of my weight. It had to look real.

I was a master of illusion, after all.

Chapter
SEVEN

Finally, I was home from the longest school day in the history of school days. I passed my father's office on the way to my bedroom. It had been my favorite room in the house—my own personal research library—until I'd been banned from entering as a kid. My father kept many intriguing books. Biographies of serial killers from Jack the Ripper to Dr. Harold Shipman, a general practitioner in England who was said to have killed hundreds of patients and even stolen their money.

When I was seven, my parents caught me flipping through the pages of a true crime book on the floor of my dad's home office. I'd pulled it onto my lap, drawn in by the shining pages of people with red-splattered skin. I was fascinated with the way the men and women looked at me in what I'd later learn were mug shots. Their eyes were different somehow, like they knew something the rest of the world didn't.

I'd jerked when my mother shrieked. She had a hand to her chest and frantic eyes. I asked what was wrong. Was there something on me, a spider? She snatched the book away and called it horrible filth. I'd tried to keep my grip, but she was stronger. She said it would give me nightmares. With a longing glance at the hardcover tight in her hands, I hoped it did. I wasn't done with those pictures yet.

Despite her disapproval, something awoke in me that winter day on the cold floor of my father's office. I was too young to know how that moment would define my future.

After being caught in there for the second time a week later, my father had sat me down and asked why I wanted to see such things.

"I don't know. I guess I'm curious." And it was the truth. I was curious. I wanted to know about the people who'd been killed. Why they'd been killed. And most of all, who'd done the killing. I knew better than to say that.

"Why would a sweet girl like you be curious about such awful things?" My dad had gently gripped my chin, tilting my face up so he could look me in the eyes. "Promise me you're finished being curious. I don't want to see you in here again. If I do, there will be consequences, young lady. Is that understood?"

He gave me a firm, no-nonsense gaze. I nodded.

He kissed me on the forehead and patted my head before escorting me out. I'd felt frustrated. Angry. My parents didn't understand me at all. No one saw me for who I really was. I realized I'd need to hide that part of myself. The part that wasn't "normal."

But I didn't want to be normal. I wanted to be exceptional.

Now, I walked over to the bookcase, no longer forbidden, and stared at the spines of the books. My fingers touched the edges of the hard covers and I let myself be overcome by the feeling of awe that had first washed over me as a child. I selected the very book that had made my mother so frazzled and flipped through its lustrous pages. Why was the experience so different for me than my father? I mean, he owned them. Was there no part of him that got pleasure from what he found inside, even in the darkest, most secret part of himself? Why else would he possess such things? Perhaps his urge to become a cop was directly tied to such an internal flicker. Perhaps it scared him and made him so uncomfortable that he decided to become the very antithesis of it.

I stopped at the page my mom had freaked out over those years ago. On the left was a photograph of Edmund Kemper. It was a black-and-white shot. He stood, staring at the camera in his prison garb and silver-rimmed glasses. His dark black mustache matched the heavy sweep of black hair that hung too long around his ears. Next to him was a picture of one of his crime scenes. A bloody room. A dead girl.

With one glance, I understood. The power, the frantic adrenaline and wild freedom, the chance of getting caught at any moment. Now that I'd tasted it, I knew I'd only want more.

Thinking I'd heard the front door, and not wanting to explain why I was reading this book all these years later, I carefully slid it back into its place on the shelf. Leaving the office, I heard my mom bustling around the kitchen and made my way over. Grocery bags covered the kitchen island.

"Hey, Mom, I just got home too. Dad back yet?"

She looked at me, frowned, and turned to put away some cans. "You want to ask him about Olivia, don't you?"

I began emptying another of the brown paper bags, placing bananas and grapes on the counter. "Well, aren't you interested in the details? It's kind of natural to want to know what happened."

My mother sighed and divided soup from cans of vegetables. "Dad should be home in the next hour. Please don't bombard him with questions. He'll be exhausted."

"Well, you must know what happened. If you tell me, I won't have to bother him."

She straightened and crossed her arms over her chest. "Olivia was found in an alleyway near her house. It was late, maybe after eleven."

Her face told me that she was holding back. "I know that much already. How was she killed?"

She inhaled, and her gaze shifted around the kitchen instead of meeting my eyes. "She was bludgeoned to death."

I let my jaw drop, pasting a look of abhorrent shock on my face. "Oh my God. Why would someone do that to her?"

"I don't know." She straightened, taking a long, slow breath. "It must've been a tough scene to be at." She closed the distance between us and pulled me to her. The smell of her coconut conditioner and body lotion enveloped me. She always used coconut-scented everything, said it reminded her of being on a tropical island somewhere even if we were only in Dungrave. "Death is always devastating, but the fact that someone went after a poor, helpless girl... It's repulsive."

"Do you think we should go and visit Mr. and Mrs. McMann? Show our respect somehow?" I'd feel closer to Olivia if I went to her house and saw her family.

My mom tucked a chunk of hair behind my ear. "That's really sweet, but they're probably still dealing with the police. Besides, we need to give them time to grieve."

I hid my disappointment and smiled, nodding my head as if I understood. "Do you know anything else? I get that you think I'm still a kid, but I'm not. I can handle it. I knew her too."

She released her grip on me. Her hand rested on her hip and she sighed. She was giving in. She always did. The tingling in my chest returned. "I think your dad said she was struck in the head... A dozen times or so. I don't know if they have a suspect."

"Oh." I swallowed and hoped my expression was appropriately solemn as she turned to put cans in the hall pantry.

A dozen? I knew there'd been a few blows, but twelve?

I could only distinctly remember four. That meant I'd driven the brick into Olivia's skull eight more times—and had no memory of them. My pulse quickened. I'd read about people so transfixed by their rage that they'd black out. Had that happened to me? A wave of queasiness hit me. I didn't like that I'd lost control. I wanted to remember. If I'd blacked out, did that mean that I was too sensitive—or too rage-filled—to stay in my own head?

My mind whirred. I needed to do something. I needed to find my dad. Figure out what the cops knew. Surely that would help me fill in the blanks.

Mom went down to the laundry room. It was the perfect time to take off. This way she wouldn't try to stop me or ask where I was going. I grabbed a granola bar and a bottle of Diet Coke, ran down the back stairs, and hopped on my bike. I had two destinations she didn't need to know about: the alleyway and the police station. I was craving the sight of dried blood on concrete. Hopefully they hadn't hosed it down yet.

I knew it was ill-advised to return to the scene of the crime, but it wasn't like I was taking trophies: a clip of her pretty blonde hair, a sock, her bracelet. I'd restrained myself.

That was how so many were caught. Someone stumbled across their loot and turned them in, or the cops searched and found their stash. Case closed. Sealed with a red, shiny bow.

But who was ever going to suspect me? I'd probably be one of a dozen other people gawking past the yellow tape. It was only natural to be curious; it had happened in my neighborhood. I had every right to be there.

Ten minutes later, I found myself in the alley. It wasn't the same in the morning light, not as intense or special as when it had belonged to the two of us.

My gaze went straight to the spot where I'd left her. Dried blood remained ingrained in the concrete. My heart pumped faster. They hadn't gotten to it yet. I suppressed a smile at my good luck, not that I was really that surprised. Dungrave had one speed: slow and I guess murder hadn't changed that.

There were still a number of police cruisers and officers on the scene. A lot of them knew me because of my dad, and I figured I could use that to my advantage.

Dismounting from my bike, I surveyed my options. Officers Shook, McLeod, and Schmidt were nearby, but they'd always babied me, probably because they'd known me my whole life. I was happy to see that Estevez wasn't around. I really didn't feel up for his particular attitude today.

I noticed Detective Marcus standing off to the

side. Perfect. She'd only moved to Dungrave two years ago and had always treated me with respect. I walked my bike over to where she was talking to a middle-aged man and writing something down in her notebook. When she finished a minute later, I made sure she spotted me waiting nearby.

"Ryann! Hey, how are you?" She moved closer to me.

I took a deep, trembling breath. "Hi, Detective Marcus. I'm okay...considering." I motioned toward the taped-off area. "Looks like you've got your hands full. Is my dad around?" I already knew that if he wasn't here he was probably at the station writing the file, but it was better to seem out of the loop.

"He's still at the station. He was helping out with a few of the interviews, but I think he's off soon. He said you guys knew the McManns. This must be hard for you."

I did my best to muster a few tears, but only managed watery eyes that mimicked mild allergies. "It's so unbelievable. I haven't seen her in a while— but it still hits you. I can't believe someone did this to her. Are there any leads?" I didn't want to press my luck with too many questions.

Detective Marcus removed her sunglasses and rubbed the bridge of her nose. "You know I can't say. It's still early in an ongoing investigation, and we aren't prepared to release any information yet."

She was so *official*. I figured I'd try one final probe. "So you guys don't have any suspects yet?"

Detective Marcus gave a small smile. "We're questioning all persons of interest…" She stopped talking and really looked at me. "Are you worried about your safety? We're going to catch this guy, I promise. We got a whole team here. And your dad is one of the best." She glanced at my bike. "Where you headed now?"

I squeezed the black, tattered handlebars. My bike was older, with a bit of chipped paint, but it still worked great and had come in very handy the night before. I'd planted it a few streets away from Olivia's house, and after the kill, I'd jogged back, hopped on, and pedaled away. My father had taught me that police dogs couldn't track someone on a bike. They follow the scent from shed skin cells, but because you're lifted off the ground on a bike, the trail goes cold.

I shrugged. "Maybe to visit my dad."

"That might not be such a bad idea. Though he'll tell you the same thing: you've got nothing to worry about." She put her finger up as if she'd just remembered something. "Question for you. Where were you last night?"

My back tensed. "Why do you ask?"

"Someone reported seeing a girl on a bike riding around at about nine. I was hoping to ask her some questions. See if she saw anyone or anything suspicious." She pointed to my bike. "You ride yours often?"

My breath hitched and I hoped it went unnoticed. "Not usually. I tend to walk or take the bus.

The hills around here suck."

Detective Marcus smiled. "What about last night? Were you out for a ride?"

"Nope. I took a walk, but not around here. I wish I could help."

She put her sunglasses back on and motioned for a woman in her sixties to come over. Behind her a handful of people waited their turn. Detective Marcus was clearly interviewing potential witnesses. "Thanks anyway."

I lingered a moment to eavesdrop.

"Ma'am, can you tell me if you heard or saw anything odd last night?" Marcus said to an elderly woman who'd missed her mouth with her too-bright pink lipstick.

Millions of tiny pinpricks ran down my arms. Was the woman going to point at me? Maybe this was the stupidest place I could be. I was fairly certain that no one had seen me with Olivia, but I couldn't be one hundred percent sure.

I imagined someone screaming, "That's her! I saw her bashing a brick into a girl's skull!"

I took one last mental picture of the rust-colored stains on the pavement and took off without looking back.

Chapter EIGHT

*T*he police station was a fifteen-minute ride from the alley, but I'd stopped at Creekside Café to get Dad's favorite bagel and cream cheese—the excuse I'd use for dropping by. There was a definite possibility that someone would tell him I'd gone to the alley, and he wouldn't like it.

Dungrave wasn't a large town; it was actually a step away from Hicksville. It was the kind of dull place where nothing happened, leaving me perpetually bored. Most people felt similarly, and rectified the tedium by spying—my neighbors were apparently desperate to tell my parents where they'd spotted me on any given day. "Oh, Liz, did you know that Ryann was at the Shopmart today? It was just after school. I hope she didn't skip." *Thank you, Mrs. Hopkins, for your account of my comings and goings for the last ten years, but your services are unnecessary.* Ugh, sometimes it felt impossible to escape everyone's staring and speculation. Especially since I was a cop's daughter.

When Bao-yu and I got our noses pierced last summer, my cell had gone off within five minutes. All because Officer Schmidt had seen us at the mall. My dad made me take it out that night.

There were people watching. Always.

Getting away with this kill—and however many more—would prove once and for all that I was smarter than this place.

As I walked into the frigid air-conditioned station with its mute palette of gray furnishings, I noticed that the usually unruffled office was lively. There were more officers on than normal, all of them bustling through the halls with ears glued to their cells, writing on little notepads, or huddling in groups.

My father's desk was at the back behind six other rows laden with phones and those huge old computers. I breezed through the aisles, returning the occasional wave or nod. Even when I was little, my dad would bring Bri and I in, show us off to his colleagues, and take us around. I, of course, never minded Bring Your Daughter to Work Day. It was the perfect opportunity to be a fly on the wall, watch the cops at work, and see firsthand how things really went down. I'd learned a lot, and that knowledge had proved useful when I needed it the most.

Like when I needed to get rid of the evidence connecting me to Olivia's murder.

After I left the alley, I rode straight to Ridgeway Park. At the back was a wooded area. There were a few spots for campfires and one or two big steel barrels that the homeless used as heaters in the winter by shoving them full of garbage and lighting them on fire. I set one barrel up the day before with bunches of newspaper already doused in gasoline.

Standing in front of my prepped steel barrel, I took the small Ziploc out, grabbed a damp rag I'd packed, and cleaned my arms. The heat and flames would have likely taken care of any evidence—hairs, fibers—but I refused to take chances. Nothing stupid was going to trip me up. I'd considered everything. I placed the shirt inside first, then the rag, and I put the rolled plastic gloves on top of the pile. Striking a match, I tossed it into the barrel.

Bright, rhythmic flames had engulfed the newspaper. They were beautiful, the way they flickered and swayed in the slight breeze. I watched as the evidence shriveled up.

There was nothing left to tie me to Olivia.

I rode off, the night air against my face.

Finally. I was one of The Greats. I pictured the conversation I'd have with Rader, Bundy, or Gacy. What they'd say. How they'd congratulate me, maybe pat me on the back and buy me a drink to celebrate.

I looked around for my father among the rest of the uniforms.

There he was, Detective David Wilkanson, aka my dad, sitting at his desk, working diligently away, I assumed on Olivia's case.

"Hi, Dad."

He stopped typing and seemed genuinely surprised to see me. "Hi. What are you doing here?"

"I wanted to check on you. Mom said you were exhausted and coming home, but not from the looks of it." I smiled sweetly, angling my body to get a better look at his computer screen. "I brought you a bagel." I tossed the package on the desk. "I thought it would tide you over."

He leaned back in his chair, running his hands through thinning chestnut hair. "Thanks, honey. I'm starving and, yes, exhausted." He dug right in to the bag and continued talking around a mouthful of bagel, a hint of cream cheese on the corner of his mouth. "This is plain. You know I like multigrain."

"I know, but they were all out." *Of course he had to comment.* "Um, so what about the case?"

"It's a tough one. We've got more officers on than normal, still trying to get a handle on it. How are you holding up? I know how sensitive you are."

I could feel the heat in my cheeks. "I'm fine. I'm not that sensitive." I tried to keep my pouty face at bay. "I feel bad for Mr. and Mrs. McMann. I wanted to stop by, but Mom said it was too soon. Do you guys know anything?" I held my breath, still eyeing the screen. There was a list of names, phone numbers, and addresses. Maybe a list of potential suspects?

"We're collecting evidence. Interviewing neighbors, friends, and family members. Anyone who knew her or could have seen anything."

I'd known her. Would they interview me? A jolt of electricity flowed through me at the prospect of being involved. It was a dream scenario. "It's just so bizarre." I shook my head. "Don't most murders have a motive, like revenge, money, or jealousy?"

"A lot do," he said between bites.

Sometimes my dad and I played this little game where we'd take turns with theories on TV cases, like *Dateline* or *48 Hours*. We'd try and see who could figure it out first. "What could be the motive for someone to go after a kid?"

"Sometimes there isn't one. There are some sick people out there."

Not what I wanted to hear, but I nodded in agreement.

I couldn't decipher much else on my Dad's monitor. But he had a bunch of paperwork on his desk, and one file was labeled McMann with yesterday's date on it. I needed to see what was inside.

"Would you mind getting me a glass of water? The ride made me thirsty."

He pushed himself away from the desk. "Sure."

"Thanks."

I wasted no time helping myself to his chair. Glancing around to ensure no one was paying attention to me, I slowly opened the file. The first thing I saw was a color picture of Olivia's body. My heart raced and I pushed down my smile. Blood had pooled around her. It hadn't been twenty-four hours since I'd put her there, but it seemed like a lifetime. Seeing the image jerked me back. I could even smell the freshly cut grass again.

That single snapshot was all I could risk peeking at. I let the file cover drop back down and stood up in time to meet my father's gaze. He handed me a small paper cup of water, which I downed.

"Thanks. Are you coming home now?"

"Soon." He reclaimed his chair. "I've still got a few things to do." His gaze was no longer on me. It was his subtle way of dismissing me.

I wouldn't be dismissed. "Her killer is on the loose and you don't have any leads, which means it could be anyone."

He sighed, his eyes moving from his screen. "Ry, I know it's scary, but we'll find the guy that did this. Until then, I want you to stay with a friend or in a group when you're out, okay? Usually these things aren't random. It was probably a kidnapping that went bad. Try not to worry."

I gave him a weak smile. "I'm on my way to B's now." I leaned in and gave my dad a kiss on the cheek. His scruff scratched my lips and I could taste the salt on his skin. He needed a shower, and I needed to plan my next move. "Don't worry, I've got my bike."

Feeling satisfied there were no serious suspects—and that I remained in the clear—I pedaled over to Bao-yu's.

I parked my bike in front of the porch, jogged up the stairs, and knocked.

A disheveled-looking B stumbled into view through the screen. She stared at me blankly. "What's up? I just saw you at school, like, three hours ago."

She pushed open the screen and I followed her inside. It was hot and muggy. The Ng's didn't believe in air conditioning until it was over ninety-five degrees. *Ugh.* B was first-generation Chinese-American and her parents were sort of old school, according to her.

"You alone?" I asked, looking around for Mr. or Mrs. Ng or B's bratty little brother, Chen. He was eight and a terror.

"No one's here, just me. Why?" She groaned and plopped herself down on the sofa. A large fan was positioned in front of her.

I dropped onto the leather chair opposite her. I was a bit sweaty and my arms immediately stuck to it. Not my favorite sensation. "Didn't you hear? That brat I used to babysit with Brianna was killed last night." I tried to say it with as little glee as possible, but B knew how much Olivia had bugged me. If I'd acted all devastated, she'd have thought aliens had invaded my body.

"What? How do you know?" B perked up, then made a knowing face at me. "Your dad, obviously."

"Yeah, I found out last night."

Her eyebrows raised and her shoulders hovered

around her ears. She was kind of a stress ball. On meds and everything. "And you're not telling me until now? What the hell happened to her? Car accident?"

I wanted to yell from the rooftops: *No! I killed her and it was awesome!* "She was found bludgeoned in an alley near her house." I liked the word bludgeoned. It sounded so much more severe than beaten or bashed.

"Whoa. That's insane. Like, an actual murder. This is like an episode of *CSI*. They have any idea who did it?"

I had to chomp down on the inside of my mouth to keep from grinning. Bao-yu was by no means a goody-goody, but murder wasn't exactly her bag. "My dad said they don't have any leads so far, but they're interviewing everyone. The investigation will likely go on for weeks, or even months."

"Until they catch the guy?" she asked.

I was already getting tired of everyone assuming that a guy was the only viable suspect. *Hello?* It was just more incentive for me to prove that, sometimes, it's the least likely suspect you should watch out for. The satisfaction of seeing their shocked faces would almost be worth spending years in prison. I was sure I'd get out eventually, being a minor and all, but there were some cases of kids being charged and sentenced as adults. One kid, George Stinney, was executed when he was only fourteen. Sure, it was 1944, but still. Harsh.

Of course, I wasn't stupid enough to get caught. I hadn't spent the last six-plus years of my life researching and studying to make mistakes.

"They won't close the investigation until they have someone definitive. And if years go by with no leads, it will become a cold case. But they won't give up," I said.

"Do you think there's, like, a crazed killer on the loose?" B clutched the throw pillow tightly to her chest like it was a stuffed teddy bear.

I shrugged. "What, like a serial killer?" I was having way too much fun with this. "You think more people are in danger?" *Little did she know.*

"It's possible, isn't it?"

"I guess, unless it was targeted. I mean, don't the cops always look at the closest people to the victim first? Which would be her family. Who else did she really know?"

B sat up straighter and ran her fingers through her long, ebony hair. "Maybe I watch too much television, but there's her teachers, her friend's parents… oh! What if she had a few coaches or took lessons of some kind?"

"I suppose, but what would be their motive?" I loved B's imagination. Playing along was fun. And making me hungry. "Hey, you got anything to eat? I'm starving." I gave her a pouty face and rubbed my belly for emphasis.

She threw the pillow off her lap at me and jumped up. "Sure, what do you want? I have leftover pizza from last night."

"Let me guess: it's loaded with pineapple," I said derisively.

"Of course. Otherwise it would be gross." She beamed and walked towards the kitchen.

"When are you going to learn that fruit does not belong on pizza?"

I could hear her giggling from the kitchen. It's not like I hated everyone, just most people. Bao-yu got me in a way that most people didn't. She never tried to change me, never questioned what I liked or how I was, and I did the same for her. She was like the sister I'd always wanted—Bri and I weren't exactly close. She'd made sure of that. She was always too busy, with no time for me. But B was there to pick up the slack.

She bounded back in the room with two plates of pizza and two bottles of Diet Coke.

"Wow, you're going to be a great delivery person when you grow up," I teased, winking at her before grabbing the plate closest to me. I began picking off the repulsive pieces of yellow mush from in between the cheese and ham.

"Shut up. It's better than nothing. So back to this insanity. I figured it out. Kidnapping. It's the only logical explanation," B said.

"Well, they really screwed it up by killing her. It's not like you can get ransom for a corpse." I couldn't remember pizza ever tasting so good before, even with the nasty residue of pineapple juice.

"I suppose. Unless something went wrong.

Maybe the kidnappers took that little bugger, and she fought or was getting away, and had to be stopped."

I laughed. "You watch too much TV. Any plans tonight?"

She shrugged before shoving the rest of the slice in her mouth. "My parents want to go out on the boat for a bit. You want to come?"

"I'd love to, but I have to help my mom clean and weed the backyard. She said I can't go to Hayden's party on Friday unless I help."

Bao-yu gave me a long, drawn-out stare. "And why would you go? You hate him."

B was referring to the fact that Hayden Cook had dumped me for Yvonne Borgdon the year before. It wasn't so much that I actually cared; it was that he replaced me with someone so heinous. At least let it be for a chick who could model or something. But Yvonne? Revolting. "It's no big deal. That's all ancient history. Bedsides, I want you to come with me."

"You know my WoW guild raids are on Friday nights. There's no way I'm going to a party." She wore such a serious expression that I nearly burst with laughter. B loved the dorkiest things and I appreciated her all the more for it—but I wasn't taking no for an answer.

"You can play anytime. I need you, and as my best friend it's your duty and obligation to help me." I put my arm around her and squeezed.

"Ugh. Socialize with people? Why do you hate

me?" Her almond-shaped eyes pleaded with me, but I wasn't having it.

"Come on, it'll be fun."

"You can't promise that. Besides, you never beg me to hang out with the jocks—or douches, as I prefer to call them. You have Mackenzie and Katie for that," she said.

I downed half my Diet Coke before answering. "I want you." I pushed her playfully and elicited a slight smile from her. "I usually let you off the hook, but it won't kill you to come out for one night."

She let out a huge puff of air. "You owe me for this. Big. And I'll collect when you least expect it. You know, you're way prettier than Yvonne. Hayden was an idiot. Her freckles and carrot mop are gross. You're gorgeous—a natural blonde and everything. Did you know that only, like, two percent of the population are natural blondes? You're really quite rare." She beamed a satisfied smile.

"You and your random facts. You're so bizarre."

"But you love it."

"I do." I cocked my head. "I know you don't like talking about it, but why don't you go out much?" I was genuinely curious. I could analyze B like an independent study on neurosis.

"We hang out all the time. I chill with Mackenzie and Lucas and Katie—"

"Whoa. Those are our *regulars*. I mean people outside of your comfort zone, outside our circle— the same circle we've had since sixth grade. It's time to expand, B." I made a grand, sweeping gesture with my arms.

"Fine, I'll go. I just don't get why it's so important for you to have me there."

"Because I'm sick of having fun without you. It's time you were in one of my memories that doesn't involve this couch, my pool, or camping. Okay?" I stood to go.

B flopped back onto the sofa pillows. "Okay."

"Text you later." Before she could change her mind, I was out the door.

Chapter
NINE

I wanted more.

It had been a very long school week. There had to be someone of interest going the party that night, and I'd find them. Maybe I'd be generous this time. I'm sure B had some enemies whose demise would perk up her day. There was that girl in chemistry class who'd blamed B for cheating last semester. What was her name? *Chelsea.* Even her name was obnoxious.

Of course it wouldn't be wise to act too soon, but I could prepare.

Then again, did I need to be so cautious, waiting months between kills? If I went about it the right way, I could absolutely pull it off. I didn't want the feeling to fade. Maybe it didn't have to.

I took my time soaking in the bathtub, catching up on the latest Stephen King novel (he inspires me so), before scouring my closet for something to wear. I wanted to look hot. It never hurt to show your ex-boyfriend what he was missing.

Three pairs of jeans, four tanks, two pairs of shorts, a long skirt, and some pink dress my mom insisted was 'cute' later, I'd confirmed I had absolutely nothing to wear. "Mom!"

My bedroom door burst open. "What's wrong, Ryann?"

"I have nothing to wear for the party."

My mother sighed and then eyed the pile of clothes heaped on the floor in front of me. "What do you suppose those are?"

"They're horrible. I look bloated in everything. My period's tomorrow and I feel like a whale." I puffed out my cheeks.

"Ryann, you're crazy. You look beautiful in anything and everything. Just pick out something and go. What about that pink dress we got you last year?"

I stared at her like she was a crazy person, which was debatable at times. "Never in this life."

"What's the big deal with tonight? Normally you're happy with jeans and a T-shirt."

I continued to scroll through the items hanging in my closet, occasionally throwing a shirt onto the growing heap. I moaned. "It's the party at Hayden's house. I told you about it last week."

"I see. Hayden, as in Hayden-who-used-to-be-your-boyfriend?"

"No, it's not that. I just want to look nice, okay?"

She put an arm around my shoulders and kissed me on the forehead. "Why don't we take a look in Bri's closet and see if there's anything you like?"

"Because she'll kill me if I wear anything she owns."

My mom waved me off. "I'm giving you permission. She can complain to me if she doesn't like it."

Standing in Bri's walk-in, I basked in the choices.

"How about this?" Mom asked, holding up a purple, sleeveless tank. "You can pair it with your black jeans. It'll bring out those gorgeous eyes."

I grabbed the tank and examined it. It was one of my favorites. "Thanks."

Heading back to my room, I got changed and finally felt half decent. I finished my hair and makeup and was ready to go. Bao-yu and her dad would be arriving any minute. He was driving us to Hayden's. I couldn't wait until I had the added freedom of a driver's license. It would make my stakeouts and hunting easier.

At the honk of a car's horn I bolted for the door, trailed by Mom's reminder to be home by eleven.

The car ride was awkward, as usual. B's dad always tried to talk to me with his terrible broken English. He'd been in this country for eighteen years. You'd think he'd pick up a thing or two. He was nice though, if a tad strict.

As we pulled up in front of Hayden's house, Mr. Ng motioned for us to wait. "I hear about murder of young girl. You two, stay inside, whole time. Yes?"

He nodded and we nodded back.

"We're going to be fine, Dad. There's only like, fifty other kids here. No crazed psychopath is going to break into the party and start slaughtering people." I had to squeeze my jaw shut so I wouldn't burst out laughing. B patted him on his arm and got out of the car. I followed closely behind, shimmying my way across the back seat.

B and I stood outside for minute, staring at the house. The place was already bustling with activity. Music was blaring, and we could see people through the windows. There were even a few kids scattered on the front porch and lawn, beers in hand.

Hayden's parents didn't care what he did. His dad was away for work a lot, and his mom liked to go to the bar for old people in the center of town to 'have a few cocktails' with her friends, which everyone knew meant she liked to get wasted and flirt with younger men.

"I can't believe you're making me do this. My palms are sweaty," B said. "I'm gross. I knew I should have taken an Ativan before I left the house."

I rolled my eyes. "You're not gross, you're just nervous. And for no reason—you look hot."

B had traded in her usual track pants and Batman t-shirt for a sparkly tank and dark skinny jeans. She was curvy and gorgeous.

"So hot! Damn," I said, slapping her on the butt and laughing. "And you don't need an Ativan. Have a beer." She swiped my hand away, giggling.

"Come on, let's go in." I pulled her forward by the arm, and she reluctantly followed, like a puppy who might get a treat at the end of some unpleasant task.

Once inside, I was assaulted by blaring music, a flashing strobe light, and the smell of weed.

"Just a little party, huh?" B said, glaring at me.

I nudged her along. "Hayden sure knows how to throw one. There's no way his mom is just at the bar tonight. He'd never get all these people out and the place cleaned up in time."

"Not our problem. Anyway, you dragged me here. Now what?"

I grinned widely. "We mingle. Let's get a drink."

We made our way past the stoners, and a few couples making out so openly on the couch that I wanted to gag, to where Hayden was pouring beer from a keg in the kitchen.

"Ladies, you made it! You're both looking ravishing this fine evening. Beer?" He held up a red plastic cup with creamy foam spilling over the edge.

"Sure," I said, taking a sip. "Thanks."

"Want one, Bao-yu?" He held out one to her and, to my shock, she took it with a smile. No sarcastic one-liners. Frankly, I was a little disappointed.

She downed almost the whole thing.

"Whoa. Our gorgeous Asian invasion is not to be messed with tonight," he slurred, before putting an arm around B. Hayden was always one for a cheesy pick-up line.

I took the liberty of redistributing his appendage, and B gave me a look of gratitude.

"Crazy party," I yelled over the noise. "Parents out of town or something?"

He nodded, bobbing in time with the music. It was some crappy hip-hop that I didn't understand. It just sounded like noise to me.

"And they left you alone, in the house, all by yourself?" B asked, clearly amazed.

"My brother's here too."

Charlie was nineteen, and I supposed that was old enough to be considered adult supervision.

"Where is Chuck?" I asked. "Doesn't he care that you have a full house?"

Hayden pointed a few feet behind us to a crowd of about eight guys. In the center of it, beer bonging, was Charlie.

"Guess not." I laughed.

While I appreciated the banter, I had other things to attend to. Namely, the delightful task of figuring out who would be number two and how I would kill them. I had to make the rounds, but I knew B wouldn't want to. I needed to distract her.

"I think Mackenzie and Asad said they'd be here by eight thirty. What time is it?" B had a huge crush on Asad but would never admit it, not even to me. It was cute, in a dork-meets-dorkier kind of way. Our group was a mix. Part geek and part jock. Somehow we all got along. Other people didn't get it, but it worked for us. Maybe because we'd been friends for so long, the labels didn't matter.

B checked her cell. "It's 8:26."

"Then they're probably here somewhere. Why don't you do a walk-through and see if you can find them?"

Her eyes narrowed. "And what are you going to do in the meantime?"

I leaned in and whispered, "There's something I need to take care of."

Chapter
TEN

*W*alking around the rooms at Hayden's, I was a hunter stalking its prey in the wild...or at least in its natural habitat. There were dozens of idiotic, unsuspecting morons ripe for the picking. The only challenge was choosing which one.

"Hey, Ryann. Looking good tonight."

Yuck. Brad Wheeler, the sleaziest guy in the tenth grade. He was, for lack of a better term, a man-whore. "Go away, Brad."

"Whoa there, Chiquita. Don't get all pissy. Just saying hello."

I crossed my arms. Glaring at his slicked back, dark hair, I tried not to inhale the half a bottle of cologne he'd thought was a good idea. "Fine. Hello."

"You know, you should really chill. You used to be nice." He stormed away. I suppose I should've felt bad, but I couldn't have cared less. In fact, he might have done well for my next kill. Would anyone miss his obnoxious repartee and greasiness? But he didn't feel like the one. I scanned the room and noticed Hayden doing shots. Off a girl. I moved closer, dying to see what pathetic female would put herself in such a degrading position, and saw carrot-colored hair hanging off the edge of the table. Yvonne. That stupid slut.

The hairs on the back of my neck and arms rose. It would be her.

It was true that I wasn't into Hayden anymore. And it didn't bother me that he'd barely blinked before hooking up with someone else. What I didn't show my friends was my fury over being superseded by that revolting redheaded thing. How dare she take something that was mine? And how could he date that after me? People would put us in the same category! She needed to be taught a lesson.

I sauntered over to the table and put an arm around Hayden. There'd been a time when I'd let Hayden touch me, but that was long before he'd taken on that disease-infested tramp. It was necessary to put my personal morals aside and play along. Anything to stick it to that little bitch. "Looks like fun. Can I have a turn?" I batted my eyelashes and grinned, hand on my hip, chest pushed forward.

Hayden looked me over and gave me a stupid smirk. I wanted to smack it off him, but I had to restrain myself. "Uh, sure. Yeah."

He nearly pushed Yvonne off the table before lifting me up by the waist. "Thanks," I whispered in his ear. Behind him, Yvonne's pouty, seething face was pure magic. I smiled at her, adding a wink for good measure.

"So what do we do?" I asked, feigning naïveté.

Hayden spoke up over the other ten imbeciles hovering around. "I lick some salt off of your stomach, pour a little tequila in your belly button, drink it, and then suck on a lime wedge." He already had the saltshaker in one hand. He motioned with his other hand for me to push my shirt up, exposing my bare stomach. I willed my hands to relax and my fingernails to stay away from his face.

Reluctantly, I did as expected, and the crowd around us erupted with *ohs* and *ahs.*

He bent down and licked an area of my stomach before sprinkling it with a line of salt. Next he took the bottle of tequila and drizzled a small amount into my belly button. It was beyond cold. My teeth clenched, but I kept my cool as he licked the salt off my skin, slurped the tequila, and bit into the lime.

Everyone cheered, clinking glasses and toasting, and I laughed like it was the most fun I'd ever had, satisfied that I was blending in with the dolts. I caught sight of Yvonne as she stormed out of the room, teary-eyed. It was a small win, but it appeased me to know I'd soon find a way to end her.

I pulled my shirt down and jumped off the table. Focusing too much on her would blow my cover. No one could see me go near her, because I couldn't be on the list of suspects when she turned up dead.

But how would I do it?

Olivia had been different. She'd been tiny. I'd known I could overcome her physically. Yvonne, on the other hand, was bigger than me. Not by much, but enough that I couldn't take the risk.

I had homework: finding the most effective way to kill her without losing the thrill. I was ready for the challenge. I'd follow her around, set up a stakeout, find out what she did after school, see where she lived…which room was hers. Considering the cops were probably still fired up over Olivia, I wanted to wait a bit before striking. I'd try to wait, anyway. No promises. I wasn't sure I could keep them.

A half hour later I'd come up with a lame excuse about feeling sick and left the party, but B was too busy hanging all over Asad to care. B's crush on Asad was cute, but the poor girl would never do anything about it. As for him? He was clueless about all things female. He technically wasn't even allowed to hang out with girls—his mother had banned him. She'd freak if she ever learned that B, Mackenzie, Katie, and I were closer to him than simply sitting in an adjacent desk.

I bolted over to the public library, which closed at ten. I couldn't use my computer, after all, to search for which murderous method I'd choose. It was always busy after school with kids doing homework, playing online, and hanging out. It was basically a place to go instead of home, but not tonight. Tonight would be the odd single woman in her sixties reading a book on quilting or gardening and a few staff members.

The fourth floor was usually my choice if I wasn't actively researching. It was the historical wing and my quiet place. No one really bothered to go up there. The computers were old, there was no wireless, and there was no reason for anyone other than history buffs to grace the halls. I went there to be alone and to study The Greats. It was usually just me and an old man named Wally, a war vet who spent his time looking at WWII books and reminiscing about the good ol' days. Wally and I had an understanding. We left each other alone.

When I got there I mostly reread histories of some of The Greats, which were peppered full of creative ideas for me to dig into before I headed home.

The remainder of my weekend I spent wondering what that whore was doing at any given moment. Hanging with Susie or Hayden? Shopping at the mall? Reading a book, carefree at a café? I was feverish with the knowledge that it would all end at my whim.

❖   ❖   ❖   ❖

Monday math class was almost welcome compared to all the family bonding I'd been subjected to over the weekend. It was my worst subject and one of the few non-advanced classes I had. I absolutely hated it, but not quite as much as I hated the teacher, Mr. Hastings. He was an asshole. He'd sit back with his feet up on his desk, call out kids in class who clearly couldn't follow one of his ill-prepared and scattered lessons, and then humiliate them when they couldn't answer. Once, he even made fun of Candace Mitchell when she panicked and began to stutter. He mocked her, stuttering her wrong answer back in her face. Prick.

As appalling as that was, no one did anything about it, or him. Not the 'renowned' Cloverdale school counselors, the vice-principals, or our principal, Ms. Rhinehart. The guy was looking at sixty in the rearview mirror and should've retired a decade ago. But still, he was allowed to stay and grace our hallways and classrooms with his arrogant sarcasm and crappy attitude.

As Hastings prattled on about exponential functions, I played out delicious scenarios for my favorite ginger. I'd narrowed it down to a few prime ideas: one, I could poison her. Two, I could set her on fire. Three, I could fake a suicide, slitting her wrists—of course I'd have to get into her house and drug her, but it was doable.

Decisions, decisions.

By the fourth time she died in my head, the sweet sound of the bell rang out, ending the period.

"I see you enjoyed class as much as I did." Ever

since I'd let Hayden stick his tongue in my belly-button, he'd been hovering.

"It's not my favorite," I said.

"Math blows. We have calculators for anything we're ever going to need. I can't believe they still consider it mandatory after the sixth grade."

I kept walking, and he kept pace. Damn it, he didn't fit into my upcoming plan. As far as I knew, he was still dating Yvonne; therefore, I couldn't risk anyone seeing us spending time together. I'd be linked to him, and he was very linked to her. "Catch you later. I'm running late." I bolted down the hall, not looking back.

Ten steps later, I was accosted again. This time it was Katie. Could I not have five seconds alone? Her hand smacked my butt. My chest tightened. "Ouch. What was that for?"

"Just a good-morning pat. Where are you headed in such a hurry?"

"I've got to get to the gym. I can't be late again, or Coach will be pissed." I continued my brisk pace. If she wanted to talk, she'd have to keep up.

She jogged to catch me. "What the hell's with you today? Skip your morning coffee?"

"Nothing, I'm just busy. Don't you have some-where to be? Like class?"

She laughed it off. "Saw you talking all intense with Hayden. What's that about?" She nudged me. Why was she walking so close? Didn't people under-stand the concept of personal space? We weren't in India. There was room here.

"If you call his revelation of hating math *intense*."
This was exactly what I was worried about. If she'd noticed, others had too.

We were in front of the gym now. "I should really go." I motioned to the girls' changing room. *Take the hint.*

"You coming to the café with us after practice? We're all going."

Tedious. "Not sure. I'll let you know later." I forced my best fake smile and prayed she wouldn't hug me goodbye. I never understood why so many girls wanted to hug every five minutes. Hug hello. Hug goodbye. Hug you're upset, sad, angry. And then she leaned in and squeezed, and all I could do was hug her back like I meant it, ignoring the yuck and the time we were wasting.

She bounded off like she didn't have a care in the world. Truth was, Katie didn't have the IQ to know any different. Poor thing.

Cheer practice. *Again.* Since our field was now under minor construction, practice had been moved to a neighboring school a few blocks away. I headed to the bus. That was another thing I hated. It was gross. Dirty, smelly, and altogether vile. Full of people who didn't bathe and forced their ripeness on other innocent riders. Not to mention the coughing and sneezing. I swear I could feel the microscopic, diseased particles splatter on my face and body. I shivered, wishing I could be like one of those little Asian ladies who wore those medical masks out in public.

Sometimes my mom or dad would drive me to practice, depending on their work schedules, and, as if on cue, a cruiser pulled up.

My dad rolled down the window. "Hey, sunshine! Off to cheerleading?" He made a show of checking his watch. "Cutting it a little close, huh? You can't be late if you want to be captain next year. Coach remembers these things."

I rolled my eyes out of view as I walked around to the passenger side. I slid in and tried not to show my annoyance by slamming the door. "I know. I would've been on time, but now I'll be early."

"Lucky I've got a few minutes to get you there."

Bonus. I could poke around the investigation *and* get a ride. Sliding into the passenger side, I buckled up. "Come on. Can we do it?" I grinned.

"Aren't you too old for that?" His tone was stern, but his eyes lit up like a kid about to do something he shouldn't. He flicked on the lights and sirens.

And I prepared my questions.

Chapter
ELEVEN

"*You* sure know how to make an entrance."

I found Lucas and Asad behind me as I made my way to the field.

"Perks of being a 5-0 daughter. What's going on?" I said, letting them catch up. I was already sweltering and practice hadn't even started yet.

Lucas jogged in ahead and turned to face me, his eyes narrowed. "Heard a little story going round the rumor mill that a certain straight-A, home-by-curfew, still-virgin someone let ex-fling Hayden Cook suck tequila out of her bellybutton on Friday night."

"What?" Asad clutched a hand to his chest. "Say it ain't so."

"You're not even on the team, Asad, so why are you here? And did one of you get an eyeful? Or does someone have nothing better to do than go running to tell you about my seedy exploits? As if a body shot even qualifies." Asad clearly wanted me to feel embarrassed, but it didn't even clock on my radar. I hadn't seen any of my friends around when that particularly disgusting activity occurred, and I wondered who bothered to blab. High school was like a diseased petri dish. Everything spread and multiplied, especially juicy rumors.

Asad and Lucas wore identically smug Cheshire grins.

"Come on, don't be a pussy. Who told you? Not that it's a big deal." Then it hit me. It was obvious. "Yvonne." Crossing my arms, I stared them down. *That little bitch.* "She just can't mind her own business."

"Why do you even care?" Asad asked. "You're not still into him, are you?"

I grimaced. "God no. Ew. I just hate *her*." *Shit.* I had to cool off, or else, when she turned up dead, my strong…*distaste* might be remembered. I tried to look bashful. "I shouldn't say that. It's not her fault. Hayden was the one who owed me something, not her."

The guys looked at each other.

"What? I'm a mature, evolving person."

"Um, sure. Anyway, why would you let his slimy tongue on your body in any capacity?" Lucas pretended to choke.

"I don't know. I was a little drunk, and it seemed funny at the time."

"But Hayden?" Asad piped up.

"Just shut it. I have two words for you: Whitney Gilmore."

His face went ashen and Lucas burst out laughing.

"I never touched her," Asad protested.

"You both just happened to get that itching, burning sensation a week apart?" I asked, happy to get the heat off me. "All I'm saying is, we've each had our unwise moments. We don't judge each other." I winked at them. "Much."

"Where's B? I thought she was coming to watch," Asad said, obviously trying to change the subject.

"She went to see Mr. Baxter. Make-up test for physics," I said. "Her dad called him, insisting she get another chance because she was sick and apparently couldn't use her full potential or some shit like that."

"Not to sound racist, but I thought all Asians were supposed to be geniuses or something, especially with math and science," Lucas said.

Asad sighed. "That is incredibly racist, asshole."

Coach's shrill voice broke through our laughter. It was time to get into formation.

I needed to nail down Yvonne's schedule so I could find the perfect window to get to her, take care of her, and get away undetected. But now I needed to concentrate on what I was doing, or I was going to land on my face again. And after last time, Coach was keeping an eye on me.

❖   ❖   ❖   ❖

Since I had to be home after cheer practice, my next opportunity to study Yvonne didn't arrive until advanced English the following afternoon. It was right after lunch. B and I headed into Mr. Rydell's room. Late twenties and a babe. Unfortunately I couldn't enjoy him, since Yvonne conveniently sat in front of me. I had the distinct displeasure of smelling her repellent vanilla body spray—which she apparently insisted on bathing in—for an hour and twenty minutes every day. And this after I'd eaten the cafeteria's mystery meat. It was all I could do to keep from upchucking in her hair.

I took my seat, keeping my eyes down. Being forgettable was better than being memorable for now.

Our desks were practically on top of each other, and Yvonne's long, nappy hair kept falling onto my desktop. I wanted to bunch it in my fist and cut it off at the roots with one of my knives or, better yet, wrap it around her throat and choke her with it. But I remained perfectly calm, quiet and studious, taking diligent notes on Shakespeare's *Macbeth*—which bored me to utter tears. I had to make myself care so I could keep my A average.

"Can anyone tell me what the trio of witches prophesied in *Macbeth's* opening scene?" Mr. Rydell asked.

Nobody raised a hand. Half the kids in here were high as hell, having smoked up out back behind the evergreens.

I could almost hear my own stomach attempting to digest the cafeteria's version of spaghetti and meatwads—they didn't have the customary ball formation.

"Come on, guys." Mr. Rydell sighed loudly. "The whole play is based around it." He dropped his worn copy of the play down on his desk. It landed with a thud. "Did anyone do the reading?"

It was time to shine. I shot my hand up and smiled.

"Thank you, Ryann." He gestured for me to speak.

"The three witches claim that Macbeth will become King of Scotland."

Mr. Rydell clapped his hands together, relief written on his face. "Yes. Good. Now can anyone else tell me how he actually gets the throne?"

Rustling was the only reply. And so it went for the rest of the period.

It was fun having Yvonne literally within my reach. Not that I could do much in class, but the power and control were intoxicating.

I watched her sneak her phone out of her desk and start texting. It was hard to see, but I managed to read the gist of it. She was messaging back and forth with Hayden. The 'I miss you' and 'I love you' grossness only encouraged me to snuff her out. He'd never told me he loved me. Sure, I didn't love him either, but *her*? *Really*? Next she texted her mom, telling her she was coming home right after school because drama club had been canceled. *Perfect*.

After school, I waited just around the corner from Yvonne's locker. The other bimbos in her slut posse flanked her. Hopefully they'd all leave together. That way they'd be too engrossed in each other's hair flipping to notice I was following them.

My wish came partially true. When Yvonne walked out the front door, Susie Wasserman was glued to her side, all giggles and hair flipping as expected. Dumb and dumber.

Staying a good twenty feet behind at all times, I tracked them to Yvonne's street. Keeping in the shadows of a nearby tree or garage, I watched as they clucked back and forth on her front yard. It seemed like hours before they (predictably) hugged and Susie went off on her own.

I watched Yvonne go inside. After she closed the front door, I jogged across the street. Scanning the area for prying eyes, I made my way around the side of her house. Careful to stay out of view from her windows, I kept low and watched for a sign of her. Minutes later, her bushy orange hair appeared in one of the first-floor windows. I inhaled a long, deep, cleansing breath. My nails bit into the soft skin of my palms, but I relished the pain. It was likely her bedroom. I decided I'd be seeing her there soon. Very soon.

❖   ❖   ❖   ❖

I thought it over that night and decided that Hayden would be the perfect in. It would be simple to get him to tell me when and where they were supposed to meet up next. Perhaps I'd get to her first and he could discover the body. It would be poetic, like *Romeo* and *Juliet*. Except this time Romeo would get a pass.

After class I headed over to Hayden's locker. He was there, talking to some of the loser jocks on the football team, but they all loved me, so it was going to be easy.

"Hey guys, what's up?" I said, pretending to stretch so a touch of my stomach would show.

"Not much," Hayden said, his eyes moving to my waistband. The other morons gave him a fist bump and me a head nod and took off.

I bit my lip and tried to look worried. "Just wanted to make sure things were okay between you and Yvonne. She looked kind of pissed Friday night, you know, with the whole tequila thing. Anyway, I didn't mean to get you into any trouble. I know I'd be upset if the roles were reversed."

He ran his hand through his hair. "She wasn't exactly pleased, but it's cool."

I gave him my best sympathetic smile. "So you guys are still together?"

"Yeah. I smoothed things over with her."

"Are you sure? We girls can be so manipulative— saying we're okay when we're not. Claiming not to be mad, then cutting up the varsity sweatshirt you lent us." I laughed and playfully touched his arm. The more he trusted me, the more he'd tell me.

He leaned against the locker. "Nah, she's wrapped around my finger. I can do whatever I want, and she'll come running back."

His smugness almost made me move him into Yvonne's place. My blade would fit beautifully between his ribs. But he didn't deserve it the way his girlfriend did. Nothing would change my mind about hunting her down.

"I hope you're right. Well, just wanted to make sure you were okay." I moved as though I was about to take off. I knew Hayden. He couldn't stand to have anyone think that he wasn't in control. He'd tell me the details to prove me wrong.

"Of course I'm right. If she was pissed, we wouldn't be seeing a movie tonight."

Bingo.

"Big date. Well, you two have fun." I pretended to get a text so I could walk away. I had what I needed.

Tonight was the night.

Chapter
TWELVE

*I*t was final prep time.

When I got home from school, I jumped in the shower. Then I carefully pulled my wet hair back into a tight bun. I didn't need my DNA accidentally showing up at Yvonne's place.

I put on a pair of black yoga pants and a black tank with my standard navy hoodie over top to obscure my face. Thankfully the weather had cooled down a bit. I shoved everything I would need into my backpack. My tool kit was ready.

This was my moment, and I knew The Greats would be proud. It was only ten days between kills. I was moving fast. And I'd pull it off. Maybe I'd set the record for the most kills in the shortest amount of time. People wouldn't know my name or my face, but my crimes would be infamous.

Dungrave had one theatre, and all the late movies began around eight, which gave me enough time to get myself in through Yvonne's bedroom window and be ready when she returned just after ten. Her uber-Christian parents were strict; there was no way she'd be allowed to stay out any later.

I rode my bike over to Yvonne's house on Warsaw Street. Her mom, dad, and little brother would likely be home. Peeking in her window earlier had allowed me a glimpse of her pink bed with teddy bears on it. Lame.

Both my parents were working, and since Brianna thought I was irrelevant and never paid attention to me, she didn't need to be managed. Half the time she wasn't home anyway, always out with her university friends or moron of a boyfriend.

I did my nightly calls to my parents at their respective workplaces around a quarter to nine. Nothing in my routine could change.

With that taken care of, it was time to go. I wanted to be there in plenty of time in case Yvonne came home early.

I wanted to *feel* the life draining from her and know it was because of me. The knife was my back-up—I was certain I could find a better way to snuff her annoying life out. Something that was quieter than her screaming at being stabbed to death. It would be fun to use something she owned, especially since I was already bringing so much.

I grabbed my bag and headed outside, careful

not to set the alarm yet. It would time-stamp that I'd left. I locked the door and jogged around back to where I'd left my bike. My blood was flowing like I'd had an IV's worth of coffee. With all the excitement, I had to struggle to keep my mind and hands steady.

The steep hills were easier to ride up than usual. Chalk it up to adrenaline-fuelled anticipation. Half a block from Yvonne's house was a row of thick bushes that continued on for about three houses. I glanced around me and saw that I was alone. I jostled my bike in between the bushes to hide it. It was old and beat up. A few more scratches from the branches wouldn't make a difference.

I reached for my hood and yanked it over my head.

It was only a two-minute walk to the house. Her parents' green Honda Civic and silver Mazda were both parked in the drive. I checked again to make sure no one was watching me and inhaled deeply, trying to center myself. I couldn't let my eagerness get the better of me. There could be no mistakes.

Yvonne's house was like any other, with neighbors on either side. On the left lived an old woman who, I'd surmised, went to bed by eight. Her lights were already out. Her chances of seeing me were slim. I ducked when I passed the kitchen window, even though it was high—just in case. I turned the corner and reached Yvonne's window at the back of the house.

The room was dark, and as I'd hoped, her window was open. The warmer weather was on my side. I peered through the glass. There was a minute chance that Yvonne had canceled their movie date, but the room was empty. I held in my squeal of excitement, my heart racing, and surveyed the dim room. There were the same stupid teddy bears and pink bedspread I'd studied earlier. Her closet was located directly opposite me. The double doors were cracked open, but the main entry to the room was shut. Good. The last thing I needed was someone in the house to walk by and see me peeping in from the yard.

I quietly unzipped my bag.

Not wanting to leave any shoe prints on the floor that could be traced back to me, I traded my shoes for socks. The sneakers went back in my bag and my gloves came out. I slid them on, then pushed up the window. The plastic frame made a piercing squeak. My heart stopped. Closing my eyes, I held my breath, as if that was somehow going to stop Yvonne's mom from hearing. I counted to sixty, and when no one came, I exhaled and slowly pushed the window up the rest of the way.

With the screen now totally exposed, it was time to use my brand-new wire cutters. I'd grabbed them from Yeardly's Hardware store yesterday—five-finger discount. The screen was fine and thin and should've been a cinch to cut. Wrong. I jabbed the pointed end into a small opening in the mesh and clamped down. Nothing happened. I silenced the nagging voice in my head pointing out that I should have tested them first.

Whatever, I could handle it.

Using both hands, I repositioned my cutters and secured my grip before giving it my all. They finally moved, and I sliced around the top and side, peeling it away like the top of a sardine can. It took longer than anticipated. All I could imagine was someone waltzing up behind me, tapping me on the shoulder, and asking me what the hell I was doing. Happily, Yvonne's backyard was really private. High wooden fences plus tall trees and bushes. No one would have been able to see unless they were standing in the yard with me or looking down from a neighbor's window, and since it was the old woman, I felt pretty confident I didn't have an audience.

I was halfway in when a ringing blared beside my ear. My grip tightened on the ledge. I nearly cried out in surprise. There was a phone on the table right next to the window. What teenager had a home phone in their room? Hadn't she ever heard of a neat little device that you can text on? More proof she was a freak.

My gaze was trained on the vibrating ancient phone in all its huge, plastic glory. Would someone come to answer it? I didn't know what to do. Should I push myself back out and make a run for it? A second later it stopped, and I heard a high-pitched woman's voice laughing in another room. Yvonne's mom.

I let out the breath I'd been holding and pushed myself the rest of the way through. Hauling my bag after me, I proceeded to carefully return the window to its original position. Yvonne would never notice the cut screen in the dark.

Standing in the middle of her room, I spread my arms wide and took it all in. I wanted to remember what it was like to be among her things. To be in her life. All without Yvonne having a clue.

She was almost sixteen, but her room could've belonged to a ten-year-old. Pink walls with lavender doors and window frames. Stuffed animals and dolls lined on the bookshelves. Even pictures of boy bands cut out of magazines and collaged on the walls.

Pathetic.

Hearing her mom on the phone comforted me. It was as if I had a tracker on her. As long as I could hear her, I'd know where she was.

I checked the time on my phone. It was 9:37 p.m. Now, to wait.

Chapter
THIRTEEN

𝒯aking advantage of the fact that Yvonne had left her closet door open, The element of surprise always appealed to me. Let her get nice and cozy in her little pink bedroom with its loser posters and her shelf of creepy dollies. From behind the closet door I could see into the room enough to know when she'd come in, but I'd still be hidden. Ever impatient, I checked my phone again.

9:48 p.m.
Yvonne would be here any time.

I'd done an amazing job at keeping calm. But I was sure if someone came into Yvonne's bedroom they'd be able to hear me panting away like a dog on a hot summer's day. My palms were sweating and the lining of my leather gloves was wet. Disgusting.

There's no air flow in a closet, especially when you're shoved between piles of clothes, getting pinched and jabbed in the back by metal hangers.

I'd cleared a spot at my feet, kicking her shoes over to the opposite end of the closet floor. My eyes had adjusted to the dimness, though I used the light from my cell to search her crap for what I needed. Talk about tacky. The girl was hopeless. I still couldn't believe that Hayden had gone from me to her. It was like giving up caviar for a can of cheap tuna.

I saw it hanging right in front of me. A thin leather belt—exactly what I'd been hoping for. I clutched it in my hands, pulling on it from end to end. It felt good. Strong. It would hold up for what I was going to do with it.

9:59 p.m.

Blood thrummed through my ears. My skin was hot.

Leaning forward, I peered between the closet doors. A figure entered the room. I pushed forward, lifting my hands up and over my head, about to strike, when I saw blonde hair. It was Yvonne's mother carrying something. I tried not to gasp from the shock and consequence of my stupid error. Her back was to me. Barely breathing, I pulled slowly back into the dark confines of the closet, feeling for the knife in my pocket.

That had been close.

Too close.

My jaw clenched. Through the crack in the door, I could see her place a pile of folded laundry on Yvonne's bed. Oh, shit. What if she started putting things away? How the hell was I going to explain what I was doing in the closet? I had no exit. No escape plan.

I'd been too eager.

My legs trembled.

Her mom straightened one of the stuffed bears—as if it mattered—before finally turning around and leaving. I felt the familiar vibration of my phone in my pocket and quickly placed my gloved hand over it, trying to suppress the sound, not knowing if she'd hear the buzzing from the hallway. I waited for the closet door to slide open and reveal me, but nothing happened.

I checked the screen and saw that B had just tried to call me. Worst timing ever.

10:18 p.m.

The bedroom door creaked open again. I held my breath. The figure walked over to the bed, alone, and turned the lamp on. The dim light highlighted the frizzy knot of hair on the top of Yvonne's head.

I watched her for a minute, taking my time, relieved she was finally here. I needed to remember every movement. Every moment. Not like with Olivia.

Yvonne went to her window and pulled down the shade. She was making this even easier for me. Now there definitely wouldn't be any witnesses. She turned around toward the closet, and I pulled back into the shadows. It occurred to me that she might put some of her clothes away. She'd open the door and find me. I clutched the leather belt harder.

Instead she unzipped her jeans and pulled them off. Standing in her underwear, her back to me, I watched her maneuver through the pile of laundry and grab a pair of ratty gray sweatpants. As she balanced, lifting a leg to slip on the worn material, I crept toward her.

This time the thrill would last.

Olivia had been a kid—too insignificant a conquest to satiate me. Yvonne was a challenge more befitting of my talents. I was in her house, with her parents only a few feet away…

Gripping the belt between my hands, I tighten it into a line.

I need to move quickly or I'll be caught. Trying to remember to breathe, I lunge forward. I wrap the belt around her neck and pull and squeeze as tightly as my arms will allow. She slaps violently at my hands. Gripping them. Scratching at them. I pray no one can hear her.

The more she fights, the harder I work to overcome her. The thin leather wears against my gloves as I battle to keep my grip. A tingling, burning sensation moves up my arms to my shoulders.

She flails, her arms swinging out. She's trying to hit me—not that she knows it's me. Which is a disappointment. I want her to know who is doing this to her. I want her to see my smiling face. I want to look in her eyes as she struggles to breathe. But I have precious little time left. She drops to her knee with a low thumping sound and I hope no one has heard it.

I'm in too far to stop now. I bear down harder. This is taking longer than I thought.

Yvonne's arms drop to her sides. But she's still moving, if only slightly. I muster my last bit of energy, feeling the leather binding tighten just a little bit more.

And then she falls. Limp. In front of me.

I release the belt. I toss it on the carpet and push her body forward, where she lands face down on her bed, knocking over her precious stuffed bears. I reach down and feel for her pulse. Nothing.

I stand, inhaling my triumph. A rush of goose bumps races across my skin, tingling, like a surge of endorphins—the kind you get after a hard run. Looking down, I admire my kill. The additional challenge she posed makes me feel all the more powerful. More alive. I toss one of the fallen teddy bears next to her body. It's pink and wearing a purple bow tie. I want it. Every time I'd look at it, hold it, and feel its soft fur, I'd remember this moment. It frustrates me that I can't have it. My memory will have to be enough. I smile, knowing I'll be able to replay it in my mind any time I want.

The thrill is back, coursing through every cell. I

want to celebrate. Scream into the sky. But I need to get my ass out of here.

I scurry to the closet, grab my bag, and then turn off the lamp again. As my eyes adjust, I make my way toward the window, pulling the shade up just enough to reach under it, open the window, and crawl through.

Carefully, I pull the shade back down, then the window. My heart is thrumming in my ears again.

My hood is back up. I run away from the house, through the yard. Stopping at the metal fence, I swing my bag over and climb. I'm still in socks. The sharp metal bites into my feet, but I push through the pain. When I make it over, I hoist my bag onto my back and sprint. The cool night air burns my lungs, furthering my exhilaration.

I don't stop for a good five minutes. I make it to my bike, where I peel off the socks, replace my sneakers, and book it, careful to ride fifteen minutes out of the way before looping home.

10:46 p.m.

❖   ❖   ❖   ❖

The lights in my house were all out except for one in the living room, just the way I'd left it. I knew Brianna wouldn't be home yet. She was never back before midnight.

I stowed my bike in its usual place by the barbecue and went in through the back. Going straight for the laundry room, I removed all my clothes, including the gloves, and tossed them into the washing machine on hot. But not the socks. They might have had fibers on them from Yvonne's bedroom carpet. I'd have to destroy them. Finding an old metal bucket, I filled it with bleach and dropped them in. Using a metal spoon, I whirled them around the pungent liquid, making sure the chemical saturated every area. I'd leave them until morning under the basement stairs, where no one ever went except at Christmas to get wrapping paper.

With the washing machine on and the socks cooking, I decided to jump in the shower. It was a preventative measure, since I was sure I had no evidence on me. With the water beating against my back, I yelled and hollered—yelps of triumph. I punched the air, like a boxer pumping himself up for a fight.

I'd fucking done it.

When I dried off and changed, I made my celebratory nightcap. I deserved it. I choked down a shot of Grey Goose, then poured myself another with a bit of Coke.

It was near midnight now. I rummaged through my bag one more time, taking inventory. My vision blurred before panic slapped me in the face, sobering me. *Where were my cutters?* I yanked everything out of my pack. My head spun. They were gone. I hadn't closed my bag in case I'd needed something at the last minute. They must've fallen out. But where? In the closet...on her floor...on the grass below her window?

I tried to breathe. Think rationally. I could fix anything. Besides, I'd had my gloves on the entire time. It wasn't as though my fingerprints would be found on them. I'd stolen them, so no receipt or credit card could be traced to me. I started to relax a bit. And then I remembered that I hadn't used gloves in the store. My bare hand had touched them. I began to shake. Surely other people had also touched them in the store: the workers, customers. Maybe my prints wouldn't be detected. There were no fingerprints on file to match them to anyway.

Yes. It would be okay.

It had to be.

Chapter
FOURTEEN

The alarm blared. Cruel morning came so quickly. I suppose five vodkas had been pushing it. In the end, my celebratory drinking had become anxiety-reducing bingeing. I hit the snooze button on my cell with my face still buried in my pillow. I hadn't crashed until three in the morning and I was wickedly hungover. I rolled onto my back and tried to focus.

I sat up. Slowly. So far so good. Both feet on the floor. I grabbed a pair of black shorts and a pink T-shirt. My head spun and my mouth watered. I rushed to my ensuite in time to puke my guts out. When I was sure it was over, I flushed and mouth-washed. Horrible could not even describe how I was feeling. Not to mention stupid. What had I been thinking? I couldn't afford to be hungover. I needed to keep my wits about me.

I forced myself beneath the shower. I was freezing, despite the hot water. I'd drink some Gatorade, eat a few saltines, and be fine in an hour. I had to be. The news about Yvonne would erupt anytime.

Another big day was ahead.

❖   ❖   ❖   ❖

I didn't even make it to school before I got the news. I barely made it into the kitchen. Not that I was complaining.

"Ryann, come here. Sit. There's something we need to tell you." My parents sat at the kitchen table, wearing the same shocked, devastated expressions they'd worn when they discussed Olivia's passing.

I conjured a nervous look. "What's wrong?"

They were each sitting at the kitchen table. My mother patted the chair next to her. "I think you should sit."

I did as I was told and looked around, as though searching for something to explain their behavior. "What? Did something happen to Bri?"

"No, I'm right here, dumbass," Brianna said, entering the kitchen and flicking me in the back of the head with her fingers.

"Ouch." My hand instinctively went to my injury, rubbing it. "Then what is it? You guys look like someone died or something." Inside I smiled. Big grin.

My dad cleared his throat. "Actually, someone did die, honey."

"Oh my God. Who?" I widened my eyes.

My dad cleared his throat. "There was another murder last night. Someone from your school." His eyes met mine, holding them as if monitoring my reaction. As a cop he couldn't help himself. He was always 'on.'

Bri seemed unfazed. She stood against the counter with a mouthful of toast. "Don't look at me. It's the first time I'm hearing about it." Crumbs collected on her lips and chin.

I searched my dad's face again. "Who?"

My mom reached out and put a hand on top of my father's for support.

"A girl in your year. Yvonne Borgdon. I think you know her." He was looking intently at me. I needed to be convincing.

Covering my mouth with my right hand, I let my body tremble and met my Dad's gaze. "I don't understand. How?"

"Somebody killed her in her bedroom last night," he said. "I was the officer called out."

I gasped (which wasn't all faked. I was pleasantly surprised to hear that). "I saw her yesterday in English class." Inside I cheered. My dad was at my crime scene. What had he thought of my work? Keeping eye contact with him, I asked, "Why would someone do that?"

"I don't know, Ry." He paused, letting a small sigh escape. "I need to ask you a few questions." He reached across the table and took my hand in his.

"Are you up for this right now? If you need some time, we can talk about it later."

"Holy shit. Two murders in two weeks. Creepy." Bri finished her last bite, seemingly unfazed by any of the drama.

"Brianna." My mother gave her a weary look.

I took an exaggerated breath. "I don't know how I'll be able to help, but ask me anything." This should be fun.

"Do you know of anyone who would've wanted to hurt Yvonne? Did she have any enemies, any rivals?" Dad had his little notepad and pen out—the one he used for work. "Was she fighting with anyone? Dating anyone?"

A cop was making me part of the investigation. Usually, we killers would have to find some clever way to insert ourselves inside—volunteer for a search or call in anonymous tips—but I was having this handed to me. Elation bubbled close to the surface. I pushed it back down. Saving it.

"I don't know. I mean, Yvonne wasn't super friendly. I didn't really know her. Sure, she had friends, and she did have a boyfriend. She was seeing Hayden."

"Hayden who?" Dad asked.

My mother placed a hand on his arm. "You remember Hayden Cook. He and Ryann dated for a while last year."

"He was that douchey little loser with the bad hair." Of course Bri had to put in her two cents.

Dad's eyebrows rose and he looked both surprised and uncomfortable. He never liked the idea of his girls having boyfriends. "Oh, really? Him? Shit. Did you girls have a fight over him?"

At his mental leap my breathing quickened, and I tried to slow it. "No, we didn't fight over him—"

"Ha! What? You think Ryann axed her?" Bri chortled, clearly overcome with delight.

"Brianna! That's enough. You're excused," Mom snapped, dismissing her.

"Whatever. I'm going to be late for class anyway." Bri grabbed her bag and left through the side door off the kitchen.

Even though it wasn't mine and it was gross, I took a much-needed gulp from the water glass in front of me.

"Now, is there anyone who would want to hurt Yvonne?" Dad asked again.

I shook my head. "I can't think of anyone. We're in high school. No one gets revenge by murder, no matter how pissed off they are. You steal a boyfriend or write *slut* on a locker with red nail polish. You don't kill someone."

"Not everyone is as innocent as they appear, and age rarely matters. There are cases where young people do pretty horrendous things." He sighed.

I bit my lip. Dad was more on the ball than I'd given him credit for. I assumed he'd go right to adult perps, not one of her peers.

"Maybe you can do me a favor. Can you jot down

a list of all her friends? Who she associated with? Where she hung out? Her known hobbies, sports, or extracurricular teams? Basically anything about her. I'll cross-check it against Mrs. Borgdon's list," he said. "Besides, I doubt it's anyone she knows. She was likely targeted by some creep who saw her walking home from school or something. Maybe some of her friends will remember if she mentioned something out of the ordinary."

Write a list. Interesting. I could point him in any direction I wanted. The police would find nothing, since I left no useful evidence, but it would be entertaining to watch them try. "Um, sure. I can do that, but I don't know much about her."

"Because of Hayden?" my dad asked, one eyebrow raised.

"No. We've only had a few classes together. Hayden was an unfortunate coincidence." I crossed my arms against my chest. "Is there anything else I need to know? This is kind of freaky. Bri's right. Two murders in two weeks. Is it the same guy?" I tried to appear anxious, which wasn't hard when I thought about the wire cutters I'd lost somewhere. I tried to stop fidgeting with my hands.

"We don't know yet. The deaths were quite different from each other. Right now it's too early to say for sure, but they don't appear to be connected." He took a bite of buttered toast.

"Was there any evidence at her house, like how they got in? Was she home alone?"

My dad wiped his mouth and took a sip of juice. "My little detective. All you need to worry about is staying in groups with your friends so you're safe. We don't know if this was a random crime of opportunity, or if she was targeted for some reason. We have a lot of good eyes on this. If there's anything, we'll find it."

"Dave, you guys don't have that new boy working on these, do you?" My mother's forehead bunched up into horizontal lines. It was so like her to be concerned about some rookie cop. But that was my mother—overly nurturing. A worrywart.

"Against my recommendation, unfortunately."

"You don't want him to help with the investigation? How come?" I asked. "Because he's young?" Dad was sort of judgy.

"No. It's because Knox is a shitty cop. He thinks he knows everything after a couple of years on the job. I've talked to him, but he just nods and does whatever he wants anyway. He's not ready to be on his own, but that call isn't up to me."

This didn't surprise me. My father was a hard man to please. He was always thinking that someone could do better. It was tiring, and part of the reason my type-A-perfect Ryann persona was so important.

"Besides, there are some rumors about why he left his last precinct."

This piqued my interest. I leaned forward. "Like what?"

"It's not important. It just doesn't look good.

You'd think he'd want to make a good impression, not ruffle more feathers."

I wondered if the only feathers he was actually ruffling were my dad's and Estevez's.

He stretched across the table and took my hand. "I know this is a lot to process in such a short time. Your mom and I have already discussed it, and you can stay home from school today if you need to."

"No, I'm fine, I already told you. I don't want to get behind."

"That's my girl," he said, patting me on the head like I was still a child who needed placating.

"Besides, I have cheer practice tonight. We're going over a new routine for tomorrow night's game." I stood. "I need to finish getting ready for school." My parents nodded and I returned to my room.

I was on to something.

If I stayed away from a pattern of any kind, the cops would have a harder time putting things together. No two murders could be the same. I smiled.

I'd have to get creative.

Chapter
FIFTEEN

$\mathcal{B}$y the time I arrived at school it was humming with the cheerful news of Yvonne's murder.

Huddled groups lined the hallways. Loud whispers and wide eyes surrounded me. I refrained from skipping while whistling a jubilant tune. I hadn't been inside more than five minutes when Bao-yu, Mackenzie, Katie, Asad, and Lucas swarmed me, all of them pale-faced and slack-jawed.

"Oh my God, Ry! Did you hear?" Mackenzie pulled on my shoulder.

Before I could answer, Lucas piped up, "Yvonne was choked last night. Dead." Then, in a very Lucas-like maneuver, he pretended to strangle himself while making gagging sounds. He loved gore. Everything from movies and TV to comics. The more graphic the better.

I held out my arms to hold them off. "Of course I know. My dad was there." That shut them up and upped their curiosity.

"Whoa. What do you know?" B asked, glassy-eyed.

I needed to be careful. I *couldn't* have too many details, or I'd cast suspicion on myself. The fact that my dad was a cop didn't always mean I had more information.. "Not much. It's not like my dad can give me a play-by-play or anything. It's an ongoing investigation." I walked toward my locker, basking in the attention, while the gang followed closely.

"Yeah, but you must have something," Lucas said, sidling up to me. "Or maybe you're keeping secrets from your friends." He put an arm around me.

I pulled away and turned to face them. "Guys, I wish I could give you the grisly details you creeps seem to want, but I don't have them. Are you forgetting that a girl was murdered? And you want to know the logistics? Nice." I spun and started walking, but I could feel them behind me. I buried my smile.

"We're sorry, Ryann," B said. "We got carried away."

Mackenzie huffed. "You didn't even like her. Let's face it. Yvonne was a bitch."

I whirled around. "Maybe she was, but she didn't deserve to die." Point for me.

Shoulders relaxing, she shrugged. "Okay, fine. But it's normal to be curious."

I looked at each one of them. "My dad said she

was strangled in her bedroom. I asked if he thought there was a connection between her murder and Olivia's, and he said it was too early to tell but probably not. He wants me to find out if anyone wanted to hurt her or if she was fighting with anybody. That's it."

"I know a few people who wanted to strangle her," Katie quipped.

We all stared at her.

"What? Too soon?" Katie laughed. "Whatever. I'm not going to pretend to mourn a horrible person. She stole your boyfriend, Ry."

I rolled my eyes. "She didn't *steal* Hayden. I don't own him. We broke up. He can date whoever he wants."

"I wonder how he's doing?" B asked with seemingly genuine concern.

I blinked. That hadn't occurred to me.

And thinking about it now, well, I didn't really care how Hayden was coping. What I did care about was getting to class. Despite how much I loved listening to everyone's speculation, I couldn't ruin my practically perfect attendance.

I was curious what they'd think about me if they knew. They probably wouldn't believe it. Which was exactly why I didn't need to worry—even if the wire cutters turned up. No one would ever think they had belonged to me.

"Hayden's probably feeling really shitty," Lucas said.

"You think he's here today?" I raised my eyebrows.

"I doubt he even heard before he got here," B said. "You really think Yvonne's parents would find her body, call the police, then call Hayden to give him the news? Come on. They're a little busy."

B had a point.

I put a consoling arm on Lucas's shoulder. "You should see if you can find him. He must be freaking out."

Lucas nodded and took off down the hallway with Asad. I faced B, Katie, and Mac, whose face fell as her gaze swept past me. I turned to see what she was looking at and found something I hadn't quite anticipated: my dad, Sergeant Estevez, and some young guy in uniform heading down the hallway toward us. Young guy must have been the rookie in question.

"Isn't that your dad, Ryann?" Katie asked. "And who's the yummy specimen that's with him?"

I managed a nod. Were they on to me after all? My arms and legs felt leaden as the trio of cops drew closer. My mouth and throat went dry and I stifled a cough.

B squeezed me in a half-hug. "You poor thing. You're shaking."

Before I could think to run they were in front of us. "Uh, hi, Dad. What are you doing here?"

"We're investigating Yvonne's death. There are

some people we need to speak with." He seemed preoccupied, scanning the hallway and hardly looking at me.

"Where's the office?" Typical Sergeant Estevez. All business. No *hi*. No *how are you doing? Dick.*

I pointed before forcing words to the surface. "Um, up the stairs and to the right."

The rookie smiled.

"Ryann, this is Officer Knox." My dad regarded Knox with a stern eye. "Ryann is my daughter."

Knox put a hand out. "Nice to meet you."

We shook, and then Estevez settled his gaze on me. "This must be difficult for you...losing two people so close together."

Stay cool. They have nothing. "I guess." I looked down at my feet. B proceeded to side-hug me even tighter, which helped with my poor innocent bystander routine.

"You guys better get to class. You don't want to miss anything," my dad said as the three of them headed up the stairs.

"That. Was. Intense," Mackenzie said. "The whole uniform thing freaks me out. How do you deal with a dad who's a cop?"

I shrugged. "It's not that bad. It's actually kind of cool. I've thought of becoming one when I'm out of this hellhole."

"Really? You never mentioned that before." B seemed surprised.

"I know, but I've grown up around it. I've been

at the station more times than I can count. I like the idea of hauling the bad guys in and getting justice for their victims." It was also a profession where no one would ever suspect me.

I opened my locker and retrieved my books for chem. "Meet in the cafeteria for lunch?"

Mac and Katie nodded.

"Sure, see ya," B said. They took off, and I was finally alone. With everyone gone, the bubble of panic in the middle of my gut burst. I pressed my fist into my stomach, hoping the pressure would ease the motion inside me, and followed them up the stairs. I needed to find out what the cops knew—who they were really here to see. It had to be Hayden. I wondered if he knew yet.

Officer Knox was talking to one of the secretaries. My dad was nowhere in sight, and Estevez… was leading Hayden out from a classroom across the hall from the office. My ex looked shattered—pale and teary-eyed. I slunk back around the corner of the nearest hallway, where I could spy undetected.

My ex was the last person to see her, well, except for her parents. And me. I smirked. Poor bastard. He wasn't equipped for interrogation. Beyond his ego, Hayden was a decent guy. His bravado crumbled to pieces in the hallway. Obviously this was the first he was hearing about his girlfriend's murder. In homicide cases, the police always look at family first, then spouses, boyfriends, and girlfriends. More times than not, the killer is someone close to the victim. Hayden would do nicely.

I could breathe again.

I was in chem for just over forty-five minutes when there was a knock on the door. Mr. Wexler went to answer it, but I couldn't see who he was talking to. He made a gesture and nodded before turning back to us. "Ryann, can I see you for a minute, please?"

I didn't have to look around the room to know that everyone was staring at me. I hoped it was my dad saying good-bye. My cheeks flushed. I had a pretty good idea of who was actually waiting for me in the hall. A knot formed in my gut, but I kept my shoulders back and head high.

Wexler closed the door behind me, leaving me alone in the hall with him.

We were face to face.

"Hi, Ryann. How are you?" Estevez's steely gaze was meant to intimidate me, but I refused to allow it.

I smiled. "Okay, I guess. What's going on?"

"Let's take a walk. I have a few questions for you."

I leaned back against the wall. "I already told my dad everything I know. I'm not sure I can help you."

He stood, his hands on his utility belt. "It's come to my attention that you used to date Yvonne's boyfriend, Hayden Cook."

"Yes. Everyone knows that."

"It's also come to my attention that there was a recent party at the Cook residence where you were seen..." He stopped to check his notepad before continuing to read from it. "Doing body shots with Hayden. Is this correct?"

My skin was hot and prickly. "I don't see how being at the party is relevant to what happened to Yvonne—"

"Answer the question, Ms. Wilkanson. It's not up to you to decide what is or isn't relevant."

I was no longer Ryann—now I was Ms. Wilkanson. He was serious. Fuck. "I let him do one tequila shot. It was stupid. Do you have to tell my dad?" All I could picture was his beet-red face.

"I have a witness that says you and Yvonne didn't get along. Was this a way to get Hayden back or just anger her?"

I put my hands up. "Whoa, I see where you're going with this. Someone told you I wanted him back, and you think that's motive or something?" I gave him an incredulous scowl.

"I'm simply collecting all relevant information from people who knew Yvonne or were associated with her in some way. Why—do you have something to share?" His thick, black eyebrows scrunched as he eyed me. He was trying to read me.

Keeping my shoulders and facial expression relaxed, I said, "I understand and will cooperate fully. The truth is, Hayden and I broke up for our own reasons. I didn't care who he dated next. I was interested in someone else. Yvonne and I didn't really know each other. I wish I could help you more." I smiled, despite my desire to make a run for it. Was he seriously suspicious of me? I was his partner's daughter, for God's sake.

He pinned me with his intense stare. "If you think of anything else, you know how to reach me."

I nodded and waited there, watching him walk away. My heart pounded against my ribs. What would he find if he dug deeper?

I was certain I hadn't touched anything without my gloves except for the damn wire cutters and if the cops found them they wouldn't be connected to me since my prints aren't in the system. My hair had been tied back, though all it took was one strand. My throat tightened. Yvonne had struggled. Was I certain she didn't scratch me? Had I checked? *No…* Would some of my DNA be found under her nails? She had swiped and clawed at my arms. Standing in the hallway, I caught myself rolling up my sleeves to check. There was one faint scratch mark. It was barely visible.

Stop freaking out over nothing.

If Estevez had anything, he'd have cuffed me.

I needed to chill out. I was getting all worked up about things that weren't real. I needed to trust my skill. Like The Greats. I doubt they ever second-guessed their performances.

Chapter
SIXTEEN

*N*o one—including the teachers—could concentrate on their lessons. They tried to move things
along as normally as possible, but by third period, the
principal announced that classes were suspended.
Grief counselors were brought in to help us deal
with Yvonne's murder. A few classrooms were set up
as makeshift therapist's offices where kids lined up
for their turn to talk about their feelings in a 'safe
and supportive environment.' *Barf.*

I went back to my locker. Might as well put my
books away. There was no sense in getting a herniated disk lugging them around. That was odd.
There was something sticking out of my locker
door. Something *green*? I put in my combination
and yanked the door open. Inside was a lavish
bouquet of flowers. My gaze traced the hallway.

Was there anyone around waiting, watching me? Was this some sort of prank?

My face warmed.

No one seemed to be paying any attention to me. Confusion was at the forefront of my mind, followed closely by intrigue and skepticism. I suppose I could have been flattered, but since I didn't have a boyfriend, and most teenage guys don't do the flower thing, I was cautious.

I felt around the petals for a card and found a small cardboard square. I pulled it out of the tiny white envelope. Holding my breath, I read: *From your Secret Admirer.*

I shoved the flowers and card toward the back of my locker. Hopefully no one had seen them.

Doing the best I could to put the creepiness out of my mind, I found Mackenzie, B, Asad, and Lucas at our usual table in the cafeteria. There was no way in hell I was going to mention the flowers from my 'admirer.'

"Can you believe what a circus our school has become?" I asked. This kind of attention was meant for a mass shooting or a hostage situation—not freaking Yvonne Borgdon.

"I know, right? It's intense," B said. "I saw your dad talking to some of the guys on the football team. Do you think they were asking about Hayden? I guess she and Hayden were together last night before she was killed, which totally makes him a suspect."

"Yeah, but he swears he dropped her off and went right home," Lucas said.

"Of course he's going to say that. He needs an alibi. He could have snuck in a few minutes later and killed her. It's the perfect cover. No one would suspect him if he dropped her off, safe and sound, in front of her mom." Asad was really worked up.

I was stunned. His amateur theory was half-right—someone had snuck in.

My turn. "You guys don't really think Hayden could have something to do with this, do you? Has anyone seen him?" I figured he'd been picked up and taken to the station. His parents would've been called before he was questioned. And the police would ask if he wanted a lawyer. If Hayden was smart, he'd say yes. But I knew the dumb, cocky ass would probably decline the option.

"Last time I saw him, a cop was leading him out of here," Asad said.

Just as I'd thought. "Of course they're going to interrogate him. He was with her last. That's a normal part of the investigation. He'll be questioned and cleared."

B made a face. "You seem sure he's innocent."

"Seriously? Hayden's a lot of things, but a killer isn't one of them. Shouldn't we be, like, supportive or something?"

"It's not like he's our friend. We only tolerated him for you. The guy's kind of a douche." Asad had a point.

"No, Ryann's right," Lucas said. "Hayden doesn't deserve us jumping on the bandwagon."

"Who else do people think might be involved?" I needed to know what the Cloverdale rumors were now that there'd been three hours to ruminate on the news. I couldn't wait to hear what fabrications people who 'knew something' had dreamed up.

B stood up from our table. "Anyone wanna take a walk?"

"And go where? School's not technically out," I said, feigning concern for the rules.

B put a hand on my head and petted me. "Sweet Ryann. No one even knows where we are. It's not skipping when there's no class going on to cut. Come on, I want to go by Yvonne's house and see what's happening. I'll be home all night playing Chinese checkers with my grandma, so I might as well have some excitement now."

"Ugh, you're so morbid," Asad said, throwing a french fry at Bao-yu. "And slightly racist." He laughed.

"It's not racist if it's about your own culture. Duh." B picked up the fry from the table and shoved it into her mouth.

"Ew, that's so gross. They wash these tables, like, once a year." Mac pretended to gag.

A chance to visit the scene of my crime without any urging from me? My insides were dancing in celebration.

The Greats were on my side, all right.

"Why not," I said, joining B. "It's not like we're accomplishing anything here. Besides, I can't watch one more stupid chick sobbing fake tears." Thank you, Bao-yu. I knew she was my bestie for a reason. I didn't need to find excuses if everyone planned expeditions to the scenes of my kills. Goes to show how everyone had a morbid, twisted sense of death. I was just honest about it.

"It's settled, then." B clapped her hands delightedly.

I wanted to cheer with her. I'd yet again get to see the scene of my crime in the beautiful light of day, albeit from afar. That was the bonus of Olivia and the alley: I could stand in the very spot I'd killed her. I knew I wasn't getting inside Yvonne's room, but at least I'd be at her house. It would have to do.

I clapped my hands together and angled my gaze at B. "Lead the way."

Chapter
SEVENTEEN

$\mathcal{L}$ucas, Asad, B, and I pulled up in front of Yvonne's house around one thirty that afternoon. Since Lucas was a year older, he had a car. It was one of the perks of hanging out with him. There were still a few police cruisers out front, and the house was taped off, including the front and back yards. I saw a few guys that I didn't know really well, including Knox. Sure my dad had a distaste for him, but it made him all the more appealing. My belly warmed. It wasn't like he was old. I think he was only twenty-one. I didn't mind older men. Maybe he could actually handle me. I wanted to adjust my bra—make the girls stand up more—but I knew I couldn't with my friends so close, so I smoothed my hair instead.

"You guys wait here while I talk to one of the officers." I got out of the car and approached him.

"Hey…Ryann, right? How's it going?"

I nodded, hands in my pockets. "Sorry, I'm horrible with names." I made a squinty face.

He laughed. "I'm Eric. Um…Officer Knox, I mean. How are you doing?"

"Kind of freaked out right now with all this stuff happening." I motioned toward the crime scene behind him.

"You knew her?"

I tried to look like a sweet, lost puppy. "Yeah. Not well, but still. It's horrible what happened to her. I still can't believe it."

"Tough break. You trying to find your dad?"

Keeping up my flirty act, I kicked a small rock on the ground in front of me and gazed up at him sheepishly. "Yeah. Figured he'd be here." I knew very well my father was at the station, but Junior Cop didn't need to know that. "Have you seen him?"

Officer Knox straightened, pulling on his belt and looking nervous. "Nah, I left the school early. I had a few things to do and then I came here. He hasn't been by yet." He glanced past me before refocusing on my face. "Those your friends lurking over there?" He smiled. "Shouldn't you all be in school?" He made a point to check his watch.

"Oh, yeah. Sorry, they're my ride. Regular classes were canceled, so they wanted to leave a little early. See if there was anything interesting going on here. I hope you won't rat on me." Peeking up at him through a wisp of my hair that had fallen over my eyes, I smiled. "Besides, we're not in the way or anything, are we?" I let my lashes flutter and watched his cheeks flush.

"Nah, you guys are fine." I thought he was going to turn around and get back to perimeter security, but he said, "Actually, if you and your friends knew Yvonne, would you mind answering a few questions? We need all the info we can get."

This was the perfect opportunity to show him I was helpful and could be trusted. "I already talked to Sergeant Estevez, so I'm not sure I know anything other than what I already told him, but my friends won't mind. Anything we can do." I put my finger up, signaling that I'd be back in a minute. Jogging over to the car, I knew they'd be thrilled to be a part of the action.

Throw a dog a bone, they say.

A minute later, I was watching B, Lucas, and Asad colorfully tell Knox every uncensored thing they thought about Yvonne. It wasn't pretty. Internally, I was elated. They were helping me more than I could have ever helped myself. Painting Yvonne in a less-than-flattering light would only make the list of potential suspects longer.

Knox was wide-eyed at their reports, scribbling away on his tiny notepad, and my friends were more than happy to keep sharing. I interjected a few times and tried to ask questions about Yvonne, but just as I'd feared, Knox wouldn't say much. Probably because he didn't know much. The only thing he said was that Yvonne's mother had found her around eleven when she went to say goodnight. I wish I'd been a fly on the wall then. I wondered if she'd screamed, cried, tried CPR. I suppressed a boastful grin.

I'd gotten everything out of Knox I was going to. We could leave now.

I faced my friends. "I think we'd better go. Officer Knox is very busy. I'm sure he has lots of important police things to do." I herded my friends back to the car. They'd had their fifteen minutes.

Officer Knox appeared almost sad to see us go. My friends had treated him like a super-cop. I knew how rookies were treated by the other officers; this was probably the first time he'd felt respected. My dad said Knox was too young and immature to have developed good judgment.

Hopefully Dad was right.

Back in the car, my friends were pumped up. I was sitting next to Lucas in the passenger seat, my feet resting on a thin layer of fast food wrappers and old fries.

"Did you see all the police tape?" B asked.

"And how many cops were there?" Asad said.

"I wish we could have seen more. I wonder if her room was ransacked or if there was blood anywhere." Lucas drummed his fingers on the steering wheel.

I cleared my throat. "Why would there be blood if she was strangled?"

Lucas gave me a pensive stare. "I don't know, maybe she was cut by whatever the guy used to choke her."

It still fascinated me the way everybody assumed it was a man.

It was B's turn to ruminate. "Do you think he was, like, hiding in her room, or do you think he broke in through her window after he saw her?"

I had to hand it to her; she was good at this too. "That gives me the creeps. Stop it." Oh, *feigning innocence and fear. Good times.*

Asad and Lucas broke out in laughter.

"Poor baby Ryann is scared. We'd better stop talking, or Precious will have nightmares tonight," Asad teased.

"Fuck off, Asad. Nice to see you're so tough. You could be next, you know," I said, smiling wide.

The others laughed.

"Seriously though, what are the odds of two murders of young girls in two weeks?" B asked.

"Bad stuff happens in Dungrave too. It's not like we live in a Disney movie," I said.

B snorted. "Yeah, but we have, like, drug dealers and prostitutes, not murderers of innocent kids. There's a difference."

We pulled into a McDonald's parking lot. "I'm starving. Let's get something," Lucas said, getting out of the VW beetle his parents had given him. He claimed that he hated it because it was a chick's car, but I knew he secretly loved that piece of yellow crap.

My appetite was ravenous. My friends had never seemed more thrilled. They clearly felt safe enough to enjoy the fear from afar, believing the murders would never touch them. They talked about the cases incessantly. Not that I minded.

It was flattering to know my work made such an impression. Were the moms inside the restaurant keeping their kids a little closer? I hoped so. They should. Most people seemed to be on high alert, waiting for the police to tie this up in a neat bow so they could go back to their safe, lackluster lives. I had noticed fewer people out and about alone. It seemed the buddy system was more popular than ever.

Through mouthfuls of a Big Mac, Asad said, "I don't think the two murders are connected. They're too different. Think about it. The first girl was killed outside in an alleyway. Yvonne was killed in her own bedroom. One was beaten and one was strangled. Plus, they're totally different demographics. That's a huge age difference. There'd be a hell of a lot more similarities between the victims if it was the same killer."

More reassurance that I was doing all this right.

"What if it's the same guy?" B shivered visibly. "What if it's a serial killer?"

And there it was. Out loud. Two beautiful words that, for years, I'd longed to hear attributed to me. I exhaled pure bliss.

"A serial killer? Isn't that a bit extreme?" I wanted to see where they would go with it. I stole a few fries from Asad.

B wrapped her arms around herself. "It's so

freaky to think that we might have two different murderers around here. The idea of one was more than enough, but now two? Shit."

"Relax. I'll protect you," Lucas said, putting his arm around her and winking.

B glared at him before removing his arm from her shoulder and looking at Asad.

"So what next? We just wait around like sitting ducks until whoever this is strikes again?" I said.

Lucas swallowed a fistful of fries. "The cops are on it, including your dad. They'll figure it out. Until then, we should stick together. I'm sure we'll all be fine."

"At least you and I will," Asad replied.

"What's that supposed to mean?" I asked, incredulous.

"Well, the victims were both female. Clearly, we don't fit the victim profile," Asad said, gesturing to himself and Luc before sucking loudly on his over-sized Coke.

I laughed. "Really? Victim profile? You've been marathoning *Criminal Minds* again, haven't you?"

Asad grinned. "It's my favorite show. You can learn a lot."

Indeed. You could.

And I had.

Chapter
EIGHTEEN

That night I found my dad sitting, watching the baseball game on TV. Three empty beer bottles sat on the table beside him. He was reclined and, seemingly, very relaxed.

I plopped myself down on the couch next to his La-Z-Boy. "Those are well earned," I said, pointing to the bottle in his hand.

He smiled and took a long sip. "Sure is. Been a hell of a summer so far. How you holding up?" Even though he pretended to watch the game, I knew he was eyeing me from his periphery.

"I'm okay. I just feel so bad for the McManns and the Borgdons…and Hayden. I saw he was taken in for questioning. Is he a suspect?"

"You know I can't tell you the details of the case, Ryann." He took another swig. The sweet, yeasty scent permeated the air.

"Why? You've told me things about cases before." I tried not to pout.

He put the bottle down and faced me. "Those were different. These are your peers. Hayden is your ex-boyfriend, which makes it a very big conflict of interest to tell you anything."

Crap. "Okay, what about the McManns? Are you guys any closer to catching the guy who did that?"

Silence.

"What about family members? Her parents? Didn't you always tell me that you look at those closest to the victim first?"

He shut the TV off. "What's this all about? You're not acting like yourself. I know these murders are scary, but you can't give them so much power. You're safe. I won't let anything happen to you." He placed his hand over mine. It was calloused, but warm.

He didn't get it. I didn't need his protection.

"Mr. McMann always seemed weird. It was him, wasn't it?" I did my best to look concerned, and Dad squeezed my hand.

"No, we don't think Mr. McMann killed Olivia. No one in the McMann family is a suspect."

"So it's true. We have unknown murderers on the loose." The edge to my voice was priceless. Maybe he'd give me more if he thought I was freaked out.

"Olivia seemed targeted. We have no reason to believe anyone else is in danger. It wasn't random, honey. So you don't have to worry. Trust me."

"Can you at least tell me why someone went after Yvonne? She sat in front of me in English class. If it's someone who knows her...maybe I know them too, or B."

"Ryann, you know I can't—"

"Please. It makes me feel better when I know what's going on."

He huffed, like he was tearing at the seams inside and waiting for something to release the pressure. I knew he wanted to tell me. I could see it in his eyes. In the curl of his lip and the way he leaned forward. And the three beers didn't hurt. "Okay, but what I'm about to tell you doesn't leave this room, you hear me?" His stern, I-mean-business look followed. I nodded. "We have someone who looks good for it. It's someone close to Yvonne. No one's coming after you." He patted my hand and reached for his beer again, downing the last bit of it.

Pretending I was too overcome with relief to speak, I nodded and kissed him on the cheek. I stood up to go, but he put a hand on my arm. "What?" I asked.

"Did you get your test back for math?"

My shoulders eased. I met his gaze and beamed. "Yup. Ninety-seven percent."

His eyes narrowed slightly. "What happened to the last three percent?"

My stomach dropped, and a wave of nausea struck me. "I got one question wrong."

"Huh. Better luck next time, then." He smiled,

turned the game back on, and leaned back in his chair.

❖ ❖ ❖ ❖

The only person I could imagine they had in custody was Hayden. The poor bastard was probably shitting himself right now. I should've felt bad, but I didn't care about him taking the rap for me. So far the cops thought they were looking at two distinct cases: one probably a kidnapping gone bad, and the other a crazy boyfriend who snuck into his girlfriend's house to kill her. I couldn't have plotted it better had I actually staged them that way.

My back pocket vibrated. It was B.

They're holding a public mourning for Yvonne at the school tonight at 8. Should we go?

Excited at the prospect, I hurriedly replied to Bao-yu. *Sure. Maybe there will be news. Wonder if Hayden will be there.*

K. Meet at school at 8, in front. Text when there.

I put my phone in my pocket with a satisfied grin. I imagined myself being interviewed about how I'd done it, about what had inspired me. I would talk about The Greats, the rush, and my urge to kill again as soon as possible so the adrenaline never ran out.

Tonight I would get to be at the center of the grieving and remembrance, all the while basking in the knowledge that I was the reason for it.

❖ ❖ ❖ ❖

My mom dropped me off at the school on the way to the diner. The lawn in front was packed with people, and not only students. Crowds milled across the grass with giant homemade cards, balloons, flowers, stuffed animals, and candles. *Shit.* I hadn't meant to make Yvonne a fucking saint! Before, everyone had thought she was kind of a bitch, and now...what? She was everyone's best friend?

Give me a break.

My fists clenched as tight as my jaw. Teeth scraping, I focused on appearing saddened and shocked—something appropriate for a memorial, that would hide the ball of rage in my gut over the attention that should have been mine.

I probably should've brought a freaking candle to light in Her Majesty's honor. If anyone deserved to be acknowledged, it was me. I was the one cleaning up Dungrave's garbage. Where were my flowers and candles for service to the community?

The journey from the street to the front doors was loud and overwhelming. People were crying, sobbing, and of course, hugging. They were rubbing each other's backs, consoling one another ad nauseam. God, I hoped they didn't try to touch me. The extravaganza seemed more for their sakes than Yvonne's. *Hey, everyone, look at me! Look how sad I am! Look how much attention I need because something happened to someone I said 'hi' to once in ninth grade.*

It was revolting. I wanted to drop-kick the

morons on the grass who were bent over lighting candles in front of a framed picture of her. Yvonne held a single sunflower and smiled that hideous smile of hers.

Checking my phone, I saw that it was eight on the nose.

Where was B? If I had to endure this pity party any longer, I wanted her with me. I texted her again, but before she could reply, I felt a tap on my shoulder.

"Can you believe this scene?" B was practically bouncing on air.

"Yeah, can you imagine what would happen if someone important bit it?" I said.

B rocked back and forth on her heels. "Wanna walk around or something?"

I shrugged, scanning the crowd to see the reactions. "If you want. Are her parents here? Sometimes people give speeches at these things." Maybe seeing the Borgdons would put me in a better mood. I should've been excited. This memorial was like an extension of my hard work, but I felt restless. All these people, and none of them would ever know they were here because of me. It was more depressing than I'd expected. The elation of the kill wasn't lasting either—at least not how I'd hoped it would.

And then something happened to up the ante. "Holy shit!"

"What is it?"

I pointed across the sea of bodies at the news

vans that were just pulling up. There were three of them. Two local stations and one from CNN.

B swatted my shoulder. "Whoa. This is big enough for national media coverage?"

"I guess so." I was a tad stunned, actually.

"I bet they'll cover Olivia's story too." B acted like she was a part of something important just by being there. It irritated me. This wasn't about her— or any of them. Seeing the news vans, people started approaching, clawing to be interviewed. Everyone wanted their time in the sun.

What I'd done was important enough to be head-line news! The knowledge would have to be enough to satisfy me, since I wouldn't get the personal recognition I deserved. Not unless I wanted to go to prison and see the devastated looks on my parents' faces.

B grabbed my arm and pulled me toward the street.

"Wait! What are you doing?" I protested, pulling my arm back and grinding to a halt.

"Going to see what's going on. Maybe we can get on camera. We can be on CNN! Come on, Ryann." She was desperate to move, but my feet were planted. Of course, I'd thought about the possibility of this moment. I pictured the lights and camera focused on me, a reporter pining for every memory or insight I had about Yvonne. They would plead with me to tell them how this sort of terrible thing could happen in Dungrave of all places. Alas, I wasn't sure if being on camera was the best idea. I had to keep a low profile. And what the hell had happened to B's anxiety? Suddenly she wanted the spotlight?

I shook my head vehemently. "No thanks. Not interested in being wrapped up in this craziness, but you go if you want."

B looked disappointed. "But Ry, this is a rare opportunity. It'll be fun."

I needed a countermeasure against the few *colorful* comments I'd allowed myself with B. "Fun? Our classmate was murdered and you think talking to strangers who are out to glorify it is *fun?*"

She deflated, and her gaze moved to her feet. "Sorry. *Fun* is the wrong word. God, why does everything have to be so moral with you? Can't you ever let yourself go? You can't always be the one trying to save the world, you know."

I forced a small smile. I'd let her have this one. "Fine. I'll go up there with you, but I'm staying back a bit. The last thing I want to do is answer questions about my ex-boyfriend's dead girlfriend."

"Fair enough." B smiled and I let her drag me the rest of the way, pushing through groups of familiar faces.

The first reporter was a local guy with Fox 7. He was tall, blond, and generally smarmy looking. His voice was fake, like you always hear with anchorpeople—a deep, over-enunciated baritone. He had his mic in someone's face, and I had to maneuver around a few people to see who was having their moment.

Hayden?

I was positive he would have been kept at the station, if he was the one my dad had been hinting about. Had his lawyer gotten him bail? Maybe he'd only been questioned and then released until his hearing date was set. I needed to get to where I could talk to him. Alone. Which would be nearly impossible in this crowd, with most of its attention focused on the bereaved-boyfriend-slash-possible-murder-suspect.

"Mr. Cook, what can you tell us about Yvonne? You must be devastated. Is it true you were with her only moments before?" Smarmy Reporter only finished one question to ask another. Hayden didn't have a chance to get a word in. He was a shell of his formerly cocky self, with dark circles under his reddened eyes. Watching him being interrogated brought something up in me... *Pity?* Maybe. Was that possible? It was hard to tell.

Hayden was about to reply when his parents rushed in. His dad stood behind Hayden with his hands on his son's shoulders and stared into the camera. "Our son has nothing to say. We are sorry for the loss of this beautiful girl, but we have no further comments at this time." Within seconds, they'd ushered Hayden away, cameras rolling and following his every step.

I needed to get to him. I glanced at B, but she was too hypnotized by the hype to care where I went.

I jogged after the Cooks and called out to them.

The three of them kept moving, but glared over their shoulders.

"I'm so sorry to bother you guys, but can I talk to Hayden really quick?"

"This isn't a good time, Ryann," his father said. "Maybe later."

But Hayden stopped.

"Hayden, sweetheart, come on. We need to get you out of here," his mother begged.

"It'll just take a second, I promise." Hayden pulled away from them and came toward me. Reporters edged in closer around us. His parents had always loved me, which was likely the only reason they were letting him give me any time at all.

"Remember what Mr. Smythe said," his mother shouted after him.

He led me a few feet out of earshot. I looked back. His dad was comforting his mother in an embrace. Things were obviously not great.

"What's up?" He barely met my gaze.

I put a hand on his arm to comfort him. "I saw you leave school with that detective. I'm worried about you. They don't actually think you had anything to do with Yvonne's death, do they?" I tilted my head, shaking it as if no one could believe such a thing.

"I'm not supposed to talk about anything." He crossed his arms tightly, his bottom lip quivering slightly.

"You can trust me."

"Your dad's a cop. You're probably not going to be my number-one choice for counselor."

I dropped my grip on him and looked at my feet. "Fine. I just want you to know that I believe you're innocent and I'm sorry you're caught up in this craziness."

"Thanks."

"Who's Mr. Smythe?" I asked, knowing full well who he was.

He exhaled loudly before clearing his throat. "My lawyer."

"Hayden, come on. We've got to go." His mother waved at him.

He turned to leave.

As I moved back toward the cluster of people, B caught up to me. "Were you actually talking to Hayden?"

"Yeah, I was checking on him."

She laughed. "You were digging for dirt, you nosy little shit." She poked me in the chest with her dagger of a fingernail. "And?"

"He wouldn't say anything—well, only that he has a lawyer." And if he had a lawyer, his parents were really worried he'd go to prison.

My senses began to realign. My body temp was cooling. I was really out of the woods, if I'd ever actually been in them. I started to relax which was great because a clear head meant that number three could be chosen.

"Hey, guys. I'm glad I found you." Mackenzie

dashed up to us. "This crowd is insane. Half the people are here for the show, same as us. You can't convince me that this many people actually knew and cared about Yvonne. She wasn't that popular."

"Small-town mentality," B said.

Mac had a point. I analyzed the faces around us, trying to figure out people's motivations for being here. And who did I see, giant white bandage across her nose and all? Melanie. I put a hand on B's shoulder. "I'll catch you guys later. I have to use the bathroom."

They nodded, and I slipped off into the crowd in *Melanie's* direction. I wanted to watch her for a minute. That was all. Or so I told myself.

Chapter
NINETEEN

$\mathcal{I}$ crept toward her, making sure to keep behind neighboring groups of people. She was with a few of the other girls from our cheer team. They were in uniform—the tacky maroon and cream colors never looked good against my skin. I'd assumed practice had been canceled, since the remainder of classes had been. My stomach fluttered. Did that mean I'd missed it? I never missed. Coach was going to kill me. And why was Mel in uniform? I was sure my elbow to the nose would have kept her out for at least a month.

Wait. Mac wasn't wearing hers. It was just like those little cliquey bitches to come here all gussied up. They even had their pom-poms. They were probably thrilled that the reporters and cameras were here to catch their oh-so-sad school spirit.

Melanie broke off from the rest of the girls and started walking toward the rear gym doors where our locker room was. She must have forgotten something. I hadn't planned to hunt that night, but when opportunity knocks, you answer.

I hustled through the crowd to the front doors. Our school didn't have cameras or anything high-tech. And it wouldn't look strange to be there, since I was a student. I jogged down the hall to the gym. The lights were off, but I'd been in there so many times, I could find my way in the dark. Same went for the locker rooms. Our team's DNA, including mine, covered it, since we used it three days a week. It was the perfect spot for my attack.

But what could I use as a weapon? I hadn't anticipated this kill, but a Great would have made do. Perhaps my initial desire to shove Melanie's pom-poms down her throat would come to fruition after all. I grinned.

Pushing open the locker room doors, I noticed the lights were on. "Anyone in here?" No one answered. I'd beaten her in, but she'd be coming any moment. I needed a hiding place. The room wasn't huge. It was an open space with lockers and cubbyholes lining the walls, and benches underneath so we could sit and get ready before games and practice. Directly behind the dressing area, in an adjoining room, were the shower and bathroom stalls.

That was the only place I wouldn't be seen. I could hide in a bathroom stall. But what if she used the toilet? Shower it was.

I'd never attempted a kill unprepared. My breath quickened. I grabbed a towel hanging beside me that had been left behind. It could be used as a makeshift noose. I got myself behind the curtain just in time.

The door opened.

❖   ❖   ❖   ❖

I squeeze the towel in both hands and steady my stance. I'm ready. My vision is sharp. My mind focused. I hear movement: a locker door opening. It sounds like her footsteps are coming nearer. I peek out from behind the curtain, but pull away quickly when I hear Melanie's voice. Who is she talking to? She must be on the phone. I don't want any witnesses, even if they can't see me. It's risky, but I look out again. Her back is to me. It's a signal to strike. I take a step out of the shower, when the door opens again. I inhale sharply and yank myself back.

"What's taking you so long?"

I know the voice. It's Whitney. Fuck.

My fists ball. My nostrils flare. No! Get out of here.

"Sorry. Tyler called me."

Melanie rustles in her cubbyhole for whatever it is she forgot. Maybe it's not too late. Whitney can still leave. I have hope.

I hear Mel's voice. "Okay, got it. We can go now."

I hear footsteps and the door. I push the curtain back a foot. I'm seething. I missed my chance. My body is halfway out from behind the curtain when the door swings again. I freeze.

"I thought I could hold it. I'll be two seconds."

"Whatever, just hurry up."

It's Whitney. She's coming back here.

I can see the bathroom stalls from the showers, which means that if she looks over, she'll see me. Pulling my body back as far as it will go, I squeeze along the tiled wall and behind the five inches of compressed shower curtain. I try to calm my breathing. My heart races. It's so loud. I panic that she can hear me.

Whitney strolls straight toward me, but veers a tad to the left and closes the stall door behind her.

I hold my breath.

The toilet flushes.

I hear the swing of the door again and wait for a scream or a "Who's there?" Nothing.

She's so close.

The faucet goes on and off.

"Finally. Let's go."

The locker room door shuts again.

I let out a huge sigh of relief and crumple forward.

My relief was short-lived. Rage took its place. I'd never failed before. I hurled the towel down, causing a loud slap against the tile. I wanted to scream out. Punch something. My eye caught Melanie's cubbyhole. It was a miniscule consolation, but it would have to do. I swung my arm through her neatly arranged crap. Lotion and perfume bottles spilled out, along with some tampons and shampoo.

Next I went for Whitney's, since that stupid idiot ruined everything, and did the same to hers. I bolted through the gym doors that went out to the field and found B and Mac—

With a friendly smile on my face.

Chapter
TWENTY

*Y*yonne's memorial was front-page news.

First it had been her murder, and now this. I read it with my morning OJ and buttered toast, which tasted extra bland this morning.

Hayden was featured in Friday's paper, all neat and tidy, his hand in front of his face to shield himself from the cameras before his parents hauled him away.

> Boyfriend Hayden Cook was the last person to see Yvonne Borgdon alive before she was brutally strangled in her bedroom. The grieving, devastated parents are desperate to find out who killed their daughter. Police are still interviewing friends and family as well as several people from the movie theatre…

Blah blah blah.

I tossed the paper across the table, wondering if the police would actually be able to find enough evidence to take Hayden to trial. What could they possibly have on him? Being on a date with her wasn't enough.

Unless they found my cutters? They obviously saw the cut screen. It might be sufficient enough to hold him.

God, I wanted to know, but there was no way I could keep badgering my dad, and besides, I knew he'd never tell me anything highly sensitive. I needed someone I could use. Someone who would be more inclined to give me the inside scoop. Someone too inexperienced to know they shouldn't keep the lines of communication open…

I smiled to myself. It was time to pay Officer Knox a visit.

❖   ❖   ❖   ❖

Knowing all I wanted to do was see Knox made the school day drag. As soon as the final bell rang, I bolted for the station.

"Hi, Ryann. You here to see your dad?" Terry, the receptionist, was always nice to me and buzzed me in no problem.

I scanned the floor for Knox. He was usually on the same shift as my dad, so it was only a matter of determining if he was out on a call or in the building.

The cubicle my dad usually worked at was empty. I made my way over. Maybe there'd be some interesting tidbits left on his desk or open on his computer.

Jackpot. The names and details of a few kids from school were on full display on the screen: Susie and Whitney, Lainey Chu, Matt Mendell, Charles Lafavere, and Pedrum Nadar. The chicks were besties with Yvonne, and the guys were close friends with Hayden. It seemed each had been interviewed. I'd have given anything to peek at those electronic files. My fingers tingled with excitement. One click of the mouse and I'd be in—secrets revealed. I was reaching out my hand when a throat cleared behind me.

"Can I help you with something, Miss Wilkanson?"

I froze, wishing I could disappear. Turning slowly, I hoped it wasn't Estevez.

Knox peered down at me, arms crossed and looking a mix between curious and suspicious. "I asked you what you were doing."

I wanted to do a small dance. It was only Junior. I brushed my hair from my face and straightened. I was wearing my new, level-four push-up bra and could tell Officer Knox was trying desperately not to notice. "Um, I was waiting for my dad. Have you seen him?" I smiled.

"He's in the evidence room. Huh. It looked to me like you were about to browse through confidential documents on a private government computer." He returned the grin. "I'd hate to have to arrest you."

"Give me a pat down," I fired back, enjoying how he blushed. "Truth is, I happened to notice the names of some kids from my school, and I thought I'd check it out. I won't tell anyone if you don't, I promise." My finger found its way up his arm. He pulled back nervously. I motioned for him to bend down. "I want to ask you something—in private."

He looked around the room, which was almost deserted, before half-heartedly leaning toward me.

I placed my hand gingerly on his back. "See, I'm worried about a friend of mine, and I was hoping you could help me understand a few things." I inched back, just enough so he could see the desperation in my eyes—and maybe down my shirt.

He cleared his throat. "Like what?"

"Do you think we can meet after your shift, say around seven, and not tell my dad?" I pouted and regarded him through my eyelashes.

He took a few small steps back, shaking his head. "No, I don't think that's a good idea. If you have questions or concerns, you should talk to your dad."

I leaned back in. "He won't talk to me. He thinks I'm just a kid, but you don't think that, do you, Officer Knox?"

"N-no."

"Please. Meet me. No one has to know, and you don't have to talk about anything that you don't want to. You're the cop here. I'm just a high school girl." He hesitated. I could tell he wanted to say yes; he just needed a little push. "Please?" I batted my lashes again.

Mouthing the word fine, he whispered, "Seven o'clock at Ridgeway Park." He walked away before I could thank him.

I snuck out while Terry was busy with someone at the counter. I had a date to get ready for.

❖ ❖ ❖ ❖

The park was busy with runners, speed-walkers, bikers, kids, and a few small, yappy dogs. It was one of those fancy parks with water fountains, towering rose bushes, and shrubbery shaped like animals. It was Dungrave's pathetic version of Central Park, at a fraction of the scale and beauty.

I sat on the edge of the main fountain and waited. Maybe I was a few minutes early. What could I say? I was excited.

Through the crowd, I saw a tall blond man coming straight for me. I stood, smoothing my skirt, and waved. "Hi."

"Hey." Officer Knox was wearing workout gear. "This is normally my run time, so we'll need to keep it quick."

"Um, sure." I knew he was brushing me off on purpose to keep our little meeting all business. He could try—he wouldn't succeed. The fact that he'd shown up told me all I needed to know. He was interested. It wasn't like he was that much older, anyway. Just enough to get into a load of trouble if we were caught. Which made it even more enticing. Part of any thrill was getting away with things in plain sight.

"Walk with me," he said. It was more an order than a request. He took off in a light jog without hesitation.

I hurried after him in my heeled platform sandals, trying not to snap an ankle. "Thanks for coming."

"What do you want to know?" He clearly didn't believe in small talk.

This was not going how I'd imagined. Did I misread his interest? "Well, I was hoping you could tell me what was going on with Yvonne's case." I did my best to keep up with his long strides.

He scoffed or grunted—I wasn't sure. "You know how this works, Ryann. Your dad's a cop. I'm a cop. I can't give you confidential information about a current case."

"What are you, a fifty-year-old grump who's already jaded by the job? Where's your donut and beer gut?" I laughed and nudged him. I needed to loosen him up or this would go nowhere.

"I do like Krispy Kremes." He smiled.

I tilted my head and twirled a strand of hair around my finger. "I don't need to know every grue-some detail. Can you just tell me if my friend Hayden is going to be arrested or charged? I'm worried about him."

He stopped and faced me. "That's huge! I can't tell you that. Besides, a statement will be released to the media soon. Be patient."

Foolish Knox, he didn't know me at all.

I stepped closer to him, lightly biting my lip. "Please. No one has to know you told me anything. I know how to keep my mouth shut. How can I prove it to you?" Ugh. I was practically begging, which was so beneath me.

"All I'll say is, he's a person of interest."

"Well, duh, he was with her minutes before. I saw Estevez walk him out of school, and he has a lawyer. What else?"

He definitely huffed. "There's not sufficient evidence to charge him. We're still waiting on the DNA results from her room."

"What about Yvonne's parents?"

"They've also been questioned and released. We're still investigating."

"So you've got nothing? Maybe the big boys don't give the hard details to the junior detectives." I snorted.

His demeanor went from hard to harder. "It's a long, difficult process. Give us a break. We have some evidence we're looking at."

I softened my face. "I know. I'm sorry. It's just scary to have these two murders happen. I could be targeted next, or one of my friends." I pretended to shudder and wrapped my arms around myself.

Knox put a hand on my back. "Are you okay?"

I forced a few tears out. "Yeah."

"Shit. Don't be upset." Seeing a girl cry seemed to panic him. Typical male.

"Sorry, Officer Knox. This isn't your fault."

He rolled his eyes and let go of a sigh. "Call me Eric."

I gazed up at him with wide, teary eyes. "Really?"

"Not around the station or in front of any other officers, but sure."

"Thanks, Eric. You're really sweet."

Was he blushing? "We're going to catch whoever's doing this. I promise."

I nodded, wiping moisture from my cheek. "What about Olivia McMann? She was an innocent little girl." I could see in his face that he saw me as a fragile flower. I bet he thought he could be my hero. My night in shining armor.

His shoulders relaxed a bit. "Both parents were cleared. We're still talking to family friends, neighbors, teachers, and coaches—anyone who'd had contact with the family, or Olivia, recently. Even the cable repair man who was at the house three months ago."

I nodded. "You've gone out of your way for me here, and I want you to know you can trust me. No one will know you talked to me, but I need one more favor."

His eyes widened. "More?"

"Yes. Meet me again another time?" I smiled, looking up at him while blocking the sun from my eyes with my hand. He laughed a little and his mouth settled into a thin smile. "I'll take that as a yes."

Before we parted, I got his cell number, plugging it in as E. I officially had an in. A very cute in. Which never hurt.

Chapter
TWENTY-ONE

𝒩ow that I knew Hayden was a serious suspect (they'd definitely find *his* DNA in her room), I was free and clear to concentrate on my next steps. I went to my favorite place. The place I went to get centered, to refocus, and to have a little alone time: the library.

The familiar rush of air conditioning swept over my body. The smell of old books, the humming of the fluorescent lights, and the faint shushing from the old biddies made it feel like home.

I cruised through the stacks until I was at my go-to aisle: True Crime. Letting my fingers run along the spines, feeling the rough edges, and scanning the titles was the perfect pastime. My finger would move until I got the urge to stop, like instinct or intuition. This time it landed on a biography of one of my favorites, Jack the Ripper—oddly fitting since, 126 years later, no one knew definitively who he actually was. I, too, was going to get away with murder. And we'd share the agonizing reality of being unrecognized. I wondered if he regretted not coming forward to claim his due. Sure, he would've gone to prison, but at least his picture would be in all the history books, and his likeness in all the movies that were made for him.

Was it so bad to want credit?

But if I wanted to remain free, I'd have to go on being the sweet, good girl who never argued or caused a problem. I would never be revered for what I'd done, for my elite contribution to our society of serial killers.

I would never be remembered.

My dad told me once that he always remembered the bad ones. Not the petty thieves or the corporate crooks, but the prolific murderers, kidnappers, arsonists, and gangsters. Those people weren't necessarily admirable, but they made an impression. People paid attention. People feared them. And people remembered.

Grabbing the Ripper book, I ambled over to the comfy chairs by the windows and slumped into the worn foam. My brain raced. I tried to read, but images of Olivia and Yvonne overpowered the words on the page. My face and neck became hot and prickly.

I tried to shake the twitchiness, wringing my

hands out at my sides and taking deep breaths. Nothing worked. I understood what was wrong with me. I needed to be productive, and there was only one thing that would make me feel better.

Another kill.

I'd been so close the night before! That little entitled bitch would have been perfect. The book in my hands made its way through the air before smacking into a chair a few feet over. An elderly man reading at a nearby table shot a shaky glance at me.

Had I just thrown a book? In a public place?

"What are you doing?" the man asked, incredulous.

Shit. "Oh, sorry. There was a bug on it. I'm a bit jumpy with them." I made my eyes big.

He mumbled something under his breath before lowering his gaze back to his novel.

I suppose I was a touch wound up. My desperation was probably written all over my face. Ugh. Drinking helped a bit, but it wasn't like I had access to it anytime I wanted. Besides, my mother was home tonight. I couldn't keep sampling my parents' stash. They'd notice soon enough that the level of vodka in the bottle was lower. Bri would know she hadn't done it, and she'd start watching me. Not that Little Miss Perfect could prove anything.

I pictured the list of my victims on the walls of every police station across the country. It would be a distinctive statement attributed to me, even though they'd have no clue who I was. The cops would have already drawn up a criminal profile. Would my characteristics match up? Highly intelligent, detailed, a true master. It would never get them close to the public Ryann. But they might catch a glimpse of the real me.

Upping the ante was part of the fun. Otherwise, what was the point?

I signed into one of the library computer stations and searched options for my next kill. Since I was a well-organized planner, I knew it would be more productive to make a list of what I'd need for different possible scenarios. But, sigh, I couldn't risk it being found.

It didn't matter, since I practically had a photographic memory when it came to that stuff. I decided to research kid killers. It was always interesting to see how others worked.

Fourteen-year-old Joshua Phillips had bludgeoned his neighbor—an eight-year-old girl he used to play with—with a baseball bat. He claimed it was an accident, but I knew better. As a teenager, Graham Young had taken a strong liking to poisoning people. He started by testing it on his family members and had at least seventy victims to his name. And then there were Cindy Collier and Shirley Wolf, two teen girls who killed an elderly lady because they thought it was fun. Hell, they even got a movie made about them.

When I'd read my fill, I logged out. I needed a coffee. My mom always told me not to drink it. She thought I was too young. If she only knew about my affection for vodka and rum.

Outside the library was a small café with a patio. B and I went there all the time, though she'd get a hot chocolate or chai tea latte. Lightweight. I let the steam from my coffee tickle the end of my nose and inhaled deeply before putting in my single sugar and cream. I took advantage of the slightly cooler temperatures, grabbed a table outside, and texted B to see what she was doing. She responded right away.

Trying to get through bio assignment. u?

I wanted her here.

Library coffee place. Take a break?

Yes, please. Be there in 10.

She lived only a few streets away. And while I loved hanging with B, this visit was a means to an end. I needed something from her.

She must have booked it, because in mere minutes she was standing in front of me, blocking the last of the evening sun. "Hey, move to the left. You're interrupting my tan." I waved her over to my other side.

"Gee, sorry, Your Highness." She curtsied. "I'm going to get something to drink." She grabbed her wallet and tossed her bag on the table in front of me. Perfect.

My eyes narrowed on my prize. I felt like Captain Hook about to pillage treasure.

I watched B walk inside and dove a fist into her

purse as soon as she was out of view. I heard the rattle of the pill bottle as I fished it out. Luckily for me, B had panic attacks and was always stocked with Ativan. Today she was my friendly neighborhood pharmacist.

I only needed about seven or eight pills and, considering the bottle was full, I was sure she'd ever notice. She was neurotic, but it wasn't like she counted them. *I didn't think.*

I quickly slid them into a tissue and then straight into my pocket. I retightened the cap and shoved it back inside the bag. Just in the nick of time too, because B was walking out.

"Got you a cookie," she said, offering me a slightly greasy brown paper bag.

"Peanut butter?"

"Of course. It's not my first day as your best friend, you know."

I smiled and took a huge bite. So sweet.

Chapter
TWENTY-TWO

On Tuesday morning I finally stopped to read the posters that had been popping up all over school. They were for the annual summer dance, lamely titled *Cloverdale's Sizzlin' Summer Party.* It was set for Friday night. The year before, as a freshman, I hadn't been able to go. Technically I couldn't go this year either, since it was for juniors and seniors—unless I went as someone's date. I needed to be at this dance. It would be great hunting grounds, and besides, it fit everyone's expectations of me.

Most freshman and sophomore cheerleaders went, since we were the most popular girls. I would go, be charming and funny, and further secure the persona I'd worked so hard to cultivate. All the kids at my school would be reminded of just how sweet I was. And I'd bring the Ativan B had so generously provided. Just in case. You never knew when you might need to subdue someone.

On whom would I bestow the honor of being my date to this pathetic soiree? Leaning against my locker, I surveyed my prospects. I couldn't pick anyone who would get handsy or hopeful. I just needed an in.

Then it hit me. It was so simple. I don't know why it had taken me so long to think of it.

I had a mission and headed straight for him. There was still some time before first period, and I knew exactly where he'd be.

"Every morning like clockwork. Hey, fatty," I said playfully.

Lucas looked up from his squat in front of his locker, his mouth full of our school's grosser version of an egg and sausage sandwich. "I'm not fat, just big-boned," he said, spraying pieces of sandwich from his mouth.

"Ew." I brushed the bits off my arm. In reality, Lucas was skinny, but the kid could eat several meals at a time. I don't know where he put it. We'd joke that he had tapeworms.

"Sup, kitten?"

"I will ignore that blatant sexism because you're about to do me a huge favor."

He finished the last bite and slurped his can of Mountain Dew. "What favor?" His eyes narrowed.

"Walk with me. I don't want to be late," I said, ushering him to his feet.

"God forbid."

"I need you to take me to the dance." I prompted my straightest face so he'd take me seriously.

He saw my expression, stopped walking, burst out laughing, and then frowned. "Shit, you're serious?"

"Dead serious. Come on, I need this."

He shook his head and walked on. "Why the hell do you even want to go? Don't you loathe obligatory school functions?".

This time I trailed behind. "I'm a cheerleader. Of course not."

"Yeah, right." He snickered. "A dance? You know I hate those things. If I was going to suffer through one, it would be for a chick who'd put out."

I whacked him on the arm. "You're a pig. Look at it this way: if you take me, I'll owe you one." He groaned, and I knew he was about to give in. "I'll sweeten the pie. You only have to be my date long enough to get me in the door. Then you can leave." I beamed at him. That was more than reasonable.

He stopped again to face me. "Before I agree to anything, I want one thing first."

I rolled my eyes. "What?"

"Who is so enticing that you're begging me to get you in the door to that snoozefest? And no bullshit. Truth." His eyes practically burrowed into me.

"Doesn't matter," I snapped. He'd buy it more if I acted like it was a huge secret.

"Nope. No outs. You want me to do this, you

have to deliver. Drop a name." He crossed his arms with a giant smirk.

I used the first name that came to mind. "Fine. But you can't tell anyone. Take it to your grave?" He nodded. "Travis Sullivan."

"Bahahaha."

I whacked him on the arm again, only harder this time. "Screw off. I'm not asking your opinion. Will you do it or not?"

"Testy, testy. Don't get all huffy. It's just...he's a dork. His hair alone is embarrassing. And don't you want a guy taller than you?" I stared him down. "What do I get out of my good deed?"

"I don't know. What do you want?" I asked, growing more impatient.

He stroked his chin in a thoughtful, smoking-a-pipe kind of way. "Hmm. Let me ruminate on it. I'll get back to you soon."

"Do you even know what ruminate means? Come on! I hate when things aren't resolved! You know that," I called out after him. He waved, his back to me. "You're lucky I have to get to class. Remember, tell no one!" Satisfied I'd sold my story, I sped off in the other direction.

❖ ❖ ❖ ❖

I tried to stay under the radar in math as much as possible. Hastings had sent a letter to my parents informing them that I wasn't 'working to my potential.' I played it off at home like the guy was just looking out for me, but I despised him just as much as every other kid who'd had the displeasure of sitting in one of his hot seats.

It didn't matter. Hastings wasn't my issue right now.

"Ms. Wilkanson, are you in there?"

I froze, realizing the old goat was talking to me. "Um, yes?"

He stood, his shoulders arthritically hunched. "I was simply asking you to come to the board and show your work for question eight. You can manage that small feat, can't you, Ms. Wilkanson?" He rolled his eyes and waved his arm like he was the freaking Queen of England and I was holding up teatime.

Every kid in the classroom focused on me. Waiting. Wondering what I was going to do. I could feel the heat bubble inside me, rising. He had the nerve to single me out? "I'm actually not feeling very well right now," I murmured. I couldn't snap. It wouldn't be like 'me.'

He made another sweeping gesture. "Isn't that convenient, Ms. Wilkanson. Would your sudden illness have anything to do with your not doing the assigned homework? Perhaps if I asked you to write me an essay on why your homework was unimportant, you would value it more in the future."

"I really am sick. I did do the assignment, but I accidently forgot it in my locker. You can check it if you—"

"Dismissed," he said, waving his hand to me as if

I was a peasant. The collective staring followed me as I gathered my books and slowly made my way out.

Needing some air so I wouldn't erupt with fury, I went to the patio area off the cafeteria and texted Mackenzie. She always skipped classes, wandering around the halls and doing anything other than what she was supposed to. I envied her. She had the freedom to be who she was without worrying about the consequences. She couldn't have cared less if she was expelled…or arrested.

"Hey, freak. Why are you out here?" Mac asked, joining me outside.

"Mr. Hastings is a dick." I smiled.

She nodded, plucking the split ends off her cascade of dark hair. "Let's blow off second period. We'll come back after lunch."

"I don't know. I have English. I really shouldn't miss it."

Mackenzie grunted and shook me by the shoulders. "Ry, do something you're not supposed to do. For once!"

She made puppy eyes at me. I really didn't want to be bugged. Why couldn't I be left alone? "Sorry, but—"

"Come on, Ry. Throw me a bone." She clasped her hands together and got in my face.

"God! Why does everyone always need something from me? What about what I need?" I realized my mistake as soon as Mackenzie's smile turned into a scowl. My throat tightened.

"Fine. Sorry I asked." She turned quickly and began to storm off.

"Wait," I called out. She stopped, keeping her back to me. "I'm the one who should be sorry. You didn't do anything wrong. I'm just mad about Hastings. It has nothing to do with you. Let's go. Take me wherever you want." I prayed she'd let me smooth things over without a fuss. Public Ryann didn't yell at her best friends, especially in public. Thankfully no one was around to see it.

She whirled around, yipping and hollering.

I exhaled. Smiled. I even put my arm around her shoulder for good measure as we headed for the doors.

Chapter
TWENTY-THREE

$\mathcal{M}$ackenzie and I got ice cream cones and sat at the beach for the rest of the school day. While we were there I got the text from Lucas that I'd been waiting for. He was in. I needed to shop.

After much begging and pleading, my mom took me to the mall after school so I could get a dress for the dance. She'd tried to insist that I wear one of her old bridesmaid dresses, which was *not happening.* No way was I wearing anything shiny, crinkly, or sequined, and I wasn't about to be seen with a huge bow on my ass.

The usual buzz of carefree shoppers was notably muted. Fewer women were on their own; instead they were shopping in pairs or groups. People were looking over their shoulders. A few moms nervously scanned the food court for a place to sit, with tight grips on their kids.

I'd caused this alarm. And it was magnificent.

I was in no mood to browse. By the third store I was antsy, so I settled on a short black dress with strappy black sandals. I figured a lot of the girls would be wearing black, and I wanted to blend in as much as possible.

❖ ❖ ❖ ❖

Three days later it was dance night and I was pumped. School had let out an hour early so we had time to get ready. Some girls went to the salon to get their hair and makeup done professionally. My mom had offered—she thought it would be a fun girls outing—but having strangers touch my face and hair and generally fuss all over me was about as pleasant as a root canal.

It only took me forty-five minutes to put my hair up in loose curls and do my makeup. I was fidgeting with my eyeliner when I heard my dad call out that my "date" had arrived. Ew. Referring to Lucas as my date made me gag just a little. I checked the time. It was 6:45. At least he wasn't late for once.

When I reached the bottom of the stairs I saw Luc. He was dressed in a pair of dark jeans, one of those T-shirts with a tuxedo print on it, and a black blazer.

I made a show of looking him up and down. "Wow. You really went all out, didn't you?"

He made a face. My mom piped in with that disappointed tone and told me to be nice.

"What? I am nice. It's only Lucas," I retorted.

"Gee, thanks," he said. "That stings, you know. At least say it when I can't hear you."

My dad snorted and went back to the TV room to catch the remainder of the baseball game.

Mom had her cell pointed at us. "Just one picture," she begged.

Lucas wasted no time flailing his arms around me in a too-tight embrace, smiling with a goofy grin.

"Fine. You get *one*. Then we have to go, or we'll be late." I pushed the corners of my mouth up to the best of my ability.

As we walked to the car, I noticed Luc wouldn't meet my eyes.

"You look pretty," he said.

I gave him a weird glance. "Thanks." He came around to my side and opened the car door. "Um, what are you doing?" I said. "I'm sure I can handle opening my own door, you freak. This isn't a real date."

"Duh. But you asked me to do this, and I'm gonna do it right."

The car ride felt more normal as Luc blared Pearl Jam. Nineties grunge rock was not my thing, but I wasn't going to deprive him of his one joy.

"So, are you just going to walk me in and take off, or what?" I asked.

"Not sure. I might check it out." He parked his yellow junk-heap in the school lot.

"Whatever." I got out of the car. "Wish me

luck," I said, smoothing my dress and making sure I had my clutch, which housed the Ativan. God, I hoped there was someone viable for me in there. It was the perfect setup: loud and crowded, and no one was dressed the same as usual. It would be harder to recognize someone—and that confusion would only be a good thing when people recounted the chaos later.

It had been nine days since I'd killed, and I'd hated every agonizing second. I was still annoyed that Mel had been a miss. It had to happen at the dance. I would make it happen. I needed it to smooth out the rough edges that had spiked up since my last fix. Between snapping at Mac and losing my cool in the library, I was on thin ice. Maybe a kill would hit the reset button.

We shuffled up to the doorway near the school gym and showed our student IDs. The teachers at the door were checking bags. The pills were wrapped in a Kleenex masquerading as a used tissue, but I still had to steady my nerves as I approached Mrs. Dowd, one of the senior science teachers. Chances were slim that she'd open up the tissue to see what disgusting substance was inside. She was looking for obvious stuff: a flask or some weed. She grabbed my ruby red bag and moved a few items around inside—debit card, lipstick, hand sanitizer—closed it, and handed it back to me.

"You have fun now," she enthused, showing me every single tooth with her grin.

I smiled stiffly, and Lucas walked me inside, where the fluorescents had been traded for flashing strobe lights. A guy in the senior class was deejaying some horrible, homemade mix. The music was so loud that my whole body vibrated, even at the edge of the dance floor. Writhing, sweaty teenage bodies bounced before me. I was in hell.

"So where is he?" Lucas nudged me in the ribs with a goofy sneer on his face.

I grimaced. "Who?"

"Don't play innocent. Travis, duh. It's why you dragged me here."

I straightened. "I'll find him. Don't rush me. Oh, I wanted to ask you...if you had any of...you know."

He started to giggle. "Are you nervous?" he asked in a playful voice, the one reserved for singing the *sitting in a tree, k-i-s-s-i-n-g* song. "Need something to take the edge off?"

I shrugged. "No, but it's a party. I want to have fun."

"Pharmaceuticals aren't your usual. You sure?" He suddenly looked concerned.

"Yes, Dad. I'm sure. I'll be careful, and I'll pay you for it later." I held my hand out, palm up.

He glanced around before slipping a tiny white envelope in my hand. "Don't. Get. Caught."

I liked Lucas well enough. He was harmless and nice, but I needed him to get lost so I could get to work. "Go scope out whatever or whoever you were going to. I'm going to take a walk around."

"Fine, but text me if you need a lift home."

"Thanks, Luc. I really appreciate it." He strolled out into the middle of the sweaty mosh pit and quickly disappeared.

The gym always smelled musty and gross, but with the added stench of body odor and Axe cologne, it was completely disgusting. I could hardly take a deep breath without bringing on a coughing fit. I made my way through the middle of the dance floor, ducking and swerving to avoid flying appendages. I wasn't having any luck finding someone worth my talents until…I spotted him. I knew by the sudden nipping in my gut that he was the one.

He was in the middle of the dance floor, tie undone, hair messy with sweat, two girls draped all over him. I wanted to gag. I wasn't sure why he hadn't registered on my radar before. Omar Murphy thought he was God's gift, and not just to women—to everyone. He did nothing in school and always got some loser kids to do his homework, which they did, to bask in his glory for the few minutes he · allowed. The teachers gave him countless free passes because he was a star athlete on the basketball and football teams. He had undeserved offers from top universities. He was cocky and, even worse, pretentious. Just the look on his face and the swagger in his step were enough to make him lucky number three.

I had to get closer, but it was going to be difficult with Whitney and Tyra grinding all over him.

I'd have to keep my eye on him until he went to the bathroom or got a drink. If I could get him alone, I could lure him away. I was charming and hot.

Keeping him in my periphery, I went over to the refreshments table and poured myself a glass of fruit punch. It was sickly sweet, which was perfect. The sugar would help disguise my little concoction of Ativan and whatever Lucas had given me.

I marched over to the corner where no one was paying any attention and removed the Kleenex and packet from my purse. I carefully emptied both into the punch and stirred it with my finger, wiping my hand with a napkin that I later tossed into the trashcan next to me.

I held the cup as I continued to watch Omar from the outskirts of the crowd. He was moving between the girls, and none of them seemed to mind. I mean, have some self-respect. You don't have to share; there are plenty of guys to go around.

Seeing him grind on them—the girls giggling like it was the biggest compliment he could give them—made me sick. I'd had enough of his display. If he didn't step away soon, I was going to have to figure out a way to help it along.

This kill would be different—more inconspic-uous, and less hands-on fun. But in such a public place, I had to keep it as low-profile as possible.

"Why are you just standing there watching everyone? You look like a loser who can't get someone to dance with her." Lucas chuckled.

I wanted to wave him off, make him go away. I was a little busy. "I'm fine." I pointed to the gross, writhing bodies. "Go. Dance. Pick up a chick or something."

He took a sip of what I assumed was punch. I wondered if he'd spiked his own drink tonight. "I thought you were looking for Travis. Where is he?"

Please go away. "I haven't seen him yet." Omar was starting to slow down. He already looked a little drunk, which would help me out immensely.

"Seriously? He's right there."

I followed Lucas's finger and saw Travis standing with a few other seniors across the room. Crap.

Lucas put his hand on my back and shoved me forward. "Come on, let's go talk to him."

I dug my heels into the floor, which did nothing but scuff my new shoes.

"What's your problem?" He eyed me closely. "Are you nervous?" A huge smile took up residence on his face.

I pulled myself from his grasp. "Of course not. I just don't feel like it."

"You're being weird. Come on."

I could see he wasn't going to let it go. But maybe I could use it to my advantage. I could have a dance with Travis next to Omar.

"Fine." I stalked over there. I was on a mission now. Lucas trailed behind me. I approached Travis's little group. "Hey."

He turned to face me, startled. "Hi, Ryann. What's up?"

"Do you want to dance?" I had no time for flirty nuances.

"Um." He glanced over to his friends, who giggled like the children they were, before he faced me again. "Sure."

I yanked him with the hand that wasn't holding the punch and dragged him onto the dance floor. Scanning the faces in the crowd, I searched for Omar. Bingo. I pulled Travis closer to Omar so I could keep my eye on him.

"Do you want to put that down or something?" Travis asked, pointing to my cup.

"Nope. I might get thirsty."

He smiled, clearly feeling awkward—not that I cared what he thought.

We danced to a slow song. Travis tried to pull me close. I could almost feel his hot breath on my face. Ew. If his hands moved any lower, I was going to introduce my knee to his balls.

A minute later, Omar stepped away from his harem, leaving the girls to dance with each other.

I pulled myself from Travis's embrace. "Sorry. I have to go to the bathroom." He stood, mouth gaping, as I walked away.

I trailed a good distance behind Omar.

I'd have bet money that Tyra would follow him, since she stalked him on a regular basis. He loved the attention. His dad had played pro for the Green Bay

Packers, so everyone thought Omar was a pretty big deal. He had his dad's money and good looks, which was why he thought he could do what he wanted to whomever he wanted.

Who better than me to teach him otherwise?

Luckily, Tyra left him alone. I studied him as he headed toward the back hallway where the locker rooms were, and rushed to get there before he did. There was an exit next to the boys' bathroom that led outside to the bleachers and football field. As soon as I spotted him, I called out his name. He looked up, confused, but then smiled. He was flattered, obviously.

I sucked in a breath, stuck out my chest, and motioned to Omar with my index finger. He glanced around as if to make sure I was really talking to him.

I gave him my best come-hither look, and on cue, he headed my way. There were a few other kids in the hall, but no one was paying attention to us.

"Hey, Ryann," he said, inspecting me up and down with hungry eyes.

I wanted to kick him in the nuts for visually violating me. Instead, I traced his chest with my index finger and whispered, "Hey yourself. Saw you on the dance floor. You looked pretty good out there. Too bad about the company you keep." I smiled playfully, keeping my eyes locked on his. Now that he was closer, I could smell the alcohol on his breath. He'd obviously pre-partied or snuck some booze in. Either way, he'd just made my mission a hell of a lot easier.

"I didn't see you. Where were you hiding?" He leaned in closer, and it took all my energy not to punch him in the throat.

"I was here all along. Maybe you should've taken a better look." Ew. The flirting was threatening to make me taste my dinner for a second time. I took his hand and stroked the inside of his palm, which was already clammy. Double ew. "What do you say we take off somewhere quieter? I feel the urge to get to know each other better." If we stayed in this hallway, too many people could see me talking to him, which wouldn't be too strange considering I was a cheerleader and he was a football player. But I didn't want to be remembered as the last person who'd seen him alive.

His eyes widened, and his smile bordered on sleazy. "Lead the way."

I hold his hand and we slip out the exit. When we're outside and the door has closed behind us, I pull him farther toward the field, the drink still in my hand.

"Where are we going?" he asks, clearly trying not to stumble. He's more wasted than I'd realized. Yay. I lead him across the field, though most of the turf is still missing since it's being replaced.

I giggle. "I thought we could...get to know each other better under the bleachers." I push my chest into his arm to illustrate my point and move things along.

This appears to excite him, because he practically

carries me there, wobbling the whole way. I steady him and insist on walking closely beside him instead.

We snuggle up underneath the bleachers, and the only faint light that filters in comes from the floods on either side of the field's end zones. I have to tolerate his germ-infested, slimy hands on me. He starts kissing my neck, cupping my breasts. Groaning all the while. The guy doesn't understand the concept of foreplay, clearly. I pull back and whisper, "Hey, hold on. Can we talk for a minute first?"

He backs up a step and I'm surprised to find he looks worried. "Oh, okay. Sorry, are you all right?" I didn't anticipate this. He seems genuinely concerned that he's making me uncomfortable, which doesn't coincide with his playboy image.

"Yeah, I'm fine. I thought you might be thirsty, so I brought you this." I push the spiked drink into his wavering hand, praying he doesn't drop it.

Omar gives me a confused look. "No, I'm okay, thanks." His lips find their way back to my neck. I shudder at the sensation of wet slobber on my skin. He's almost sucking. He better not give me a hickey, I think, unexpectedly tense. I can picture my parents' faces after seeing that. I'd never be let out again. Besides, who would I say they were from when my friends asked? It's difficult to keep track of too many lies and stories. This needs to remain as simple as possible.

I gently put my free hand on his chest, pushing him back again. "Oh, I think you're going to love the drink I prepared. I made it special for you." I pull him close and murmur in his ear, "It will make what we're about to do a hundred times better. Are you up for it?" I tease his ear with my tongue, and before I know it, he's grabbing the punch and downing it in two swallows. Within seconds, he's all over me again. I have to figure out a way to get him off of me and get back inside the gym. Sure, I could let him die here, but I want the drama of an audience. I let him kiss my neck—no sucking—for a few minutes more to solidify the ruse.

Omar backs away, swaying a bit, and fans himself. "Is it really hot? I feel really hot." Sweat is beading up on his face and neck. I can feel the heat radiating off him.

Crap. My cocktail is taking effect faster than I'd imagined. I need him in the gym.

"Come on. Let's get you inside. You can splash water on your face and get a drink of water. You'll feel better."

He nods and starts walking with me back to the door. "Ryann, I feel really weird."

I have my arm around him. The sweat is seeping through his clothes. More of his foulness is on me. "I know, but you'll be okay soon."

Getting him to the door is no easy feat. The guy is tall and heavy, but we eventually make it, and I'm able to open the door and push him inside before gently shutting it behind him. Still outside, I book it around the corner to the other doorway. No one can see me with him.

❖   ❖   ❖   ❖

I needed to get inside before I missed the action.

Omar was pretty disoriented, but I was hopeful he'd make it back to the gym. I wanted to see it unfold with my own eyes, not hear about it through the grapevine later. I deserved to watch him take his last breath.

I deserved to see the light extinguish from his brown eyes.

Chapter
TWENTY-FOUR

The first yell carried beautifully across the dance floor. Whoever that screech belonged to could've had a promising future as a horror-movie scream queen. Other panicked shouts followed. A pack of scurrying teenagers formed a circle around whom I could only guess was Omar.

Like any innocent dance participant, I joined the herd of kids, pushing and elbowing my way toward the center of the action. Being small had its advantages, and I needed a front row seat. Poor Omar was on the floor. Foaming at the mouth. Eyes rolling back. Convulsions. All classic signs of a drug overdose.

I knew that Lucas had given me some kind of opiate, but I wasn't certain which one. Probably Oxy. That was his usual choice. He'd grind it up and snort it or drink it, claiming it worked faster. All I'd needed to know was that the alcohol, downers, and Ativan would suppress Omar's system and put him into a permanent sleep. My research said that the eight Ativan pills would be lethal when mixed with alcohol. The stuff I got from Luc was insurance. It was the ideal crime. Lots of kids did drugs and drank, especially at parties and school dances. Everyone would believe it was an accidental overdose. No one would trace it to the supposed serial killer in our midst.

Of course, it didn't have the same pizzazz as my other kills, but I had a plan to keep things lively. It was going to be a busy night.

I suppressed a toothy grin and checked my phone to see if Lucas had texted me during the commotion, but there was nothing. Hopefully he'd already left, thinking I was cozy with Travis. I didn't want anything to interrupt the spectacle that was deliciously unraveling before me.

A few of the teachers rushed over, and a school liaison police officer told people to stand back. Someone turned the music off. I watched Mr. Baxter dial 911 and announce that the paramedics were on their way. The strobe lights were off and the regular gym lights on.

As I inched nearer, other kids jostled me as they too tried to get a closer look. I jutted my elbows out, aiming for ribcages. The smell of putrid teenage sweat surrounded me, and I swallowed back my instinctive gag.

Omar was flat on his back on the floor with sweat beads running down his face. His eyes were fluttering and he looked much paler. Mr. Baxter loosened Omar's tie and opened his shirt. He put his ear to Omar's mouth to see if he was breathing. I was practically holding my own breath, wondering if he was dead yet.

Whitney and Tyra appeared. They were hysterical and trying to get to Omar, but Mrs. Jacobson and Mr. Rydell held them back. It was kind of funny the way they carried on, as if Omar actually meant something to them. They were notorious for, shall we say, spreading the wealth, and Omar was simply tonight's conquest.

Mr. Baxter started doing chest compressions, shouting, "Stay with me, Omar! Come on! Breathe."

I wanted to shout, "Go to the light, Omar!"

The ambulance arrived quickly, which displeased me. Omar had only been down about seven minutes. The thought that he might be revived stirred bile in my stomach. The paramedics worked on him, but Omar hadn't moved the entire time, so maybe there was hope. Half the people in the gym had been cleared, against their will; somehow I managed to stay on the side they hadn't evacuated yet.

There's nothing teens enjoy more than drama and gore. Lucas would eat this up, especially since Omar used to rag on him about being on cheer.

Some of the kids had their phones out and were taking video and pictures. The teachers were yelling at them to put them away, but there was too much going on to control everyone. A few people were crying, some with shocked faces—mouths gaping, eyes wide—that sort of thing.

Omar's normally ebony skin was looking more grayish. And other than the paramedic hammering on his chest, he was absolutely still. He stopped to check for breathing and shouted that Omar was unresponsive. My fists relaxed a bit.

I watched in horror as the woman paramedic pulled out the defibrillator. The guy ripped open his shirt and she put the pads on his bare chest, yelled, "Clear," and then shocked him. Omar's body jolted, coming off the ground slightly. The guy looked at the machine and called out a number, and the woman did it again. And again. She shook her head. He was not coming to.

I was so happy I wanted to grab my pom-poms and cheer right there in the middle of the gym floor.

They moved him onto the gurney and rushed him out past the remainder of the crowd. I looked around me. People were clinging to each other. Bawling and shaking. Half of them didn't really know Omar. It reminded me of Yvonne's memorial. Nonetheless, it was contemptible.

Figuring that there was nothing left to see, I called my mom to come get me. I told her that Lucas hadn't been feeling well and had gone home.

My mother didn't do well with stress. She babied me the entire drive, stroking my arm and telling me how frightened I must have been, how traumatized. I got ice cream out of it. It was as though I was five again and had skinned my knee. She did anything she could to soothe my stress, and apparently witnessing an overdose merited a stop at Dairy Mart.

Good news must travel fast, because my phone wouldn't stop lighting up with texts. Mackenzie, Asad, and Lucas were all vying for the horrific details. That was one thing I enjoyed about my friends—they weren't squeamish. They wanted to meet up and hear all about it in person, but I was too busy making other plans.

I wasn't giving up an opportunity for another kill when I had such a solid alibi. I'd been seen at the dance. I'd never be a suspect. I felt inspired. And fate owed me one. Melanie would never know how close she'd come or how lucky she was.

A Great named Gary Ridgway killed between seventy-one and ninety people in the United States over an eighteen-year period. He was one of America's most prolific serial killers. How was I supposed to compare myself with someone like him if I sat back and took my sweet time? I needed to jump at every opportunity. Would Gary have waited around? I don't think so.

And neither would I.

Warm, adrenaline-fueled tingles coursed through me. This kill would be epic.

My mother assumed I needed an impromptu therapy session when all I wanted was to get a move on. Finally, she left. I fired up my laptop. It wasn't hard to find out where Mr. Hastings lived. I knew I shouldn't have been looking up something as specific as his address on my personal computer, but I was too impatient to wait. Besides, no one was investigating me.

I was a bundle of energy, and time was of the essence: I had a curfew. I'd give my mom an excuse about going over to B's. I knew B was at home. She hated dances and social functions in general. It was her gaming night. And I was at her house a ton, so it wasn't likely that mom would check up on me. She never did. If she needed me, she'd text or call my phone.

The prick was in the online yellow pages. You'd think he'd be unlisted, considering how many kids detested him. In his long career, there must have been a lot of haters. I was happy to be the one to dispose of him.

I changed out of my dress, threw on a pair of jean shorts and a black T-shirt, and shoved my tool kit and hoodie into my bag. Grabbing an elastic, I smoothed my hair back into a ponytail. I was ready to go.

"Hey, Mom!" Our house was small enough that my voice carried downstairs. She hated when I yelled, but it didn't stop me.

"What?" she called from the kitchen.

"Can I go meet B for a few hours?"

It was quiet for a minute. "Are you sure that's the best idea? You've had a pretty eventful night already."

I grabbed my bag and ran down the stairs to find her doing the dishes. "I'm fine. How many times do I have to tell you?" I put my arms around her, squeezing her gently, knowing she had a soft spot for that kind of thing.

She hugged me back. "Fine, but not late, okay? Make sure you stay with Bao-yu the entire time. And in well-lit public places. You girls shouldn't be out alone."

"It's only nine o'clock."

My mom pinched my chin lightly and kissed me on the cheek. "I'm your mother. I will tell you to be careful until I die."

"We'll be fine, I promise. I'll call if I need you." I hurried out before she could change her mind.

I grabbed the shed key from the back hall on my way out and made my way into our backyard. I needed a few extra provisions. The backpack-and-biking routine was getting inconvenient. Things would be a whole lot easier when I could drive.

No matter. Burning Hastings's house down and watching that bastard try to save himself would be the icing on the cake.

In the garage there was a small can of gasoline that my dad used for the lawnmower, but he wouldn't miss it tonight. I shook it. It wasn't full, but it contained enough. It wouldn't be too heavy to sling on my back and bike with. I placed it in a garbage bag, tying a knot at the end to contain the smell, then put it in my backpack. Dad also kept a few packs of matches for the fire pit in our backyard. I slipped one into the back pocket of my shorts.

As I made my way out of the shed, I noticed something colorful on a table on our back porch. Whatever it was hadn't been there when I'd come down those steps minutes before. Had it? The hairs on my arms stood on end. My eyes traced the yard and the fence line. I was alone.

I walked closer and realized that it was a flower arrangement. It was much like the one that had been in my locker, only this one was twice the size and in a glass vase. Butterflies plummeted in my stomach.

I searched the arrangement, but there was no card this time.

Two bouquets from a secret admirer seemed unlikely. This one was probably from Bri's loser boyfriend. He bought her flowers sometimes, but she was too much of a bitch to be grateful. She'd probably just left them outside. Besides, the flowers in my locker had a card. These ones didn't. They couldn't be for me.

Satisfied that I was being stupid, I hopped on my bike.

It was a good twenty-minute ride to Mr. Hastings's house on Seventh and Riverside, but I had so much energy from my Omar high that I could've pedaled for hours. I was positively humming. It was as though every cell in my body was individually charged with electricity.

Maybe a tiny part of my brain feared that Omar would make a miraculous recovery, but it was fruitless concern. I'd given him enough drugs to finish the job. Although...the ambulance had gotten there really quick. Fuck. Why was I doing this to myself when I was feeling so good? He was dead. I had to stop worrying. Everything had turned out just fine with the last two.

I tried to fall back into the glow of my many successes. Olivia, Yvonne, and Omar. Soon Mr. Hastings would join their ranks, and he deserved to.

He thought he could treat us like dirt simply because we were young. He had no respect for others, no remorse for his behavior, and I was happy to be the one to give him his penance. I didn't know if Mr. Hastings was a God-fearing man, but he'd better be prayed up.

Some of his bitterness was probably because he was lonely; his wife had been dead for twenty years. The guy could've gone on a date or two. Maybe a lady friend would have softened the edges.

As far as any of us at school knew, Mr. Hastings lived alone. Not even a cat or a bird. He was too mean to care for another living thing.

I rode toward his house and stopped at the foot of his front yard. I could see the flickering of his television from behind a sheer curtain. I checked around me for prying eyes and into the windows of the nearby houses. No one was around, and I was grateful. The night was too humid for the hoodie. I walked my bike over to a row of bushes that separated Hastings's yard from his neighbor's and laid it down on the grass before creeping back to peek inside the window. He was fast asleep in his recliner, drooling out of the side of his mouth. My belly fluttered in anticipation.

The task of tossing gas from a canister didn't require extra precautions like gloves. It was nice. My hands could breathe. I needed to make sure that once Hastings smelled smoke or heard the crackling of flames, he couldn't get out—otherwise it would be a whole lot of effort for nada. I racked my brain on what to do next. I checked the side of his house and found a broom. Perfect. His door had a screen and one of those metal handles that stuck out a bit—just enough, in fact, to stick the broom handle through. If he tried to get out, he wouldn't be able to open it. But I had nothing for the back door. Hopefully with enough gasoline in the front, where he was sleeping, he wouldn't have the time or presence of mind to make it to the back. Maybe he'd sleep through most of it. I'd heard of that before. Still, I wanted him to know exactly what was happening and why. Karma, as they say, is a glorious bitch.

❖ ❖ ❖ ❖

I open my bag and quietly untie the plastic, removing the gas can. Twisting off the lid, I try not to fumble with my shaking, adrenaline-filled hands. Getting caught is a huge risk, since I'm on Hastings's porch. The shrubs over the railing shroud me a bit, but if anyone walks by they'll see me, and how the hell would I explain being on my math teacher's porch with matches and a can of gasoline?

Peeking inside the window, I double-check that he's still snoozing in the chair. He is. I'm elated. I crouch and slowly pour the gasoline along the bottom of the walls, around the windowsill, and finally over the frame of the front door. Hopefully the broom handle will burn before the fire trucks get here and realize that someone's trapped inside. I know they'll figure out that an accelerant's been used, but the broom will make them investigate harder. It points to murder versus simple arson.

I sneak around to the back of the house, impressed with my own stealth, and splash the last of the gas on the back door. The house is old, with a wood frame and, most likely, highly flammable insulation. This thing is going to light up like the fourth of July.

I put the canister back in the plastic, tie it up, and zip it in my bag. Hoisting it securely on my back, I reach into my jeans pocket for the pack of matches I'd taken from my house.

It's time.

I strike the match and immerse myself in the swooshing sound the tip makes when it catches. The sweet smell of sulfur tingles my nostrils and I breathe it in, long and hard, before finally tossing the single burning stick into a small pool of gasoline that's puddled in front of the door. He's not getting out.

The fire whooshes and sears as it speeds along my design. I want to stay and watch it burn, but I know I need to run. I see movement and realize that Mr. Hastings is staring, panicked and horrified, at the back door. We both freeze, separated only by a pane of glass.

He puts his hands out and screams my name for help. He looks so desperate. So terrified. I could help him—change my mind—get him out. Maybe even become a hero if I rid myself of the evidence in time. But as I watch Mr. Hastings fumble with the locked door, fighting for release and rescue—screaming at me to help him—I do the only thing I can.

I swipe a second match along the bottom of the pack and throw the flame onto the accelerant. Fire spreads in an instant, rushing inside the doorframe. I watch his panicked face as he tries the handle, yanking and turning it, but it doesn't open. It doesn't take long before the flames lick up the old, dried wood, which is like kindling.

Before I can register what's happening, Hastings is on fire, and I watch him burn. I study his scream, the way his body thrashes, the orange flame flickering from behind the glass. It mesmerizes me.

Hastings meets my stare.

It is the first time one of my victims has known I'm the person responsible for ending their lives. Me. It's a high in its own right. It fills me up so completely that I don't feel like anything is missing anymore. I am meant for this.

His hand slides down the glass door, as does his body. And he's gone from sight.

Sirens wail in the background. Someone has already called 911, which means neighbors are already crowding around the house in front. If I want to escape now, I have to leave my bike and make a run for it through the backyard.

My mind sputters with what to do. I've never made a mistake before. Everyone saw him humiliate me in class. It wouldn't be a far cry to think I could have done this if my bike is found on his fricking front lawn.

I need to come up with a plan, but first I need an alibi.

B.

I text her that I'm coming over and run, not stopping until I get there.

Chapter
TWENTY-FIVE

$\mathscr{I}$ went to the back door where Bao-yu was already waiting for me. She yanked me inside. I was jittery, incensed that I couldn't enjoy my kill. All I could do was picture my fucking bike on his lawn! My heart thrummed and my legs quaked. Hopefully my smile hid my panic.

"What's up?" B was wearing her pajama bottoms and a tank top, her hair piled in a messy bun on top of her head. She was staring in apparent confusion through her thick, black-rimmed glasses.

Closing the door, I kept my bag with the gas can on me and ushered B down the basement stairs to her room. "Nothing. I was bored, so I thought I'd come by. Why? Got a hot date hidden here some-where?" I faked a laugh.

She hurried up and got in front of me. B always

liked to be in charge. "You're acting weird," she said.

This was the perfect opportunity to plant the seeds for my alibi. "I'm having a bad night. My bike was stolen from my front yard." I lazed on her bed using one of her stuffed animals as a pillow.

She sat next to me. "Shitty. Sorry, Ry, that sucks. Did you call the police to report it or tell your dad?"

My blood iced. *Of course* I would've called my dad. "Um, he's been so busy at work. I didn't want to bug him, but I should call it in." I made a big scene of taking my phone out and dialing. "Hi, this is Ryann Wilkanson and I'd like to report a stolen bike." I waited while the night receptionist realized who I was. "No, don't bug my dad. I'll just do a regular report like everyone else." This seemed to impress said receptionist, who then transferred me to a non-emergency worker. I went through my story: *I was inside for a few hours and then when I came out, my bike was missing from the front yard. I didn't call it in right away because I didn't think of it until my friend suggested it.*

The guy finished getting my details and I hung up, turning to B. "He said they rarely get bikes back once they're stolen. They usually get broken up for parts or driven to neighboring cities where they're sold. They're not going to get much for my piece of crap."

"Well, hopefully they find it. But I know you, Ryann, and something besides your bike is bugging you, so out with it. What's up?" She eyed me intensely, biting her lower lip. "It's Omar, isn't it? You're still in shock?" She grabbed me and squeezed me tight, which surprised me, since we had an unspoken hands-off policy. I had to let her, despite my worry that she'd feel me trembling. "You poor thing. Was it horrible and traumatic and everything I wish I'd been there to see?"

"You're so morbid, B! God! It was horrible, if you really want to know." I didn't even have to try to look upset. All I could think about was being yanked for Mr. Hastings. I could imagine Estevez slapping handcuffs on my wrists in all his haughty glory. I suppressed a roar. How could I be so stupid?

"Ry, you're shaking. Want to tell me about it? It might make you feel better." She continued to stroke my arm while completely invading my personal space. What was up with her?

My nerves were frayed. I had already ignored a handful of texts from Lucas. Looking at her I knew I had to give her something so she'd back off. "I saw a crowd and went over. I managed to squeeze through, and saw Omar twitching on the ground—convulsing. The paramedics tried to save him, but he didn't make it." I looked down in an effort to seem overcome.

"You mean…he's dead?" B's voice raised a few octaves.

I was reminded that I didn't actually know for sure. "I think so. I heard a paramedic say they'd lost him when they were carrying him out. Wait. How did you hear about that? That was only like…two hours ago."

B pulled her knees to her chest. "I talked to Luc. He told me what happened."

My mind was a gridlock of thoughts. Had he stayed at the dance after all? "I didn't see him after he dropped me off. I had no idea he saw." That explained the half a dozen messages from him.

My palms slicked. Was there a chance that Lucas would put together the drugs he'd given me and Omar's overdose? I'd been careful, but had anyone seen Omar with me?

"I know it's a freaky thing, but you're acting really weird, even for you. Are you sure there's nothing else wrong?" B stared so attentively at me that I thought she was going to read my mind and uncover all my dirty secrets.

"Seriously? In the past three weeks, there's been two murders and an overdose. I think I'm due for being a little weirded out. Why are you so calm?" I was practically shouting. "You need Ativan to watch a scary movie. Don't you have any feelings or empathy at all?" I glowered at her.

"Not particularly."

"Bao-yu Ng! Be serious. You're not that heartless. I watched you cry at both *The Notebook* and *101 Dalmatians.*"

She pointed a finger at me. "The Notebook is sad—and I was having my period which means it doesn't count—and *101 Dalmatians* gets a pass!"

I crossed my arms and stomped my foot playfully. "Why?"

"Because we were eight!"

This broke the tension and we both broke into hysterics. It's one of the things I liked most about B. She could always get my mind off things that bothered me.

"Seriously though, you think Omar died?"

I'd been sure, but now I wasn't. If he wasn't, I was in deep shit. "I don't know. Is there anyone we could text who would?"

She shrugged. "I can see if Lucas has any more details."

"Yeah, okay. Try him."

I attempted to relax. This was not all crumbling down around me. I was in control. I would be okay. "Well, what'd he say?"

B glared at the lit screen. "He hasn't heard anything yet."

"Where is he now?"

B typed. "At Asad's."

"Let's meet them somewhere."

B shook her head. "I can't go out now. My parents won't let me. You know their rule. If I haven't gone out by nine, I'm in for the night."

"So don't tell them. Come on," I pressed. "Who's the Goody Two-shoes now?"

She huffed and pouted, making a show of it, but I knew she'd cave. "Fine, but be quiet. You're not exactly known for being light on your feet."

She texted the guys and we agreed to meet them at the late-night café on Mills Street called Strange Brew. "Fifteen minutes," I said.

B finished her text to Luc and went to get a sweater.

"Seriously, you're going to go out like that?" I laughed, pointing at her pj's and hair.

"Oh yeah, I forgot." She motioned to me. "Give me two minutes." Even though she'd die before admitting her feelings for Asad, she'd never let him see her looking like she just crawled out from a coma. She rushed to her bathroom, which was also in the basement.

Grabbing my phone, I looked online for any news on Omar. Nothing yet. How long would it take? I could call Dad. I hummed and hawed for a minute, but my curiosity got the better of me—and so did a much better idea. I scrolled through my contact list until I saw the name, or rather the initial, I needed: E.

I texted Eric and instructed him to call me, but I didn't want to talk to him in front of B. I tiptoed over to the bathroom and heard the water was running. Two minutes to B were ten in reality. My phone vibrated. "Hello," I whispered.

"What's up? You know I'm at work right now— with your dad." He sounded a tad annoyed.

"I know, sorry. Have you received any reports about an overdose at Cloverdale Secondary tonight?"

"Yeah, I heard something about that earlier. Friend of yours?" he asked.

"I knew him and heard about it. Do you know the status on him?"

Eric was breathing heavily. "Like, is he dead?"

I swallowed hard, clutching the phone with a sweaty hand. "Yeah."

"Let me check."

I could hear Eric tapping on a keyboard and other people talking in the background. A lot of other people.

"Busy tonight?"

"It ain't a slow one," he said, pausing again. I heard the clicking of the keys once more. "Looks like he was taken to Mercy General Hospital. He was unresponsive when they brought him in. That's all I got, unless you want me to call the officer posted there."

"No, no, it's okay. Thanks, though."

"Hey. You okay, Ryann?"

"Yeah. Why do you ask?"

"Just checking. It's my cop intuition. Let me know if there's anything else, all right?"

"Thanks."

Bao-yu finally emerged, looking much more presentable in tight jeans and a fitted white top. "Ready?"

I nodded. We crept up the stairs and out the back door. It was only a few blocks to the café, and if the guys were already there—well, they could wait a little longer.

Chapter
TWENTY_SIX

$\mathcal{A}$sad and Lucas were on their second cups of coffee by the time we strolled in.

"What the hell? You ask to meet us and you're ten minutes late," Asad barked.

I elbowed B in the chest. "Blame it on princess over here."

Her face twisted into a scowl. "Hardly. This one walks so slow I'm surprised we made it here this month." She sent me an elbow right back and I laughed.

I focused on Luc. "I didn't see you after we split up. I thought you left. Where'd you go?" My stomach was a solid mass.

He took a huge gulp of his coffee before answering. "I met up with someone."

Asad, B, and I exchanged questioning glances.

"Would you like to elaborate on that?" I smiled a nervous smile. He fiddled with his cup and avoided eye contact with all of us. "Who?" I pushed.

"It's not a big deal," he protested.

B piped up. "Oh my God, was it Natasha?"

Lucas's reddened cheeks blew his cover. We all burst into congratulations and crude jokes, which only seemed to make him more uncomfortable. Natasha was a girl he'd liked for over a year, but she'd had a boyfriend until a week ago.

"You don't waste any time, huh?" Asad joked.

Lucas laughed, relaxing a little. "I've waited so long, and that girl is never single for more than five minutes. I had to get in there and make my move."

That made us bust out even harder. "Make your move? Oh, wait. That must be why you agreed, and so willingly, to take me. I guess I don't owe you after all." I smiled and punched him in the shoulder.

"Wait, what about you? Did you play kissy-face with Travis? That was the whole point, right?" Lucas made fish lips and disgusting sucking noises.

I placed my palms over my eyes for a second. "We danced. But by the time I returned from the bathroom everyone was standing around Omar..."

"Overdosed in front of the whole gym," B said excitedly.

Asad groaned as he stood. "Does anyone want anything? I'm getting a cookie."

B reddened. Asad was a softie, and sometimes B's brazenness was a little too much for him.

"I'll take an iced coffee, if you don't mind?" I said.

Asad nodded and went to the counter.

B leaned in toward Lucas and I. "So, Luc. Did you see it all go down too?" Her eyebrows rose in anticipation.

"Not much. Me and Natasha were sitting on the gym bleachers...distracted." He cleared his throat. "And then we saw a rush of people run to the back. We joined in to see what the big deal was. Omar was already on the ground getting CPR."

"What did Omar look like? Was he foaming at the mouth?" B asked, practically on her haunches.

"Eww, B. That's gross...and heartless," I said.

She rolled her eyes. "I have to get it all out of my system before Mr. Sensitive comes back and judges me." She motioned toward Asad.

"Not that I noticed," I continued. "He was unconscious and was getting worked on. His body did stiffen a bit, though, so maybe he was having convulsions. Whatever he took, it was obviously way too much."

I tensed.

B reached over and took a sip of Luc's coffee. "I wonder if he's dead," she added after swallowing.

I too wondered that very thing and cringed as the minutes passed without confirmation. If he woke up, he might remember, and even if he was brain-damaged he could give me away. The memories of amnesiacs can come back years later. I couldn't live the rest of my life waiting for the cops to come banging at my door. As long as Omar was breathing, I'd be in jeopardy. "Could we find out?"

Lucas looked at B. "Could you ask Asad if he knows any of the numbers of the guys on the football team? They might know."

"Sure, be right back." She made her way over to the counter where Asad was putting cream and sugar in his steaming cup.

Lucas snatched my arm from across the table. I let out a light gasp. "Did you take the stuff I gave you?" His nostrils flared.

And there it was. "Um, no. I lost it. I must've dropped it somewhere in the gym. I went to check my pocket and it was gone." The lie was necessary. It felt like Lucas already suspected me of something, but I wasn't entirely sure what. "Why?"

He pulled his hand away. "I'm wigged out that any of it could get traced back to me." He sat back, running his hands through his hair.

I leaned in, watching Asad and B from the corner of my eye. "I didn't give it to anyone, and I didn't even get to sample it myself. Besides, if anyone did find it on the floor, how could it be traced back to you? It could have been anyone's. It's not like you left your name on it."

"I know, I know. It's just...I've distributed to some of the guys on the football team before, and if the cops start interviewing everyone and asking for names..." He looked inconsolable. "I could get arrested, Ry. My mom will go to an early grave." He paled in front of my eyes.

B and Asad sat back down, and an iced coffee appeared in front of me.

"Wow, why do you guys look like someone kidnapped your kitty?" B said.

I smiled. Luc tried to.

"It's nothing. We just feel bad for Omar," Luc said.

"I'm waiting to hear back from Tyra," Asad said.

I snorted without meaning to. "You actually talk to her?"

Asad put his hands up. "I don't have enemies. You never know when you're going to need something, and thanks to me, you'll be getting the info you want. I don't know why you guys are so concerned, anyway. Yeah it sucks, but Omar isn't our friend." He continued to stir his coffee.

Thank God Luc took this one. "You weren't there. You didn't see him. Sure, we're not friends, but that doesn't mean we don't care if the guy dies."

I nodded but stayed silent. And then Asad's phone went off. I braced myself on the edge of the table and held my breath. *Please be dead. Please be dead. Please be dead.*

Asad's eyes grew wide and I watched him swallow hard. "Omar's alive."

Chapter
TWENTY-SEVEN

*M*y usual deadpan face was failing me. I prayed that I'd shrink into a ball and slip under the table so my friends couldn't see my expression, which I was sure would give me away. But before I could ask questions or even process what I was hearing, my phone rang. It was my dad.

"Hello."

"Hey, Ry, are you at Bao-yu's still? It's kind of late, kid."

"She's here with me at the café. Mom filled you in, obviously."

"Yeah. Are you all right?"

"I'm okay. It was pretty upsetting, but I'm with B and everyone. They're helping me keep my mind off things." I played it up a touch, but I was really upset—that Omar was still alive.

I could hear something more in my dad's tone. Then he said, "Do you know a teacher at your school—a math teacher named Mr. Hastings?"

I thought I would pass right out. My vision became spotty and I put my hands out to steady myself. He was asking me about Hastings. Was I going to get caught by my own father? I wondered if he'd turn me in or help me get away. He loved me, but… "Uh, yeah. He's my teacher." It took everything to keep my voice steady and strong. "Why?"

"He died in a house fire tonight."

I had to play this the same way I had the others— shocked and innocent. "Oh my God!" There was a discernable tremor in my voice for good measure. My friends looked up in alarm and motioned to me with wide eyes. I ignored them to the best of my ability, trying to focus on my father's words instead of my heartbeat thrumming in my ears.

"Ryann, a bike was found on Mr. Hastings front lawn. I identified it as yours. Why would it be there?"

This was it. It was happening. "It was stolen."

"Did you report it?"

"Uh-huh. I didn't want to bug you, so I phoned the non-emergency line and made a report with them a few hours ago."

He sighed. "You should have told me. Then I wouldn't be caught off guard like I was."

It wasn't my intention to make him feel guilty, but I'd take it over suspicion, or worse, accusations. "I know, but there's been so much going on lately.

My bike's not important. It was a junker anyway. Wait. It was at Mr. Hastings's house?" I tried to sound alarmed.

"It was, but since you reported it, it will be easy to add that to the file."

"File?"

"The arson file. Mr. Hastings's house was intentionally set. Gasoline was poured all over the porch and the front and back doors. You don't know anything about that, do you? Have you heard about any angry students?" He sounded genuinely concerned.

"Nothing. I was at the dance, Mom picked me up, and then I went to see B. My bike was gone when I got home, so I walked." I paused, taking a much-needed deep breath. "Why are you asking? Do you think I had something to do with it?" I allowed my voice to rise.

"Calm down, honey. No one is accusing you of anything—especially not me. You don't have a bad bone in your little body. Now, I've got to go. You get home soon."

"Or I can stay over at B's. I'd rather not be alone. Mom has to go in to work soon."

"Okay, but call your mom and let her know."

"I will."

We hung up. I discerned three sets of eyes burning into me and demanding details.

Asad straightened up. "Why was your dad asking you about Mr. Hastings?"

I couldn't lie. Everyone was going to find out soon enough, so I might as well be the one to tell them. Divulging the gory details was the next best thing to actually killing, and this way I could control the delivery. "Apparently my stolen bike was found on his front lawn."

"That's weird," Lucas said.

B shrugged. "And?"

"And his house was on fire." I swallowed the gigantic lump in my raw throat with a mouthful of coffee. "He's dead."

"Holy shit," Asad said.

"Seriously?" B slapped her hand on the tabletop.

I jumped. My nerves were beyond frayed by that point. "Seriously," I managed to say.

"Was it arson?" Luc asked.

"That's what my dad said. I know a lot of people didn't like Hastings, but burning his house down, with him inside? That's insane."

B waved her arm in the air to get our attention. "How do they know it was arson? Maybe the old grump fell asleep with a cigar in his mouth, or the oven on. There are ten ways a fire might have started. It could've been faulty wiring."

I shook my head. "My dad said there was gasoline. It wasn't an accident."

"I wonder how badly Hastings was burned," Luc said.

"This can't be related to the other murders. Those were young girls. This doesn't fit," Asad said. He was

the Sherlock Holmes of the group—he always had a
theory going.

"I guess. But someone wanted him dead," I
added.

"All of this is crazy. Murders…overdoses. All in a
month! This is seriously screwed," B stammered. "It
could be any one of us next."

I placed my arm around her back. "None of us is
getting murdered, so calm down." My friends weren't
on my hit list. I wished I could've reassured them.

B was internally flailing. I knew her well enough
to tell. She was about to shift into full panic-attack
mode. I leaned in to whisper to her. "Take one of
your pills. You'll be okay. Oh, and no more coffee for
you." I pushed all drinks away from her.

She reached into her purse and fumbled for her
pill bottle with shaky hands. I had to help her open
it. They were small and green and melted under the
tongue. Best of all, they worked on her in a matter
of minutes. B loved the drama and gore…until her
mind reached capacity. She usually had no idea it
was coming, and then—wham! I'd known her long
enough to see the signs. I was like one of those
service dogs that warned people of an oncoming
seizure, but I didn't mind. We were all pretty used to
her issues by now, so it wasn't a big deal.

I stared longingly at her pills as I tried to push
my own anxiety down. Omar was alive, and my bike
connected me to Hastings.

"This is so surreal. First Olivia, then Yvonne,

now Mr. Hastings. But they're all so different. If it's the same killer, wouldn't he use the same signature or something?" I asked.

I could tell that Asad couldn't wait to jump in. "It's unlikely that one murderer would use three different killing methods. I doubt they're related."

"So every guy is a suspect? Great," B remarked.

"Why does everyone assume these killers are guys? A woman can kill just as easily as a guy," Lucas protested.

I would have appreciated his open-mindedness, but all the wind had left my lungs. At first I'd wanted a woman to be equally suspect, but that was before things had become precarious. My insides spasmed. If my friends were making these deductive leaps, then the cops might be too. "Asad knows the most about this stuff. How likely is it that a woman committed one of these crimes?"

"Anyone can kill, but yes, traditionally, violent murderers are male. Statistically speaking, men are more likely to use their hands to kill—they stab, choke, beat, et cetera. Women tend to be more hands off: shooting, poison, and arson."

While they worked on their conspiracy theories, I had more important things to worry about, like if Omar had regained consciousness and named me as the one who'd given him the laced punch. It would be his word against mine—unless someone had seen us, but even they couldn't prove I'd actually given him drugs. He could've taken them on his own. He did drink it willingly—it's not like I'd choked it down his throat. He'd known there was something in it, and he'd swallowed it. Not my fault.

But I didn't want to argue my case. There was a way I could finish the job.

Bao-yu had calmed down. "Ry, let's go. I'm tired, and I want to get home before my parents notice I'm gone."

"Sure. I told my dad I'm spending the night at your house, okay?"

She nodded and we both rose.

Lucas and Asad stayed parked.

"I'll let you guys know if there's any updates on Omar," Asad said.

B and I left the café. I texted my mom quickly to tell her I was staying at B's, and we managed to sneak back in undetected. I watched her crawl into bed and pass out. It wasn't so easy for me. My stomach knotted and I was wobbly. Why was this happening to me? The Greats hadn't panicked, and neither would I, especially since there was no evidence to link me to anything. I didn't want to behave like an amateur—not after I'd come so far.

I just needed a little something. Raiding her parents' liquor cabinet would have been too risky, so I helped myself to one of B's little green friends and passed out next to her.

Chapter
TWENTY-EIGHT

When I woke up, B was snoring like a chainsaw beside me. It was a big sound for a wee girl. We'd had countless sleepovers, but I never got used to the foghorn she called a nose.

I was still tired. But I couldn't wait to find out what was going on with Omar and Mr. Hastings so I could decide my next steps. I rummaged through the sheets for my phone. No messages. My relief would likely be short-lived, but at least my dad hadn't called to question me again.

I wasn't in the mood to chit-chat, so I grabbed my stuff and took off, leaving Bao-yu drooling on her pillow. I had to get the gasoline canister back to my house undetected. It wasn't as if my parents would be looking for it. Saturdays were reserved for inside chores and grocery shopping; outside chores were typically Sundays. My immediate problem was refilling the can. My dad might notice if I shoved it back empty. He most likely wouldn't remember how full it was, but as with everything else, I couldn't take the chance.

Walking sucked, even though B lived close. The police would have my bike in evidence, because it was found at the scene of a crime.

I made it to my house around ten and went straight for the back, pulling the plastic out of my bag and placing the gas can in the shed where I'd found it. I hadn't had any cash on me, and I sure wasn't going to carry a ten-pound can of gas three blocks to my house, where anyone could see me. I'd take my chances and claim ignorance if Dad asked about it.

I dragged myself inside, where Mom was doing dishes. She asked the typical 'Mom' questions about my night. I answered quickly and retreated to my room, going straight for my laptop and searching every social media site for news of Omar.

I had to look no further than Tyra's feed. She kept posting poem after cheesy poem, framing each with hearts and angels. What an attention whore. But it led me to a thread where a few of his teammates had posted that Omar was expected to "wake up anytime." My blood chilled and my vision blurred.

I couldn't let that happen.

Some of his friends had posted that Omar's parents had kicked them out of the hospital and were only letting in immediate family. At least there would be fewer people to sneak past. I knew just how to prevent Omar from ratting me out.

Luckily for me, Brianna was diabetic, so I had easy access to syringes. I'd read about how injecting air into a vein could kill someone. The air bubble travels to the brain, heart, or lungs and causes a heart attack, stroke, or respiratory failure. It was the perfect solution to my problem, because there would be no trace of foul play. It would look like the overdose had simply shut down his system. Besides, I'm sure the doctors and nurses were shooting him up with all kinds of meds. It can take a while for an air embolism to show up. In the meantime, the staff would think they'd made a mistake. Case closed.

I needed a way in to his room, preferably unde-tected. The hospital would have surveillance cameras in certain areas. I considered wearing a disguise but figured that could raise even more questions. I was worried that someone would see me, of course, but I'd have to risk it. As far as I knew, the hospi-tal's surveillance cameras were automatically erased every forty-eight hours. They'd mentioned it on the local news once when a patient had escaped from the psych unit.

I hurried to shower, dress, and catch the bus.

The front information counter at the hospital was busy with people. Two crabby-looking blondes manned the desk. One of them had the over-pro-cessed hair of a 1980s groupie. It looked like hair-sprayed cotton candy. For five grueling minutes, I waited in line for my turn.

"Can you tell me what room Omar Murphy is in, please?" I smiled wide, showing as many teeth as possible. Teeth were supposed to indicate an honest smile, or so I'd read.

The woman typed away on her keypad and said, "Room 447," without looking up. "Go to the fourth floor and turn right. It's down the hall to your left."

I was almost too startled to speak. That was easy. Didn't hospitals consider confidentiality or safety? I could've been a crazed killer. Ha ha. Seriously though. It couldn't have been easier if she'd drawn me a map in crayon. I thanked her and headed to the elevator. It might have been easy to get his room number, but getting past his parents would be a much bigger problem.

I felt the syringe in my pocket. My safety blanket. Simply knowing it was there relaxed me. If all went as planned, it would be over soon. My failure to complete Omar's kill wound a nagging sickness through my body. It even stunted my celebration of Hastings. Two kills should have doubled my excitement and enhanced my euphoria, but I only felt like a failure. I'd thought it was bad after the miss with Melanie. This was far worse.

Now I had a chance to set it right.

When the elevator dinged, I stuffed myself inside the metal box with about ten other people who, luckily for me, carried balloons and flower arrangements that obscured my face from the security camera. I couldn't have planned it better.

I was walking down the fourth-floor hallway as instructed, reading the numbers beside the doors, when a realization hit me. Hard. What if Omar didn't have a private room? What if his roommate saw and identified me? My breath hitched.

But I was out of ideas, so I kept going. Two rooms away from Omar's, I surveyed the situation. Standing outside was a middle-aged man with Omar's dark skin—likely his football star father. I didn't see a woman, which meant that either his mother wasn't there or she was keeping vigil at his bedside. My throat tightened and I choked out a cough.

The man's phone rang, and I watched as the sheer majestic force of our great universe caused him to walk away to take the call.

The doorway was clear.

I gave my surroundings a quick three-sixty and casually sauntered over. If I pushed open the heavy door and peeked my head through, I'd hopefully see his mom before she had a chance to spot me.

The coast was clear. Omar had a roommate, as it turned out, but that bed was on the far side of the room with a privacy curtain pulled all the way around it. The only way they'd see me was if they walked around and took a peek. Considering that we were on an ICU floor, I didn't have to worry about that.

Feeling more secure, I walked closer to Omar's bed.

He looked normal except for the breathing tube taped around his mouth and the machines rattling and humming around him. He was hooked up ten different ways. If I injected him, there was a risk that the air embolism would affect him in a matter of seconds and I'd have to get the hell out of there. Instead I hoped it would be minutes or hours before the air bubble fully blocked his artery.

I knew I had to get the hell out of Dodge, but a huge part of me wanted to stay and make sure I finished the job this time. That was the problem with public places: too many good Samaritans were ready to rush in and save the day. And this was a bloody hospital. What if they revived him again?

The hum of the machines lulled me. I had experience with needles. I'd learned to give Bri her insulin a few years before, because she absolutely hated doing it herself. I had to do it when my parents weren't home. It didn't bother me at all. I enjoyed the whole process: grabbing her skin, intruding upon it with a dainty instrument. It was fun.

But it was also easy, because the needle pierced fat. There was no precision needed. Omar would be much more challenging. I had to get it directly in the vein and hope to hell that no one caught me.

The prospect practically paralyzed me, but I had to get my shit together. I was already running out of time.

Chapter
TWENTY-NINE

I pull the slender syringe out of my pocket and pop off the plastic cap. Slowly, I retract the plunger, filling the entire tube with air. More air generates a bigger embolism. The machines beep around me. The smell of cleansers and bleach make my lungs spasm. I move closer to his bed and stand over him. Part of me wonders if he'll open his eyes. What will he think if he sees me? That sweet Ryann is visiting—or would he piece it all together?

He's probably a vegetable.

Omar is hooked up to so many things, but when I see the IV, I realize I have a direct line. I take a relief-fuelled breath, grab the IV attachment, and push the fine needle into it, pressing slowly on the plunger. Quickly, I withdraw the needle, secure the cap, and jam it back into my pocket. I'm about to leave when a weak voice *speaks from behind the curtain. My legs turn to lead.*

"Is somebody there? Hello?"

I turn on my heels and bolt toward the door. I make it into the hallway before I hear a man yell, "Hey! You!"

I turn—God! Why do I turn?—and spot Omar's father. I speed-walk as fast as I can with my back toward him until I'm on the other side of the hospital. Thankfully he doesn't chase after me, but it doesn't stop my body from vibrating and my stomach from churning. That was too close.

I don't stop moving until I find an exit door and swiftly make my way into the stairwell. Four flights of stairs is nothing with this much anxiety flowing through me. I don't mind the temporary panic, because after the fear comes the exhilaration of having gotten away with it. And that rush satisfies me. It's worth this risk and the next.

I make it back to the first-floor lobby and head straight for the front doors without looking back. All I can do now is wait. It's uncertain how long before the air bubble will effectively block his artery. If there's any justice in this world, I won't have to wait long.

I figured that the news about Omar's untimely demise would probably be around school by Monday, which meant I had to occupy myself Saturday night and Sunday.

As soon as I left the hospital I stopped by the café

again and grabbed an iced cappuccino and bagel. I was starving, and it would help explain where I'd been—my mom was going to ask when I was five seconds in the door.

But Brianna was the only one home when I got there, which was a relief. I hunkered down on the living room sofa, stuffing the pretzel bagel into my mouth and slurping the cappuccino.

"Could you be louder or more disgusting? Ew." Brianna hovered over me, her arms crossed, her typically snotty expression full of judgment.

With my mouth full, I said, "Well, hello. And how are you?" A piece of soggy bread fell from my mouth, which prompted another indignant sneer. I smiled and batted my eyelashes.

"You're so gross."

Taking another bite, I said, "What do you want, Bri?"

"Dad was looking for you. He needs to talk to you."

"Why didn't he just call me?"

She rolled her eyes. "I don't know and I don't care. Just call him." She stomped off the same way she'd stomped in.

My phone had been on silent and there was a voicemail. I pushed away the remainder of my breakfast. What did he want? Was it about my stolen bike story? I dialed, heart fluttering. I swallowed hard to push down the last bite of doughy bagel lodged in my throat.

I prayed it would go to voicemail.

He picked up after one ring. "Ryann, where were you?" No hello or anything.

I could hear my breathing, which meant that he could too. "Sorry, my phone was on vibrate. What's up?" I kept my tone light and normal. It seemed like five minutes before he spoke again.

"Ry, I need to know where you were last night."

I swallowed hard, griping the phone tighter. "You already know where I was—"

"Tell me again," he interrupted.

My hand quivered lightly now. "At the dance, and then I came home for a bit before I went to B's."

"What time did you notice your bike was missing?" he asked in his work voice. It sent shivers up my spine. Was I being questioned?

"Um, I don't know. Before I went to B's. I had to walk over."

His breathing grew heavier. "I need as exact a time as you can give me."

"What's this about, Dad? You're scaring me." It was the truth.

"What time, Ryann?" His voice took on an edge that he rarely used with me.

"I don't know. About 9:45 or so. What's going on?" I was practically begging now.

"An eyewitness claims to have seen a girl matching your description in front of Mr. Hastings's home just before the fire." Tension coated his voice.

"That's ridiculous! I was with Mom, then B. You

can ask them both. They'll tell you." I paused. It was now or never. "Wait a second. You think I had something to do with what happened to Mr. Hastings! This isn't the first time you've questioned me. I know the drill," I said, practically yelling. I figured I'd amp it up and give him the expected reaction: righteous indignation.

"A witness described seeing a girl nearly identical to you outside his residence around 9:30 p.m. And your bike was found at the scene. So I'm going to ask you one more time. Where were you last night at 9:30?"

"At B's house. I promise. How could you even ask me that?"

His razor tone softened. "Look, honey, an officer is going to be talking to you. Just answer his questions the same way you did for me."

I could hear how hard it was for my dad to get the words out. He doubted me. I could feel it in my bones.

"Once they interview B and get an alibi for you, you'll be cleared."

Cleared? My body practically seized up.

"I'm going to be interrogated?" My vision was fuzzing. I couldn't focus.

"I'm going to pick you up and bring you down to the station. Everything's going to be fine. Just tell the truth. I'll be there in fifteen minutes, so be ready." He hung up before I could argue.

I needed something to take the edge off.

Bri had locked herself in her room as per usual. I went for the liquor cabinet and poured a single shot into a glass. Downed it in one go. I poured a second and did the same, then brushed my teeth and mouthwashed.

I stood at the window and waited for the cruiser, practicing my story in my head. This couldn't be it. I had so much more to prove.

I shook off the unwarranted worry. I could do this in my sleep. I'd spent the last ten years successfully manipulating people to believe I was a kind and innocent girl, and I could do it again today. I calmed. There was no way my own father would let anyone railroad me because of a bike. And they had nothing else. An eyewitness? *Prove it.* It was my word against theirs, and their mighty witness was probably a half-blind old lady who thought teenagers all looked the same.

Besides, a witness couldn't testify if they were dead.

Chapter
THIRTY

*W*ithin minutes my dad was out front. At least the lights weren't flashing. This was not the way I thought I'd be spending my Saturday.

I met him in the driveway. He'd sounded so freaked out on the phone that I knew he wouldn't want to wait for me. That bothered me too. If he believed me, why had he sounded so anxious? He should have been outraged that someone would even *suggest* his precious daughter could do something so heinous. (That fact that his precious daughter had done it was beside the point entirely).

I opened the cruiser door. My father's face was paler than normal. He smiled at me anyway. It wasn't his usual toothy grin, but a forced curl of his lips. "Hey, how are you?" he asked, staring into my eyes, probably checking for obvious signs of guilt.

"I'm okay. Mostly worried about you."

"No, no. Everything's going to be fine. We'll clear all this up. No one could possibly think someone as sweet and harmless as you could have anything to do with an arson investigation." He put the car in reverse and pulled out of the driveway. In less than ten minutes, we would be at the station, and I would have to put on the best performance of my life.

The car ride was quiet and awkward. I didn't like this development. As I rehearsed what I'd say in my head, I received a text. It was Asad. Tyra had just told him that Omar's condition was unchanged: stable and unconscious. In her expert opinion, he was going to be a vegetable.

So, nothing yet. I knew from my research that it could take hours for an air embolism to strike, so this news didn't surprise me. I texted back: *Thanks 4 letting me know. Ttyl*

"Who was that?" my dad asked.

I shoved my phone back in my bag. "Just Asad. He's giving me an update on that guy from my school who overdosed last night."

"And?"

"He's still unconscious in the hospital."

"That's too bad. Drugs are an evil thing. I see it all the time. Did you know him?" His hands tightened on the wheel.

"Not well. He's on the football and basketball teams." Chewing on my nails, I thought about what to say next. I wanted to ask who their eyewitness was, and who would be questioning me at the station, and if I was a suspect. But just as strongly, I didn't want to know any of those things.

We pulled into the station and my dad escorted me inside. I did my best to exchange the normal pleasantries with the staff, but I wondered if they all knew why I was there. Were they silently weighing my guilt or innocence? My dad ushered me past the secure double doors and cubicle area to a small inter- rogation room in the back. I stopped before entering and glared at my father. "Is this really necessary?"

He patted me on the back. "It's just for privacy. You're not being formally questioned."

"Sure doesn't feel that way." I rubbed my temples, and continued to do so as I sat down at the single table. There was a chair opposite me for the interviewer, whoever that would be. I hoped for Detective Marcus, or better yet, Eric. But I had a sinking suspicion of who I'd get. And if that was the case, *bring it.*

"Just sit tight for a few minutes. Do you want a glass of water?" Dad asked.

"Sure, thanks. Don't you have to be in here with me, like, legally? Or get me a lawyer?" I wanted to see him squirm a bit for putting me through this.

"It's not like that. Just answer the questions and you'll be done. I'll be watching from the other room. No big deal."

It certainly felt like a big deal. Otherwise why didn't someone come to the house or simply call me?

But I supposed police protocol had its particulars. I nodded.

"I'll go grab you that water." He kissed me on top of my head before leaving.

I smiled weakly.

Within a few seconds the door opened again. My father couldn't have been back with the water already. Maybe he'd forgotten to tell me something. Instead I found myself staring into dark brown eyes topped by thick black eyebrows.

"Hello, Miss Wilkanson. How are you doing today?" He didn't smile. He just sat down, straightened a pile of paper in front of him, and took a swig from his coffee cup.

My stomach wound into an angry ball. "I'm okay, I guess. A little curious as to why I'm here." I smiled, keeping a twinkle in my eye for him.

He folded his hands on top of the pile of papers. "Ryann, where were you last night at 9:30?"

Cut to the chase, why don't you? "At my friend B's house. Bao-yu, that is."

"Let's backtrack a little bit. Why don't you go through your entire evening for me, minute by minute?" His eyes glinted back at me. *Touché.*

I did my best to sit straight and maintain steady eye contact. There would be no fidgeting or tells in my body language. He was reading me every second I sat in front of him, and I was going to give him my innocuous voice, which I had on reserve for special moments like this. "Okay, I'll try, but most of the time I can't remember what I ate for breakfast." I chuckled softly. Nothing. His face was stone.

"Your father said you went to a school dance. Why don't you start there?" he said coolly.

"Sure. My friend Lucas picked me up around 6:45 and we drove to the school. We got there maybe ten or fifteen minutes later. I was at the dance for about an hour before there was an emergency. I didn't really feel like staying any longer, so I called my mom to pick me up."

"Why didn't you leave with your friend Lucas?"

"We split up at the dance. We were both interested in other people, so we went our separate ways for a while. I'd thought he'd left by the time I called my mom for a ride."

"Then what?" He tapped his pen lightly on the table. Tap. Tap. Tap. I wanted to grab it out of his chubby little fingers and stab him in the throat.

I smiled instead. "She took me for ice cream, and then we went home."

"But you didn't stay home. You said you went to Bao-yu's house. What time was that?"

"I don't know. We got home and I left maybe fifteen minutes later. So around nine, nine fifteen."

"You called in a report that your bike had been stolen. What time did you make that call?"

"Probably around ten o'clock."

He was trying to intimidate me, staring without blinking. Did he practice that? "At what time did you notice that your bike was missing from your house?"

"When I left to go to B's. It wasn't there, so I walked." *Shit. Shit. Shit.*

"Do you own a cell phone, Miss Wilkanson?"

"Yeah."

"So why didn't you call it in right when you noticed it? Or call your father to tell him?" His eyebrow arched, deepening his stare.

I crossed my arms on the table and leaned in. We were as close to nose-to-nose as I could manage without being overtly hostile. "I don't know. It was a piece of crap, so I wasn't really worried about getting it back. My dad always told me how hard it was to find stolen bikes again. I wouldn't have even bothered reporting it, but when I got to B's house, she told me I should. I didn't call my dad because I know how busy he's been with everything that's going on." I gave him a knowing look, which he ignored.

"Don't you often phone your father on shift? There have been many occasions when you've called him while he was working—many of which I've been present to witness. Why not this time?"

He was really starting to piss me off. "Like I said, he's been busier with the murders. In the past there wasn't as much going on."

That satisfied him enough that he moved on to the next question. "I spoke with Bao-yu, Ryann." A rush of panic flooded through my veins. I could feel my breathing intensify. "And she said you texted her close to ten to ask if you could come over." He paused. "You know what I'm thinking, Ryann? Your mom can attest to you leaving around 9:00 p.m., but Bao-yu doesn't have you at her house until 10:00 p.m. You only live a few blocks from each other, so if your bike was missing and you walked there, you should have arrived at your friend's house by 9:15 p.m. at the latest. So where were you for the other forty-five minutes?" He clasped his hands tightly in front of him again, a silent checkmate.

I resisted the urge to take a huge, gasping breath as the air around me thinned. Forcing my body to relax in my chair, I leaned back and gave a small grin. "I must have been looking for my bike longer than I realized. I thought that Mom or Bri had moved it into the backyard, so I went around the sides and the back, then around to the shed." I congratulated myself on the subtle, placating tone in my voice. "Then I looked around the alley. I suppose I took more time than I'd realized. I didn't check my phone. I didn't realize that I would need an alibi." I stared him down this time. He wasn't going to win.

He looked pissed. "Ryann, are you sure you didn't ride your bike to Mr. Hastings's house in that time? Your bike *was* found in his front yard."

"I'm positive. I don't even know where Mr. Hastings lives. I don't make a habit of knowing my teachers' addresses." He seemed to like that response even less. *Where was my dad?* Had he really left me to get grilled like this? He said he'd be watching.

Sergeant Estevez smiled at me, and it was anything but genuine. "Wasn't Hastings your math teacher this semester? It's my understanding that something happened between the two of you last week. He kicked you out of class. That must have embarrassed you. Possibly even made you angry." He leaned onto his forearms, attempting a stare-down.

The guy really did his homework. "He was my teacher. And yes, he had me leave class because I didn't have my homework with me. But he did that with everyone. There was no reason to be embarrassed."

"I have an eyewitness that puts you at Mr. Hastings's house at the time of the fire. Can you explain that?" He kept his eyes locked on me while he sipped his coffee. I was about to answer when he put a finger up to stop me. "You may have been told that a person was seen riding a bike around the Chesterfield area on the night of Olivia McMann's murder. Funny—the person was identified as a blonde, teenage female on an older-style red bike. Isn't your bike red, Ryann?"

I inhaled slowly. He wouldn't rattle me. "You have a witness who says she saw a girl. I'm sure that there are a lot of blonde teenage girls in Dungrave. If you don't believe me, just take a look at my high school. As for bikes, I'd say the vast majority of them are red. Is that everything?" I was pissed now, and I didn't give a shit if he knew it. That was all I was going to give him without a lawyer, and he knew that too.

"That will be all for now, but if you think of

anything else, please give me a call." He slid his business card across the table toward me.

I stood and pushed the small square of paper across the table toward him. "I'll let my dad know if there's anything more. But thanks anyway."

Chapter
THIRTY-ONE

*E*stevez stayed behind in the interrogation room, sipping his coffee and reflecting on the interview. There was more to Ryann's story. The nagging pull on his insides told him so, not to mention the evidence that was slowly accumulating around her.

This was more than a delicate situation. She was his partner's daughter. It was obvious that Dave thought something was off too, but he couldn't bring himself to admit it.

They'd worked the recent murder cases side by side, and Estevez had witnessed the change in his partner as soon as Ryann's bike was recovered and more than one eyewitness described a girl that looked just like her. Dave had gone quiet and pale. The stress twitch under his left eye started acting up, and he ate Tums like candy. Of course Dave couldn't acknowledge it. It was his kid. Estevez was a father too, and he understood that his partner wasn't about to hand her over. He could only imagine what he'd feel and do if their situations were reversed. Dave was in denial. Any explanation or excuse for Ryann was good enough for him. It had to be.

Estevez found himself wondering how an honorable guy like Dave could have such a manipulative and calculating child. How could she set a fire and kill someone? And, if his suspicions were correct, how could she smash a child—one she used to care for—twelve times over the head with a brick? A shiver ripped down his spine.

He wasn't certain about the Borgdon girl's death yet. Ryann knew her. Hayden *had* dumped Ryann for Yvonne, yet Amelia seemed sure it was the boyfriend. Hayden Cook didn't seem like the kind of kid to do something like that, but, a month ago, Estevez would have said the same thing about Ryann.

The picture of Stanley Hastings's burnt corpse was ingrained in his mind. The only way he could make sense of it was to assume that Ryann had thought the house was empty when she torched it— that she'd been completely unaware Hastings was still inside. But that didn't explain the other two.

He knew the truth in his gut.

There was something cold about that girl. Her eyes were flat. She didn't look shocked or upset that her teacher was dead. She looked…satisfied.

Another chill swept through him. He sipped his coffee.

Maybe having a cop for a father had taught her too much. She'd grown up around it, and she'd clearly paid attention on her many visits to the station, listening when her dad spoke. She was too good during the interview. Most adults would have trembled. She was a fifteen-year-old kid, and she barely batted an eyelash during his questioning.

Olivia, Yvonne, and Hastings had one person in common. Her. He remembered Warren stating, back in the alley, that the angle of the strikes indicated that the killer was not much taller than Olivia.

Ryann was not much taller at all. And she was right-handed, he'd noticed. According to Warren, the wound patterns indicated that McMann's killer had been right-handed. He couldn't tie her to Yvonne yet, but if he didn't rectify it, that poor Cook kid was going to go down for it.

Deep down, Dave had to see it too.

The specifics weren't enough to hold her or get a warrant for any of the files. So he'd have to wait her out.

She was bound to mess up, and he'd be there when she did.

He'd have to get as much information on her as he could. Follow any lead, no matter how small, and keep it out from under Dave's nose. He'd likely have to hide it from everyone. The unit wouldn't appreciate him investigating one of their own, but Ryann hadn't left him any choice. She was dangerous. She had to be brought down.

He was sorry he'd be the one to do it.

Chapter
THIRTY-TWO

*A*ngry wasn't the word. I was irate. How could my father abandon me in there to practically be accused of murder? Leaving the small, suffocating interrogation room felt good, but not as good as facing my dad would. I looked around, figuring he'd be out of the observation room by now, but he wasn't. I stood, arms crossed, waiting. I wanted him to know how furious I was.

A few minutes later, the door opened. Another man came out first, then Dad. He spotted me, and I swear he was gray. He headed straight for me and grabbed me lightly by the shoulder. "You did great in there, kid." He feigned a smile, which boiled my blood further.

"Did I? Because I felt ambushed. Where were you? How could you let Sergeant Dick do that to me?" My face was so hot that I probably looked like a beet, but I didn't care. "Don't you have anything to say?"

He tried to shush me and ushered me over to the corner by my arm. "Keep your voice down. We'll discuss this when we leave. Now is not the time." His breath was hot on my face, and it smelled like rancid coffee.

I pulled away, squaring my shoulders. "Then take me home."

❖ ❖ ❖ ❖

The car ride from the station felt much the same as the one on the way there: quiet and awkward, until I couldn't take it anymore. I would not be ignored again. "Seriously, Dad. What was that about? How could you let him grill me? I didn't do anything." I had softened my previously enraged tone and added a pinch of *poor me.*

"You handled yourself extremely well. If I had come in to stop it, it would have looked like you had something to hide. And if I'd thought you were digging yourself a hole, I would have jumped in."

"I can't dig myself a hole if I didn't do anything wrong! What about...oh I don't know...*believing I didn't do it?*"

"Don't you think I know that, Ryann? You don't have it in you to be a calculated killer. You're not shrewd enough to evade police manhunt. But there is circumstantial evidence that needs to be cleared up, and the law doesn't make exceptions for cop's daughters," he snapped.

He might as well have punched me in the stomach, though I scoffed it off. "Evidence? What evidence? A bike? What—and a blonde girl? They've got to do better than that."

He breathed deeply. "It's obvious to me that you had nothing to do with it, and when Estevez runs into a dead end any minute, he'll know it too. We've been partners a long time. He's not going to come after you when there's nothing to substantiate further investigation, especially when you're my kid."

My arms were tight across my chest. "Well, he seemed pretty convinced."

He reached for my hand in a rare show of affection, but I yanked it away.

"You did fine in there, and I can't see any reason why he'd need to speak to you again. We can put this all behind us."

My phone vibrated. Ignoring my dad, I read the text from Asad.

Bad news. Omar's dead.

I felt the weight of a thousand bricks lifted. He was dead. I'd done it, and I was almost happy enough to forgive my father for his betrayal.

"Who was that?" my dad asked.

I tried to look shaken. It was difficult, considering the relief fluttering inside me. "Remember that guy at the school dance who OD'd? Asad just texted me that he died."

"Shit. I'm sorry. You weren't friends with him, right?"

I shook my head. "It's still weird. I saw him collapse and watched the paramedics work on him. I thought he was going to be okay." I bowed my head and felt my dad's hand cradle the back of my neck. "I can't handle any more. Just tell me if you think I'm a suspect." I sniffled into my arm.

"What they have is circumstantial evidence. It's not enough to prove you had anything to do with Mr. Hastings's death." He turned down the radio and cleared his throat. "I do have to ask you one thing. Where were you between the time you left home and the time you got to B's?"

"I already told you. I was looking for my bike around our house. I even checked the alley behind. I gave up and walked to B's. It wasn't like I was paying lots of attention to the time." I stared him directly in the eyes. "I've never done anything wrong—do you think if I did, I'd start with something like *this?*" I needed to be finished with this tedious conversation. I teared up, right on cue.

"Like I said: you don't have it in you."

A few hours later I met up with B, Katie, Lucas, and Asad at Ridgeway Park. It wasn't the most exciting place in the world, but we didn't have much money and there wasn't a lot for us to do. So we'd hang out, sit on the picnic tables, eat candy and chips, and loiter.

"I still can't believe Omar's dead," Lucas said, wide-eyed. "And Hastings. Holy hell."

"I thought for sure Omar would pull through," Asad said.

I passed the bag of salt and vinegar to him. "Yeah, a lot of people are going to be devastated."

"That's a lot of funerals this month. And they were all so young…well, except for Hastings," B added.

We nodded in unison. Gripping my drink, I took a long, refreshing swig.

"I still can't believe you were in jail," Katie said, staring at me.

B smacked Katie. "She wasn't in jail. She was being questioned." B centered her attention on me. "Sorry again if I made things worse for you. I didn't know you'd tell them a different time."

"It's not a big deal. I thought I'd left the house later. Honest mistake."

"What was it like? Did they put a huge spotlight on you? Did they videotape it?" Katie's eyes were fixed, her head propped up on her hand. She looked mesmerized.

"No and no. It was a few questions and that was it. It's not like I'm a suspect."

Asad wiped his greasy hands on his jeans. "I wonder who that witness saw anyway. Half of Dungrave's girls fit her description. Hey, I wonder if they'll do a lineup and call her in to take a look at all of you." He laughed, thinking it was all a joke, but he'd brought up a very real concern that hadn't crossed my mind until then. My insides stiffened.

B and Lucas laughed it off, and so did I.

Asad gasped suddenly. "Did you guys hear? Hayden has been officially charged with Yvonne's murder."

Our collective mouths gaped. "Seriously?" B asked.

Asad nodded. "Yup."

"I still don't think he did it," Lucas said. "We know him. He's not capable of something like that."

"Then you didn't hear the latest," Asad announced. "Apparently Hayden and Yvonne had a fight at the movies."

"So?" I said. "A lot of people argue."

"Yeah, but more evidence was found at the scene. Hayden's brother told his friend, Josh, that some of Hayden's blood was found in Yvonne's bedroom. I guess it was just a trace amount, but still. He also told Josh that the cops think it was a crime of passion, because one of her own belts was used to strangle her. It doesn't point to premeditation."

I thought about the cut in the screen. Maybe the police found the wire cutters and thought they were Hayden's. It was one piece of evidence not publically released. Sometimes cops purposely kept certain facts about the crime out of the media so that when a viable suspect turned up, they could see if the person knew the confidential information.

But how did the cops explain Hayden sneaking

back in just after he'd dropped her off? Apparently I wasn't the only one with that question.

Lucas ran a hand through his hair. "If it wasn't premeditated, then why wouldn't Hayden just knock on the front door and ask Yvonne's mom to let him in?"

"Maybe he knew it was past her curfew and snuck in through her window. Everyone knows how strict her parents are. I wonder what's going to happen to him now," B said. "I guess he'll go to trial, right?"

"Looks that way," Asad said.

I stayed mum. It was better that way. With so much going on in my head, I wasn't on my A game. Why was my father so sure I wasn't capable? He didn't know me at all! If he opened his eyes, he'd see the truth, though I was relieved he was blind to me.

"There's nothing we can do about Hayden right now. Is anyone going to Omar's funeral?" Katie asked.

"One at a time. Can we focus on Yvonne's first? It's tomorrow, you know," B said.

That got my attention. With all my scheming, I hadn't noticed that there hadn't yet been a funeral for Yvonne. There'd been one for Olivia. My parents went, but my mom claimed it was far too upsetting for Bri and I to attend. She'd insisted we stay home. I'd really wanted to go and see her one last time. But I wouldn't let Yvonne's funeral pass me by. "Are any of you going?" I asked.

Lucas and Katie shook their heads, but B and Asad said they were.

"Can I come with you guys?"

Everyone stared at me like a third eye had popped out of my forehead.

"You didn't even like her," B said.

"Neither did you. But I'm still friends with Hayden. We should be there on his behalf. Show support."

"That's honorable." Asad patted my hand. "I wonder if Yvonne's parents would even let Hayden into the funeral, considering he's the number one suspect."

"Wait. You're not trying to get back together with him, are you?" Katie's eyes, wide before, had grown even bigger.

"No. That's the last thing on my mind. But I know what it's like to be 'questioned' by the police." I cringed. "Is Hayden seriously going to be charged with murder?"

As usual, Lucas didn't let a mouthful of food stop him from speaking. "Heard he's got a big, fancy lawyer. He won't talk to anyone about it. We've all tried, but his lawyer told him to keep it zipped."

"Yeah, I heard at Yvonne's memorial."

"Standard protocol," Asad piped in. He looked hungry for more drama. "On *Law and Order*, the cops have to establish motive and opportunity. They can either arrest and question, or question and find enough evidence to arrest later, which is what I suspect is happening with Hayden."

"What was his motive?" I asked, pretending to be clueless.

"I don't know. The oldest motivation of all time. Jealousy," Asad said.

Katie laughed. "Jealousy over who? No one was interested in Yvonne *but* him."

Lucas whistled. "I don't know. There were a few guys who wanted a piece. I heard she was in the bedroom with Shane at Hayden's party. If Hayden got wind of that—*boom*." Lucas pounded his fist into his open palm. "That might've been enough."

B grunted in disgust. "You're a pig."

I liked playing along with their little theory games. It was entertaining. "Okay, then what about opportunity? Hayden dropped her off. Yvonne's mom said she saw her come into the house alone."

Asad cocked a knowing grin. "That's simple. He parked nearby, ran back to the house, snuck into one of the other rooms—maybe her room—and killed her. Maybe she snuck him in and he thought they were going to mess around. Then when she didn't want to, he killed her for being a tease." He gloated as if he'd just won some kind of trivia game. And I had to admit that he wasn't too far off. He really was good at this.

I looked at the time. "Shit, guys. Gotta go. Catch up later," I said. Really, I needed to get home and pick out my best funeral attire.

Would red be too tactless?

Chapter
THIRTY-THREE

$\mathcal{I}$t was touch and go for a while with Omar, but now I was back. My concentration was operating at one hundred percent. I was sure Estevez wanted another go at me, but I'd handled him well enough. He had nothing substantial. He was bluffing, trying to scare me. But I knew his game, and I was one step ahead. And I was smarter than either he—or my father—gave me credit for. I'd be more careful next time. The whole bike thing was still tearing a hole through my stomach.

I decided to put my feet up for a while and try to relax. It was Sunday evening, which meant *Dateline* was on. My bed felt softer than ever. My thoughts drifted to all I'd accomplished. I knew I had to cool it for a while and lay low, but it's amazing how quickly one can develop a taste for something. I lusted for it. All I

could think about was who would be next and how I
would do it. My mouth watered at the prospect.

I imagined the conversation that would have
passed with Estevez once my dad had gotten back to
the station last night. But why imagine when I could
ask? I reached for my phone and called my dad.

"Ryann? Are you okay?" His tone was strained.

"Yeah. I just haven't seen you much. I wanted to
know if anything else happened. Does Estevez still
think I'm guilty of something?" I struck a perfect
balance between anxious and choked up.

"I already told you. No one thinks you're guilty
of anything."

I laughed haughtily. "Of course he does, or else I
wouldn't have been questioned like that."

"You've been through a lot, but you have to calm
down and stop worrying. Nothing is going to happen
to you. I promise." He sounded so sincere. But I
hadn't forgotten the way he'd practically handed me
over to that prick. Or all the other criticisms he'd
voiced over the years.

"I know, but Estevez seemed so angry. It was
like he had something on me. But that's impossible,
because I didn't do anything. I'm scared, Daddy." I
threw in a sniffle for good measure.

"Don't be afraid. I'll always protect you, my little
lamb."

I hated when he called me that. "Yeah? Like you
did earlier, when you put me in a room with a cop
who thinks I'm guilty?"

"I had no choice. Besides, you have nothing to hide."

"No I don't, so do you think you can call off your partner?"

"Estevez won't harass you. He's a good cop."

I held in a derisive laugh. "Never mind. Can you at least tell me if there are any updates in the other cases?"

"Ryann, you know I can't—"

"Not about Hayden, I know. But what about Olivia? You guys must have some leads by now. It's been nearly a month since all this insanity started."

He was quiet for a minute, and then he began to whisper. "Actually, we have a suspect in interrogation. Right now, in fact. That's all I can say."

"That's great news. At least there's one sicko off the streets."

"He's being questioned, but he hasn't been charged with anything yet. He's a registered sex offender. He'd been out about three months before her murder. Did you make yourself some dinner?" he asked suddenly in the same ultra-calm tone. It was almost comical that he could shift so seamlessly.

"Not yet, but I will. Talk to you later."

"Good night," he said softly and hung up.

Hearing that they had a suspect made me perk right up. It was time to shift gears.

I threw on my shoes, grabbed my bag, and went out back. My sister had a bike in the shed that she never used. To my chagrin, it was bright pink, but beggars can't be choosers. I knew she'd be livid if she caught me with it, no matter that she hadn't set her bony ass on it since she was thirteen.

My destination was Mom's diner.

I was hungry, and it was a great place to people watch, especially on a Sunday evening, one of the busiest nights. Perhaps I'd be inspired. Scoping was half the fun. Just contemplating who would be next on my list was the perfect distraction.

I locked up my new ride against the metal pole beside the front entrance and headed inside. I knew my mom would be surprised. I hardly ever visited her at work. She thought I was embarrassed that she was a waitress. I wasn't. It was just upsetting that she had to serve those assholes who looked down their noses at her and gave her the change from the bottom of their purse instead of her proper due.

I pushed open the heavy glass doors, triggering the familiar jingle of bells.

My mom looked up, her arms full of dirty plates, and her eyes brightened.

"Hey, you! To what do I owe this pleasant surprise?" she asked, dumping her armful into a bus bin.

I tried to match her huge smile. "Thought I'd pay you a visit. Hope that's okay."

"Of course." She made her way over to me and kissed me on the cheek, motioning for me to grab a seat at the bar. "Get you anything?" She put a tattered menu before me.

"Apple pie and ice cream?" I let my smile grow bigger.

"Nice try. Eat some real food first. How about a turkey sandwich?"

"Pie is real food. There are multiple food groups represented. Fruit, dairy, whole grains."

She eyed me as she poured me a glass of apple juice. "How did you get here?" I could tell she was nervous that I was alone, but she was trying not to show it.

"I took Bri's old bike. I'm okay, Mom. No boogeyman is going to get me."

She smiled faintly, but the creases around her eyes gave her away. "Turkey sandwich first. Then pie."

While she put the order in and brought a table their orders, I took the liberty of scoping out the place.

There was a family of four. Mom, Dad, and two bratty kids, both under five. Nope. Another couple sat in the corner, sharing french fries and gravy. They looked to be in their mid-twenties. I hadn't given much serious thought to a double kill. Besides, I'd have to watch them for a while to see if they fit the profile. Another table housed four people in their thirties. What a lame place for a double date. Alas, no. Finally, there were two women with strollers— this was clearly a little post-playdate snack. *No way.*

And then I saw him in my periphery, sitting at the far end of the bar. He had definite potential.

He was alone, eating his burger and onion rings,

drinking a beer, and reading the paper. I figured he was in his early sixties. Gray hair, gray beard, plaid shirt tucked into dark denim and—for the love of God—suspenders. My mom had gone over to see if he needed anything, and he'd snapped at her. Grumpy bastard.

For the next half hour, I watched him eat painfully slowly and sip on a second beer. It was light beer, which didn't help his case. Pussy. He waved down my mom and yelled for his check. The diner had grown busier. Four new tables had come in within the last twenty minutes. I watched my mother run around like a chicken with no head. She could barely keep up. And then the bastard stood up to go to the bathroom. Mom went over to collect the check and sighed.

"What is it, Mom?"

"Nothing. This miserable old man never tips. He always barks at me and doesn't even leave me a dollar." She shoved the change into her apron and forced a smile. "It doesn't matter, sweetie. It's my job."

"Yeah—to bring food, not to be treated like crap."

"It's okay, Ryann." Just as she was cleaning up his disgusting mess, the old prick came back over.

"What in the hell are you doing?" he barked.

"Just clearing your dishes."

"You'd better have left my beer. I ain't done with it yet." He smacked himself back on the stool, inspected his beer, and took a long swig, staring my mom down.

My face flushed with soothing warmth. Soft tingles trickled through my extremities, quickening my breath.

It would be him.

I didn't care who he was, if he had a wife, a husband, kids, pets, sick parents, or a good job. I only cared how and when I'd kill him.

I scarfed down my sandwich. I needed to be finished in time to follow him out. He was folding up his newspaper, and his beer was almost empty. I stood, readying myself, when my mom came over. The muscles around my lungs squeezed in torment.

"Still want that pie?" She nudged me playfully.

"No thanks. I'm stuffed." I reached for my bag, keeping the man in my field of vision.

My mom stood back up. "Leaving already?"

"Uh, yeah. Sorry, I said I'd meet everyone. Thanks for dinner, though. It was much better than cooking."

"Oh, okay. Well, call your father when you get home so we know you're safe." She backed up to let me by.

"Have a good shift." I leaned in and hugged her, smelling the sweet fragrance of her hair and the baby powder she always used before she went in to the diner. She said it acted as a barrier between her skin and the greasy smell of diner food.

I was walking toward the door when she called back to me, and when I turned around the man walked past me. I heard the jingle of the bell as he left. He was getting away. My whole body tensed.

"Yeah, Mom?"

"Love you."

I forced out a smile. "You too." This time I turned
and bolted.

The man had only gotten about fifteen feet
down the stairs. He was driving a red Subaru station
wagon. I quickly typed his license plate into my
phone. I wasn't sure how I was going to follow a car,
but I got on my bike and tried anyway.

He pulled out of the parking lot slowly and drove
the same way. Maybe he was tipsy. Dad always said
that people drove extra slow to hide that they'd been
drinking.

I didn't have to ride hard to keep on him. Four
turns later he was pulling into a driveway.

I stopped my bike a house away and watched
him walk up his front steps. Judging by his house,
he lived alone. The front yard was a disaster. There
were overgrown weeds and grass, chipped paint on
the fence and arm rails, and dead bushes along the
edge of the yard. If a woman lived here, she was as
much a pig as this guy.

When he was inside, I sidled up the lawn. The front
window was low and only half-covered by a shitty
sheer curtain. It was easy peeping. A dim light went
on in the front room, making it much easier to see.
It was just starting to get dark. I couldn't do anything
now but watch. I needed to see what I was up against.

The man disappeared for a minute and came back
with another beer in his hand. He situated himself in

his recliner: feet up, remote in hand. Did every man over fifty live this way? It was like watching Hastings in his heyday. My own father wasn't far off.

I walked around to the side of the house, spied his trash and recycling bins, and decided to peek. I didn't need any surprises when I came back. I half-expected to find some evidence of a woman: discarded makeup cases, used body lotion containers, empty fruity wine bottles, something. All I found was a bag full of generic waste, including bologna packages, milk containers, and a variety of snack wrappers, and a recycling bin overflowing with empty beer cans. I backed away toward my bike and added his address to my phone, under his license plate number. Not that I'd forget.

Chapter
THIRTY-FOUR

The library was open for another hour, which was enough time to get started on Subaru Guy. I logged on to one of the giant, old-fashioned computers. The sound of the system coming to life always made me silently giddy. Unsure exactly what to look up, I decided to browse a few of my favorite websites that honored people like me. One was called *Killers Among Us.* It featured stories and statistics about killers in the United States. So far I'd murdered by bludgeoning, choking, poisoning, and arson. But I wanted to do something outstanding.

I never understood killing with guns. It was far too impersonal. I didn't want to be a literal arm's length away from my victim. Even the murders of my last two victims had their charms. I'd still felt connected. I'd practically fed Omar the drink. It had gone from my fingertips into his mouth. I'd half-carried his limp, sweating body across the field. And when that hadn't worked, I'd injected him.

And Hastings was a bonus. He should have treaded more lightly around me, but he was a fool, and he'd paid the price. He was the only one to look me in the eyes and grasp what I was capable of.

What were my options this time?

Subaru Guy was a sizeable man. On the plus side, he was probably a drunk, and, of course, I had the element of surprise. He'd never suspect me, and that was half the fun. The other half of the fun would be watching his eyes fill with utter fear before the lights went out. I craved that look of recognition, that realization that his killer was a cute, blonde, teenage cheerleader.

I needed to figure out the when and where. I could sneak into his house, like I had with Yvonne. Wait for him and ambush him. Or I could simply ring his doorbell with a box of Girl Scout Cookies and force my way in when he went for cash. Why not utilize my sweet face?

My purse buzzed. It was a text from B. She was with Mackenzie. They were bored and wanted me to entertain them, which would have been a decent idea if I wasn't already so gosh darned busy.

I texted back my denial and fired off a message to Eric. *Hey E, What's up?*

Not much. You okay?

Little upset. Can u get away? Meet me?

Not a good idea.

Please? Need to talk.

Fine. Quick though. Same place as last time. Still on shift.

K. 15 min?

Sure.

He was closer to twenty minutes. I hated waiting. I was busy too. "Why are you late?" I asked, arms crossed and huffy.

He was in uniform, looking very official. He gazed at me, seemingly unimpressed. "You're lucky I came at all."

I was sitting on the edge of the fountain. He stood in front of me, shoulders broad and squared. He was almost intimidating. "You can sit if you want to." I patted the marble bench. Eric stared before taking a small step back.

"I'm on duty. I can't be seen sitting around, at night, with another officer's underage daughter." He kept his arms behind his back, as if he were standing at attention in the army.

"Would you relax for five minutes?"

"You said you were upset. What is it?" he asked coolly.

I huffed. "I feel all pressured, like I'm on the clock or something. What's your going rate for a counseling session?"

"Look, Ryann. I came here because you said you needed help, not to play games."

"Walk with me over there, so we can have some

privacy?" He stared at me dubiously. "Please?" I begged.

"It's probably better to stay here."

I stood and grabbed his arm, yanking him toward the bathrooms and behind a row of bushes. He came with me willingly, which was unsurprising. He wanted me to force his hand, and I could play along—be the bad guy.

"Why do we need to be over here?" he asked.

Still holding on to his arm, I leaned in until my breasts grazed his chest and whispered, "Because I don't like it when strangers see me cry." I pressed against him longer than necessary. Eric didn't push me away.

"What happened?" he asked, more softly.

I backed up just enough to look up at him. "I thought you'd know by now."

He shook his head.

"Yesterday my dad brought me in to be interrogated by that asshole, Estevez." He stepped back in surprise. "Seriously? How could you not know? Gossip travels fast. The juicy scoop that your coworker's kid was questioned in connection to arson—*homicide*—didn't make the rounds yet? I find that hard to believe." I smirked as though I'd forgive him anything.

His hand landed on my shoulder. "I promise you, I didn't know. Your dad actually brought you in? What evidence do they think they have?" His eyes narrowed, the skin on his forehead creased slightly, and if I wasn't mistaken, his cheeks flushed—an odd response, perhaps, to learning that I'd been questioned in a murder investigation.

"They don't have any evidence, because I didn't do anything, but Estevez has it out for me. You should have seen the way he treated me. He grilled me like I was a low-life thug. I was humiliated."

"Where was your dad?"

I gave a wry laugh. "That's the best part. He was watching from the observation room. He didn't come in once. He didn't even try to help me. Instead he let me get ripped apart in there." Like the professional actor I practically was, I burst into tears, and before I knew it, strong arms were around me. I leaned in, letting him console me.

"I can't believe your dad would do that."

I pulled away hurriedly, wiping my eyes on the sleeve of my shirt. "Of course you don't believe me. I'm just a silly little girl to you." I kept my gaze down and waited.

Eric swooped in as expected, tilting my chin up. "I don't think that."

I placed my hand on top of his, bringing his fingers to graze the outer edge of my lips and 'gazing' into his eyes. "What do you think of me, then?"

He kept his hand steady at first, then traced my mouth and cheek with his fingertip. "I think you're very beautiful and a lot smarter than people give you credit for." He stared at me for a minute and leaned in closer. I closed my eyes, anticipating his lips against mine, but instead his hand left my cheek cold. I opened my eyes to see that he'd taken a step back.

I tried to reach for his hand again, but he pulled away. "What's wrong? I thought you liked me."

"This isn't right...for a lot of reasons. You're underage, you're my coworker's daughter, and... shit, hundreds of other things that I can't think of right now."

He was clearly flustered, which meant that all was not lost. I took my own step back. Two could play this game. "You're right. I'm sorry, Eric. I almost ruined your career. It's just that I feel so comfortable with you. I forget about our age difference." I managed a devastated look.

His hand found mine again. "If the situation were different, or the timing...I don't know. But right now, nothing can happen between us. No matter how badly I want it to."

I smiled, wiping away the streaks of tears from my cheeks. "Really? You want something to happen?"

"I'm not allowed to like you, Ryann. So please, don't ask me." He looked away.

I moved in closer again, as close as I had been moments ago. "I'm asking you," I said. I put my hands on either side of his face, pulled his head toward me, and kissed him.

Chapter
THIRTY-FIVE

$\mathcal{I}$t had been four days since I'd followed Subaru Guy home, and tonight he was going down. My mind kept wandering to him during classes and cheer practice. It was my subconscious telling me that I wanted him. Badly. Waiting it out was pointless. No one, not even Estevez, was looking for me.

I packed my bag with all the necessities for my evening ahead, including the very sharp hunting knife that I'd 'borrowed' while shopping with my dad.

It felt like wearing my hoodie—hood up—was my trademark, but it was hot, and I didn't feel like sweating all over the place. I decided to wear my black baseball cap instead. I didn't have any distinguishing marks on me, like tattoos or moles, but I'd been sighted by two people and couldn't afford to add another.

I still had Bri's bike. She hadn't even noticed I'd used it. I loaded up my backpack and slipped out the back door. It was a little after nine. Mom was at the diner, and Dad was asleep. He'd just gotten off and was exhausted. He'd been doing a lot of overtime lately. I would've felt bad, had he not subjected me to Sergeant Asshole the week before.

Subaru Guy's address was still in my phone, but I had his place memorized. It only took me twenty minutes to get there, and during my ride all I could think about was the multitude of ways I could make him feel glorious pain. Playing out all of these scenarios helped settle the beast within me. The moments before were special.

I figured he'd be home. What did a single man his age do after nine anyway, besides drink and watch TV?

I stowed my bike a few houses away this time in case I had to make a run for it. I couldn't risk leaving it in the yard of yet another dead guy.

My heart and breath were steady as I walked the half block to his front door. I could already see his car in the drive. I was right. No life.

It was like a strange ritual or placating habit, but I needed to feel the weapon in my pocket. In this case, my fingers traced the container of bear spray. According to my dad, it makes you feel like your face is on fire; you want to dig your fingertips into your burning flesh and rip the pain away. You can't breathe, can't see, your eyes and sinuses are in indescribable agony, and you want to die. If it could subdue an eight-hundred-pound bear, it would destroy old Subaru guy.

Making sure the coast was clear, I snuck up the pathway to the front door then did one more sweep of the area from under my baseball cap. The street was abandoned except for a few parked cars and a stray cat, whose soft meowing played out in the distance.

❖ ❖ ❖ ❖

I knock on the door and wait. I hear the release of a deadbolt and hold my breath as the heavy wooden door creaks open, revealing the man's darkened face. The room behind him is dim except for a tiny lamp in the far corner and the flickering lights of the television. He's holding a can of beer and gives me a rotten glare.

It's just how I've imagined it, and it thrills me.

He stares me down, takes a sloppy swig from his can, and says, "Yeah. What do you want?"

What I want is to kick him hard in the jewels. Instead I smile and try to look helpless—not an easy feat. "I'm locked out of my house and my battery is dead." I quickly produce my phone and sigh. "Would it be all right if I used your phone?"

He drains the beer, single-handedly squeezes the can, and tosses it behind him on the floor. Charming. "Where do you live?" he asks, looking past me down the blackened street. "Never seen you before."

He makes me think on my feet and I like it. "I just

moved in with my dad and his wife a few houses that way." I point vaguely. "Look, can I use your phone or not?" I huff. I should have brought the Girl Scout Cookies. He'd let me in then. Fat bastard.

He backs up, extending his bare arm—he's wearing a gross white sleeveless undershirt—into the front room. "Fine, come in."

I glance around once more to make sure we have no witnesses and kick the door shut with my foot. I don't need an audience, as fun as that would be.

As I step inside, the smell gags me immediately. Cat piss, old man sweat, and some sort of odorous luncheon meat? I want to wave my hand in front of me and spray us both down with a bottle of air freshener.

I smile. "Thanks a lot. My dad's at work, but he should be able to come and let me in."

He grunts in his eloquent way before making it to a small table and handing me a cordless phone. I haven't used one in years. It feels massive in my hand.

He stares at me under a heavy brow. "You gonna call or what?"

I flash him another grin. "Crap. Would you believe that I'm blanking on my dad's number? It's programmed into my phone. I usually just scroll through my contacts and click. Can't remember the last time I've actually dialed." I laugh, but he doesn't look amused. "I'm sure it will come to me, just give me a minute." He turns around. This is my chance. I rush into my bag for supplies.

With his back to me, he begins fiddling with some-

thing on the end table. "I'm kinda busy, so could you
hurry it up?"

I don't respond.

He turns around, and surprise registers in his
eyes. He's likely trying to figure out why I have goggles
on and a bandana wrapped around my nose and
mouth. I reach up, bear spray in hand, and press the
nozzle directly at his face. His arms fly up violently as
shrieking sounds force their way from his throat. His
hands rush to his face and his fingers desperately rub
at his eyes. He goes down to his knees with a blood-cur-
dling howl. His shrieks warm my flesh, and I allow
myself a moment of ecstasy as I watch him writhe on
his grimy floor.

He won't stop screaming and making a ruckus.
While I enjoy the torment he's suffering, he needs to
be quieted. My foot finds its place in the middle of his
hunched stomach. It stifles him a little, but not nearly
as much as I hope.

"Shut the fuck up, or it's going to get worse for you,"
I say, putting on my gloves.

He rolls back and forth on the cat hair–covered
carpet, moaning. Grunting. Saliva and snot make his
face and neck wet and shiny. It's fascinating. His eyes
are swollen, red, watery messes. I sympathize, just not
enough to help or have a change of heart.

I know that he won't be immobile for too much
longer and it's safer for me to subdue him. I bind his
hands in front of him with duct tape as he lays on the
floor. He can't see me through the tears and puffiness

of his eyes, but he tilts his head up, like he's staring me in the face.

"Why?" He sobs the words. This large, grown man is reduced to a crumbling mess because of me. I feel like I can do anything. I'm Godlike. "Why are you doing this to me?" he asks through choking coughs.

I put my hand against his cheek and stroke his face as a mother would her sick child. "Because I can."

Reaching into my pocket, I pull out my knife and squat down so I can be closer to him. I trace the blade lightly against the moist skin of his cheek. He yells out again.

"Please, please don't do this. I'll give you anything you want. You want money? Alcohol? Drugs? What?"

Laughter escapes my lips and I let the tip of the blade slowly pierce the underside of his jaw. He yelps. "The only thing I want is your blood on my knife."

He gasps. I know he'll beg, which never looks good on anyone. And while I'd like to hear how creative he'll get, I need to get this going.

My knife cuts through his grubby, stained under-shirt. I wad it up in a ball and shove it in his mouth. He begins to flail harder. I admire his fight, but this will not do. I slap him as hard as I can across his face. It's enough to quiet him a bit more. Clasping the knife handle firmly with one hand, I grasp his sweaty, greasy hair in the other, pull back his head, and expose his neck. Staring him in the eyes, I smile. In one quick motion I slide my blade across his throat. A dark, crimson line emerges from the slash, slowly at first, then quicker. It gushes. I should have known he'd be messy. Ugh.

The man has stopped moving now. I drop his head back on the fur-laden floor and survey my work through my unfashionable plastic goggles.

My gaze traces past a picture of him with a toddler, a few books on a shelf, and a pack of smokes and a pocketknife on the table next to his chair. I resist the keepsake yet again and take a mental picture to remember this moment. Our moment.

Glancing at the small clock on the fireplace mantel, I realize that I've been here for fourteen minutes. I need to get the hell out.

It isn't until I stand up that I realize I have blood splatter across my shirt. Shit. I thought I'd been so careful, and now I've got the guy's DNA all over me.

Observing out the front window, I see that the street is just as deserted as it was when I charmed my way in. There's no way I can take off my bandana or eye protection in here. The chemicals in the bear spray will end up choking me. I have to get outside in my current attire and not run into anyone. I'd look like a murderer.

I collect my stuff in a sheet of plastic wrap, crack open the door, and take a peek. A loud ringing blares out, and I think my heart will stop. I'm on edge more than I realize. There's no way I'm answering Subaru Guy's phone.

There is, however, one more thing I want to do before I leave.

With my gloved hands, I wipe down the phone to get rid of my prints, then push over the guy's limp and heavy body just enough to reach into his back pocket and pull out his wallet.

I let go of him and he plunks right back down. I open the wallet. I need to know his name, so I can look for him on the news.

I slid out the white plastic card. Marvin Dodson. Aged 57. Huh. He was an organ donor. Who knew a guy who drank enough to pickle his own liver would bother? Too bad he wouldn't be found in time for any organs to be viable. I pushed the license back into the brown leather wallet and tossed it onto the couch cushion.

I gazed one last time at my masterpiece. There'd been no sign of the cat indoors, except for the hair on everything. I wondered if it would start eating him. I'd heard about things like that happening, and I didn't think it was an urban legend.

It was time to go. The shaking in my body was not nerves this time. I felt more alive than ever before. This kill had been everything. The others were satisfying in their own ways, but Marvin had encompassed all my dreams. My knife. My hands. His eyes meeting mine. Him begging and knowing I was his god.

My celebration would have to wait. What mattered now was getting away and destroying the evidence that I was currently carrying—and wearing.

The coast was clear. I made my way out.

Chapter
THIRTY-SIX

$\mathcal{G}$rabbing my bag, I jogged down the stairs to the side of Marvin's house protected by tree and shrub cover. I removed the bandana and goggles, careful not to transfer any residue to my skin, and laid them on the plastic wrap. I dropped the knife and gloves, peeled off my blood-splattered T-shirt, and added it to the pile. I was left in only a dark tank top. That was why I layered. Squeezing the sides of the plastic together, I tied the edges into a knot and shoved the whole thing in my backpack.

It felt like I had a ticking bomb on my back, ready to go off at any minute. My bag would get me life in prison, maybe even the death penalty. It was rare for someone my age, but Colorado still had lethal injection, and it wasn't impossible if I was tried as an adult. I shivered, but immediately shook it off.

I couldn't think like that. My head needed to be on straight if I was going to keep getting away with it.

I wished I had spent more time on old Marvin. But alibis and timelines were crucial, and I needed to keep it as simple as possible. At fifteen, it wasn't as if my hours were unaccounted for. Between my parents and friends, someone was constantly checking in with me, asking me questions, keeping me up to date, or texting a play-by-play of whatever they were doing. It was exhausting. And annoying.

I casually walked back to my bike, aware of every bird fluttering its wings, every squirrel moving a twig, every leaf falling. But I was distracted by the smell of food that wafted from one of the houses.

I was hungry.

My pocket vibrated. I pulled out my cell and saw that it was my father. I stopped to look around, like I expected to see him in my   sightline, pink bike in hand and his cuffs out. But no one was there. I considered not answering, but I knew that he'd get worried and I'd have extra explaining to do—you know, seeing as there was a murderer on the loose.

"Hey, Dad. What's up?"

"Hi, honey, where are you?"

"Just out for a walk. Everything okay?"

"Yeah, everything's fine, except I woke up and you weren't here. It's after ten, Ryann. It's a school night. *Where* the hell are you?" The tone of his voice made me uneasy. Ever since the police station he'd been acting funny. If I hadn't known better, I'd think that he agreed with that pig Estevez, despite his protests.

"Oh, sorry. I just needed some fresh air. It's been a hard couple of days." I hoped he felt like a guilty piece of crap for putting me through five rounds with his buddy.

"I know, but you need to come home. I'll come pick you up. Where are you?"

"Don't worry about it. I'm not far from the house. I'm surprised you're up. Aren't you exhausted?" Maybe his guilty conscience kept him awake.

"Ever feel like you're too tired to sleep? I think I need to unwind a bit. But I'll feel a whole lot better when I see you walk through that door. Be here in ten minutes or I'm coming to look for you." He tried to sound lighthearted, but we both knew he wasn't kidding around.

"Fine," I said before hanging up.

Double shit. There was no way I could ride someplace, burn the evidence, and make it home in ten minutes.

I made it to my bike and rode as fast as I could to burn off my nervous energy. I'd have to bring my bag—and all its criminally damning evidence— home with me for now.

I made it in fifteen minutes, which was damn good since it was a twenty-minute ride with a few hilly spots. I stashed the bike in the backyard since I'd said I'd been out walking. With my bag still over my shoulders, I let myself in the back door. It was dark. I was about to call out to my dad when the overhead light turned on. I raised my arm instinctively to shield my eyes. "Geez, Dad, what are you doing?" My knees quavered. *Had I gotten all the blood off me?*

I wished I'd had a chance to see myself in a full-length mirror. There hadn't been any way to check outside. Why hadn't I used one at Marvin's house? Stupid! My breath sped up. Hopefully my dad wouldn't notice. I was already under his microscope.

His face was void of expression. He stared blankly at me in a way he never had before. In a way I couldn't read. I was about to say something when he smiled and pulled me in for a hug. Squeezing me, he said, "I was worried about you." He drew back to meet my eyes, which unnerved me. He'd alleged that he could tell a lot from someone's eyes, especially if they were lying. I'd always thought it was crap—part of his cop persona—but at that moment I couldn't risk him seeing any hint of guilt, so I pulled away.

"I know things have been difficult. Do you want to talk? I hate it when you're angry with me." He tilted his head, his right hand still cupped around the upper portion of my arm. A knotting sensation invaded my muscles as I thought of the bloody evidence only inches from him.

"Thanks, but I think I'm okay." I walked past him, but was jerked back. Terror gripped me as I realized his hand was on my bag. He was pulling it from me.

"This thing feels heavy. What the hell you got in here?"

I whirled around, keeping the pack on me. "Nothing. Just some books and my cheer uniform. I'm really worn out. I'm going to head to bed." I leaned in and kissed him on the cheek like it was any other night, but I was petrified he'd follow. My heart pulsed wildly. Between the excitement of the kill and the fear that my dad would catch me with the blood-soaked shirt and knife, my body didn't know what to feel. I wondered for just a second if my dad would pat me on the back for this kill, had he known how badly that guy had treated Mom.

He let me go and wished me a good night's sleep. I shut my bedroom door and dropped my bag on the floor. I paced the small room. *What the hell was I going to do with it?*

I'd have to wait until he fell asleep again, sneak out, and get rid of it all.

Chapter
THIRTY-SEVEN

$\mathcal{I}$ changed out of my clothes, inspecting them for blood or even cat hair—anything that would link me to Marvin or his house. I didn't see any, but I still wanted to throw them in the wash right away. It would have to wait until morning, since my dad would wonder why his teenage daughter suddenly had an interest in late-night laundry.

I shoved my contaminated clothes in a plastic grocery bag. Next I cleaned my bedroom carpet with a lint roller—in case any hairs or fibers had gotten loose. It wasn't like I could whip out the vacuum. The roller paper went into the plastic bag with the rest of the stuff and behind a row of shoes in my closet.

My celebratory beverage would have to be put on hold. There was no way I could fully enjoy my success with that ticking time bomb in my closet.

I could hear the television on in the living room. Maybe I could dose him with some Dramamine so I could get on with things. Unlikely. My father often fell asleep in his La-Z-Boy in front of the TV. It was only a matter of time.

So there I was, sans drink, too nervous to check the news feeds, and waiting to rid myself of damning evidence. My window of time was shrinking. I needed to get out of the house, destroy my bag's contents, and return before my dad woke up again and Mom made it home from work.

My cell beeped. Now what?

It was B. *What the hell? Where r u? Haven't talked in days. U ignoring me?*

Course not. Just been busy. Sry.

With what? What's so busy you can't talk 2 me?

I texted back. Hopefully she'd let it go. *Parents are crazy right now. Stressed out about everything going on. Meet tomo?*

Fine but then u have 2 tell me everything. U ok?

Ya. Talk soon.

B was great in her own way, but sometimes she was so needy. I put the phone back on the bed and switched on my laptop. Maybe the distraction would relax me. It was way too early to see anything about Marvin, but there might have been updates in the press about my other kills.

I put the television on in the background, just in case something popped up there. It was the local news. The male anchor seemed unimpressed, while his female counterpart appeared stoned. Her perox-ide-blonde bob grazed her chin and her blue eyes stared vacantly into the camera lens as she read the prompter with the enthusiasm of someone getting a tooth pulled.

Refocusing on my laptop, I began with a general search: *Murders in Dungrave.* Olivia came up, and Yvonne of course. They still seemed to be the talk. Scrolling down, I saw something that piqued my curiosity. It was a video clip. I would recognize that over-gelled hair anywhere. I watched as a barrage of reporters swarmed Hayden, calling out question after question. He was walking from the courthouse. I could see his parents and his lawyer, Smythe, trying to shield him from the microphones and cameras.

I'd been so wrapped up, I'd all but forgotten about him.

A female reporter shoved her mic at him. "How do you feel about Yvonne's death?" Another one shouted, "Why did you kill your girlfriend?" And my personal favorite came from a male reporter with particularly bad hair plugs: "Did you also murder Olivia McMann?"

Poor Hayden was ashen. I could practically see the sweat trickling down his forehead.

His shark lawyer pushed in front of the camera, putting his hand over the lens to block the vultures from getting any more shots of Hayden. "My client will not be answering any of your ridiculous and insulting questions."

I hit pause on the clip and read the headline: JEALOUS BOYFRIEND SLAYS GIRLFRIEND IN HER OWN BEDROOM.

A wave of indignant bitterness washed over me. I hoisted my computer above my head but restrained myself. Scrolling down to the comments section, my fingers began typing, claiming ownership. But again, I succumbed to rational thinking and deleted it.

It seemed Hayden had been officially charged with first-degree murder, let out on bond, and given an upcoming court date. That was what I wanted, right? Even if he wasn't found guilty, his life was ruined. He'd always be that guy suspected of killing his girlfriend. Sure, OJ had been acquitted, but we all knew he did it. Hayden's life would be like that: eyes on him, judging silently, telling him that they knew what he'd done to that poor girl.

I scrolled further down the page, but there was nothing new. Olivia's case was still under investigation. I was about to close the window when I caught Omar's name. When I clicked on the link, my breath hastened.

Omar Murphy was at a high school dance when he suddenly collapsed from an apparent drug overdose on June 15. Teachers and students acted quickly, calling paramedics who worked on the youth at the scene. He was rushed to nearby Mercy General Hospital, where he stayed in a coma until his passing the following afternoon. Police are looking to speak with anyone who knew Mr. Murphy or might have information about how he'd accessed the deadly drugs. He was a well-liked, popular athlete at Cloverdale Secondary and will be greatly missed.

My blood chilled. Omar's father had seen me leaving his room. What if he'd identified me? I was already being questioned for one murder. How long before I was linked to this, and what the hell would I say if they ask me? The plastic bag in my closet might as well have been a nuclear bomb. I had to get it the hell out of here. Immediately.

I raced toward my closet and snatched my hat and jacket. As silently as I could, I removed the bulky bag and zipped it into my backpack. I turned out my light and slowly cracked my bedroom door. It would creak, it always did, but I figured my dad would be asleep by now and too far gone to hear it.

Closing the door behind me, I slunk down the hall, barely breathing as I moved. The flicker of the TV was reassuring, and the volume level was loud enough to comfort me as I passed him. I poked my head out and spotted him, passed out in the dark with his head back and mouth open.

I released a pent-up breath and scurried past him and out the door. A rush of cool air hit my face.

I didn't have a lot of time. He could wake any minute, and knowing him, he'd check on me to make sure I was asleep. Considering the day's events and the suspicions he already seemed to have, I doubted I'd have any plausible explanation for my absence.

I bolted down the front stairs. No bike tonight. I couldn't waste the time dragging it out from around back. Running, I made my way a few blocks down to a small park. It wasn't as ideal as Ridgeway, but it would have to do until I found something more permanent in the morning.

I glanced around for signs of people. A man was walking a small dog that had stopped to pee.

Hurry up. Hurry up. I tried to seem just as casual, like I was on an evening stroll. Stopping to check my phone, I tilted my face so he couldn't see me. I didn't need another 'eyewitness.' The man finally strode off, and I speed-walked to the jungle gym, searching for anything I could use to hide it.

The only way to truly get rid of it was to burn it, but this wasn't the kind of area where a fire—even a small fire—would go unnoticed. I'd have to improvise. The sandbox. It was the best I could do for now.

The wood beams bit into my knees as I knelt over the edge. I began digging in the middle of the sand with my bare hands. Desperate times and all that. The hole went deeper than expected. It was big enough to comfortably hide my plastic bag of goodies.

The bushes rustled behind me. I had to do it fast, so I shoved the whole backpack in, pulling the mound of sand back as fast as I could and covering my secret. I stood up and looked around me as the bushes crackled. If someone were watching me, they'd wonder what I was doing. Why was I burying something in a kid's sandbox? There was nothing I could say. My heart raced as the rustling intensified. I tensed, fists ready in case I had to fight.

With a loud cry, a cat ran out from behind the shrubs. I just about pissed myself.

Then I was back on my knees in the sand, flattening it out. But it was too smooth, so I messed it up a bit so it appeared played in.

I stood, dusted myself off, and was about to sprint home when I came face to face with Officer Knox.

"Jesus, Eric! You scared the shit out of me. What are you doing out here?"

"Patrolling. And I could ask you the same thing." He shifted his weight on one leg and crossed his arms with a suspicious look on his face.

"Nothing. I'm on my way home actually, so if you'll excuse me..." Heart hammering, I tried to walk past him, but he put his arm out, effectively blocking me with his giant meat hook. "What?"

"You didn't answer the question. What are you up to in the park, alone, at this time of night?"

"I lost something earlier and was searching for it, okay? Can I go now, Officer?"

"Did you find it?"

"No. And why are you working right now? I know you should be off, because my dad is."

"I took some overtime. Do you want a ride home?"

It was one of the last things I wanted, but I needed to get back as soon as possible. I was haunted by visions of my father standing at the door, demanding to know where the hell I'd been.

"I sort of snuck out while my dad was sleeping. I wanted to find my lost necklace, but he's been so overprotective. I knew he'd never let me out. It would be good to get home quickly—as long as my secret stays between us?"

"I guess I can agree to that. But only this once." He backed down and turned, walking in the opposite direction. "My car's parked just over here."

Eric dropped me off a half block away from my house. I'd been out for a total of fifteen minutes. When I hit my front lawn, I slowed to a walk so as not to thud on the stairs. My hand turned the front knob and I let myself in. The TV was still on. I prayed he was still asleep. So far, so good. I snuck down the hall and peeked in on him. He was passed out, his mouth still wide open.

I let my shoulders loosen as I tiptoed back down the hall to my room. Carefully closing the door, I dropped to my knees, my heartbeat slowing. I crawled to my bed, exhausted from the stress, and set the alarm on my phone for six thirty in the morning.

I'd been desperate to get rid of the evidence, but now I was second-guessing myself. I knew the sandbox was a stupid place to hide it, but I had no other options.

My stomach was still twisting. I closed my eyes. Maybe if I could sleep, morning would come faster and I could get back to the park, remove the bag, and dispose of it properly before some snot-nosed brat unearthed it and showed its bloody contents to Mama.

I might as well have wrapped it in a nice little bow and hand-delivered it to Estevez. I tried to relax, but images of being arrested kept dancing around my head. I wished I had one of B's little magic pills to help me sleep.

Chapter THIRTY-EIGHT

The blaring of police sirens got closer. Bent over Marvin, knife in hand, I glanced down and gasped. I was covered in a mess of sticky blood. Bounding up, I tried to think of what to do next. I wiped at it with a towel, but it kept smearing over my skin until I was almost completely red. How was I going to get out of there? I ran for the door and was about to open it when a booming voice came over the loudspeaker: "Ryann, we know you're in there. Come out with your hands up." It was Estevez. "It's over, Ryann."

"Ryann… Ryann…" The voice changed, but I recognized it. "Ryann, wake up."

I jumped up and felt arms around me.

"It's okay. It's only me. You were having a nightmare."

"Dad?" I realized where I was and attempted to

gain my composure. My alarm was ringing. I clicked the button and tossed my phone next to me on the bed, still gasping.

"You normally don't get up for another half hour."

I pulled myself upright, smoothing my hair with my hands. "Uh, yeah. I have to meet B. We're presenting a project in first period and want to do a quick review."

"Need a ride?"

The dread from the nightmare still coursed through me, quickly accompanied by panic. *My backpack was at the bottom of a sandbox.* "No thanks. I'll be fine." I tried to get up but he blocked me.

"My daughter? Refusing a free ride somewhere? That's highly unusual," he said in a singsong voice. "You sure you're okay?" He put his hand on my forehead. "You're not feverish."

I swept his hand away and laughed it off. "Nope, I'm fine. Are you working today?"

"Nah, but I'll be popping by there anyway. I have a few things to sort out. You have a good day at school." He kissed me on the head and left.

I was up in two seconds flat, throwing on whatever clothes were clean enough. I brushed my teeth, threw my hair up in a ponytail, and was out the door. Mom was likely still in bed. She usually slept in when she worked the late shift.

My father was in his home office with the door shut. I knew I should've said goodbye, but every second counted.

I rode Bri's bike straight to the park. School started at 8:15 and it was 6:58. I had to grab the bag, bike with it somewhere secluded, burn its contents, and get to school in an hour. Good luck.

It was light out, which made it a whole lot easier for people to see me and wonder what I was doing digging frantically in a kid's sandbox. I'd have to worry about that later.

I dropped the bike onto the grass; the clatter of the frame against the ground reverberated through the quiet Friday morning. Except for a guy in his twenties walking his golden retriever and an elderly lady pushing her walker God knows where, I was alone…if you didn't count all the cars driving by.

It would have been so much easier if I'd had a dog or a little brother to explain away my actions.

My hands dug deeper and deeper. I moved a little bit left and a little more right, but there was nothing. The acid in my empty stomach churned. I turned over the entirety of the sandbox—which must have looked crazy to anyone watching me—but there was nothing in it but a tiny toy car, a small green plastic shovel, and a few army figurines.

I was frozen on my knees in the middle of the sandbox, my pants covered with filth. Muck and grains of sand filled the undersides of my nails. Where was it?

My mind raced at the prospect of who in the world could have the one thing that would end me.

There was a flutter in my stomach. What if my

dad knew, and he was playing some sort of game with me? Testing me? Maybe he'd finally realized who his daughter truly was... But no. He'd clearly stated that I didn't have it in me.

Wait. Eric had been patrolling around there. I shook my head. He was no seasoned detective. And if the lovesick way he behaved around me was any indication, he didn't suspect me of anything. I was being ridiculous.

But somebody had that bag.

Fighting with the horror of what that could mean, I stood and dusted myself off. Then I backed up, out of the box, and stared at the half-dozen holes I'd left in my search. A wave of dizziness swept through me and I stumbled onto a small, grassy hill next to Bri's bike. Tucking my grimy knees into my chest, I rested my head on them and closed my eyes. I sucked in a lungful of much-needed air.

I had no idea what to do next.

The ride to school was a blur. If someone had seen me the night before, maybe they were planning to turn me in. Maybe they were plotting my take-down that very moment. Just as I locked the bike along the fence at school, my phone went off. It was B. She and Mackenzie were in the cafeteria and wanted to meet before first period.

I wasn't prepared, physically or mentally, but I went, unsure of how to explain the state I was in. Dirty clothes, greasy hair, muddy fingernails. I'd gotten sloppy. I hadn't even showered when I'd gotten home the night before! Did I want to get caught? My nausea intensified.

I was beyond angry with myself but did my best to act normal as I approached them at our usual table.

"Well, looky who's finally gracing us with her presence," B said. Mackenzie laughed.

"What the hell happened to you?" Mac eyed me from my shoes to my hair.

"I was riding Bri's bike through the park and I fell—in the dirt." It was a lame excuse, but I wasn't at my peak.

"Ouch. You okay?" B scrunched up her face.

I took a seat across from them. "My knee's a little tender but I'll live. What are you guys talking about—or should I say gossiping about—this morning?" I had a feeling I already knew. Maybe it would refocus my shock.

"Seriously? Hasn't anyone told you?" Mackenzie asked, wide-eyed.

"Told me what?"

B leaned forward and with a sly glance. "Rumor is that Omar's death looks suspicious." She had a satisfied smile. B always liked to share the juicy details. I think it made her feel important.

I didn't need to put on a face, because I was actually shocked. I was expecting her news to be about Marvin. "Huh? What are you talking about? Omar died of an overdose. I saw him at the dance."

Mac took a sip of her coffee, which smelled

amazing, as Bao-yu continued, "That's what everyone thought, but turns out the coroner or medical examiner or whatever did an autopsy. I guess he was stable, and then he just died. Apparently Omar died of an embolism."

"Yeah," Mackenzie added. "I guess that's not caused by an overdose."

"What causes it, then?" I asked, resting my head on my arms.

"It's some sort of air bubble. I guess it can happen after surgery," B said.

"Or from injections," Mac added. They were practically finishing each other's hyper little sentences.

"Duh, they injected him with all kinds of stuff when they were trying to resuscitate him. Why is that suspicious?" I could hardly keep my attention. All I could ruminate on was the empty sandbox.

Where. Was. My. Bag?

Beads of sweat dripped down the back of my neck.

My jacket pocket vibrated again. Why couldn't people just leave me alone already? I pulled my phone out slowly and clicked the screen. I had a text from an unknown number. That was odd. I'd never had one before. I let B and Mac chatter on as I pulled up the text.

Found your bag of naughty things.

I gasped.

"What's wrong?" B asked.

She and Mackenzie stared at me with the same questioning glance.

I had to think. Quick. "Um, nothing, sorry, just a text from my mom. It's a family thing." I shoved the phone back in my pocket before either of their snooping eyes could glance at the screen. "I've got to go. I want to get to class early..." I stood.

Mac reached out and put her hand on my arm. I wanted to swat it away. I hated being touched a hundred times more when I was stressed.

"What?" I asked, trying not to stare her down.

"You all right? You seem kind of jumpy."

I sighed. "I'm fine. I promise. It's just family stuff. I'll catch you guys later." I stormed off, knowing that they were watching me as I made my way out of the cafeteria and down the hall. I needed a private place to figure out what the hell was going on. As I opened the door to my still-empty first-period classroom, I felt the buzz in my pocket again. My stomach clenched.

Closing the door behind me, I ambled over to my usual desk and pulled out my phone.

What did you do, Ryann?

They knew my name? My heart raced in my ears, so loudly that I didn't think I'd be able to hear someone screaming beside me. Shock was setting in, but not enough to shut my mind off.

I'd been caught. But by who? And why were they sending me anonymous texts instead of turning me in?

Whoever it was had seen me at the playground last night, waited for me to leave, and then dug up the bag. Maybe the cat wasn't the only thing in those bushes? They had my name and phone number. Now they were going to…what? *Blackmail me?*

Everyone who knew me was well aware that my family had zero money. A waitress and a small-town cop didn't exactly rake in the bucks.

But what else could they want? The only two things even remotely viable were sex and revenge.

And I wasn't going to let them have either.

Chapter
THIRTY-NINE

$\mathcal{S}$itting in my desk, I shook, from both nerves and a chill, despite the eighty-degree weather. I forced my fingers to text back. *Who is this and what do you want?*

It's none of your concern. Yet.

It is if you think you're going to get something from me.

I'll let you know what that is when I'm ready. Don't go far. xoxo

Fuck you.

I waited but received no reply. Who did that asshole think he was? No one toyed with me.

I must have sat there, completely still, for another ten minutes before others started trailing in. My first instinct was to get the hell out of there. How was I supposed to sit in class and listen to some crap about photosynthesis when someone could dismantle my life at any moment? I shot up from my seat to run out, but slumped back down just as quickly. What if the anonymous texter was in class with me? It could easily have been a student. In fact, it would explain a lot: how they knew me and had my number, for a start.

My focus narrowed on the faces of everyone in the room. I examined everything from the color of their hair and eyes, to the shape of their faces, to what kind of clothes they had on. But my class was only forty kids out of a school of hundreds. I was never going to figure it out randomly. I needed more.

Had I pissed anyone off lately? *No.* School-Ryann was frustratingly perfect. But maybe that in itself was enough motivation. Maybe someone was so jealous of me that he—or she, to be fair—jumped on the opportunity to take me down.

On the other hand, maybe someone who lived close to me just happened to be out the night before, and they'd seen me at the park.

Unknown hadn't broadcasted their intentions, so I was at a standstill. I was also at the little prick's mercy until they decided to contact me again. Patience was a virtue I didn't have.

The teacher was droning on about the sun's ability to do something or other. It jolted my memory of the flowers in my locker. And the anonymous typed note. What if it was the same person? Secret admirer, my ass!

I snuck my cell onto my lap and texted Unknown. *Who the hell are you and what do you want from me? Money?*

There was no point in denying that the bag was mine, since my DNA was all over the thing. Well, mine and Marvin's.

I'd have to use persuasion and charm to get it back. I was willing to pay almost any price, because I had everything to lose. And they knew it.

I waited and waited. When I wasn't staring at that black screen, I was glancing around the classroom to see if anyone was watching me.

The class bell startled me. The hour was over and I still had nothing. No one had bothered with so much as a squint in my direction. I wanted to pull my hair out in one big chunk.

Walking down the hallways drove me crazier. Everyone was a suspect. I tried to gauge who was looking my way or staring a little too long. Who had it in them to go against me, knowing what I was capable of? If they'd looked inside the bag (and I'm certain they had), they'd know that I wasn't to be messed with. The only teenage girl who buries a bag with bloody clothes and a knife in it is a murderous psychopath. Which begged the next and more pertinent question: what kind of person uses such evidence to taunt said psychopath?

A warm, fuzzy glow spread through me. My answer was swiftly evident.

Another psychopath.

I tried to suppress my sadistic smile. It was all becoming clear. If the person who'd found my bag had been 'normal,' I'd already have been arrested. Unknown was their own kind of twisted, which meant that they wanted something other than simply to turn me in. Maybe they admired my work and wanted to trade war stories. There are between thirty-five and fifty active serial killers in the United States at any given time. Surely there could be another one—active or prospective—in Dungrave.

Maybe I had someone who actually understood who I was. The thought fluttered through me, awakening each cell. But I had to contain my enthusiasm until I was sure I could turn this person into an ally—or quiet them permanently. It would be nice to have someone to talk to. An admirer. Perhaps I could keep them around for a short time.

Whoever this was had some balls. Not only were they smart enough to find my bag, but they were bold enough to taunt me with it. Their antics would prove either extremely irritating or interesting. In any case, I was still safe.

"Hey, what are you daydreaming about?" Lucas put his arm around me and squeezed, sending me into the lockers beside us.

"Shit, Luc, you scared the crap out of me." I clutched my chest and took a deep breath. "What's up?" I backed up, out of his grip.

"I was asking you the same thing. You looked lost in your own little world. What's on that naughty mind?"

I cleared my throat. "Just thinking about all the craziness that's been going on. Aren't you the least bit freaked out? Dungrave used to be such a quiet, dull place. Now it seems like every other week brings some traumatic...something."

"Well, I guess I shouldn't ask if you've heard the latest then." He stared at me intently.

I slammed back against a locker and put my hands dramatically over my face. "What now?"

"An old guy over on Clarke was found dead in his living room last night. His neck was sliced ear to ear. I guess a few of his buddies went over for late night poker and found him."

If I hadn't known better, I'd have thought that Lucas sounded excited. Thrilled even. Hadn't he seemed overly interested in the details of the crimes? He sure wasn't distraught. In fact, he was exceedingly fascinated with the kills.

"Earth to Ryann. I said, what do you have next block?" Luc asked.

"Oh, uh...English. You?"

"Physics. Catch you at lunch?" He'd begun to walk away, gawking at me for my answer.

I gave him a thumbs-up. He turned and scurried down the hall. *Could it be Luc?* Of all people, was it one of my (and I say this with a very big grain of salt) best friends?

It was probably just my overactive imagination coupled with my desire to wrap up the mystery nice, neat, and fast. I'd known Lucas for years, and it takes one to know one. I was pretty certain he was not one.

At any rate, Marvin had been found. That was quick. I'd speculated that it would be days before anyone discovered him. He had friends? Huh.

I pulled up the news on my phone:

Man Found Dead. Throat Slit. Fourth Murder in Four Weeks.
Does Dungrave Have a Serial Killer?

I read through the article. The journalist was linking my crimes. Finally, someone with insight and intelligence. Not every crime has to have the same signature. People have to put everything in neat little boxes. It doesn't always work that way.

I cleared the screen, not wanting to face what this could mean for me. It was only a matter of time before whoever dug up my bag connected me to Marvin's murder.

The question was, what were they going to do about it?

Chapter
FORTY

$\mathcal{L}$unch was far worse. I was silently going out of my mind. I was so used to being the one with all the control, and now the only thing I could do was wait and see what Unknown's next move would be.

I sat at our usual table while Mac, B, Katie, Lucas, and Asad blabbed on about the typical bullshit.

"Are those new shoes?" Katie asked, staring at Mackenzie's feet. "Sneakers? Since when have you ever owned a pair? Where are your heels?" Katie looked almost disgusted that Mac would commit such fashion trauma.

"Ugh, right? My father banned me from wearing anything with a heel until this psycho is caught. He said I couldn't run if I needed to get away. He even hid them from me. Hello! Exaggerate much?"

Asad broke into hysterical laughter. "Oh my God.

I love parents. Does your dad know you? The only way you'd run is to a huge sale at Bloomingdales."

I smiled and nodded the best I could, all the while judging everyone near me. I was certain each of them had a knowing look in their eyes or a teasing grin—my brain was playing games with me. I felt helpless. Much like my victims had.

Stupid haunting symmetry.

Maybe Unknown was betting on that; maybe he wanted me to feel what it was like to be at someone else's mercy. But I was no victim, as whoever was fucking with me was about to discover.

"—Ryann?"

How long had I zoned out this time? It was Luc. I looked up to find all four of them staring at me.

"W-what?" I stammered.

B playfully tapped my cheek. "Wake up. What's with you? You're here, but not really."

Ten eyeballs gawked. "Nothing! I'm fine. I didn't get enough sleep last night. My house is super hectic right now. All these cases are wearing on my dad, and then my mom gets all worried and starts to hover. It's a lot to take."

"Sorry. We didn't know it was that intense," Asad offered.

I wasn't even eating, just pushing around the pasta on my plate.

"Speaking of Dungrave's recent murder spree, any news about that old guy?" Lucas gratefully changed the subject, but pinned me with his stare.

I swore I saw something different in his eyes, in his face—an air of satisfaction...of *playful enjoyment?* "Not sure why you're asking me. The first I heard of it was from you." I stared back at him, hard and cold, hoping he'd back down. What was his game?

He didn't drop his gaze. "Your dad's a cop with access to all the case files. He's bound to know something. Besides, how do I know what's discussed in the Wilkanson household over morning Cheerios?"

I'd known Luc a long time, and he'd never seemed this particular kind of strange before. I definitely felt some hostility.

"I dunno, Luc. It doesn't seem like appetizing breakfast conversation." I stood abruptly—playing it up a tad—grabbed my books, and said, "If you'll excuse me, I've lost my appetite." I turned on my heels and was almost out of the room when I felt a hand pulling the back of my arm.

"Ryann, wait."

It was B, so I slowed down. "What?"

"What the hell? In all the years we've known Lucas, I've never seen you guys act like that. What gives?"

I stopped and faced her. "Maybe I'm just tense, but it feels like he's got some sick, perverse interest in all this stuff and he's using me to get the gruesome details. It's like he doesn't care who I am anymore, just how much I know." I bit the inside of my mouth until my eyes watered. Tears helped the whole fake-crying thing.

She wrapped her arms around me. "It's okay. Don't let him get to you. He's just being an ass."

Her words struck me like lightning. Was that what Lucas was trying to do? Get to me? It would make sense. The text messages, the probing questions. Maybe even the flowers. He did live near me. It was well within the realm of possibility that he'd been the one to see me burying my bag, the one to become Unknown. It was the why that baffled me.

"Are you going to be okay?" B asked, interrupting my brainstorm.

"Uh, yeah. Don't worry. I'll be fine. I just need some air."

"Want me to come with you?"

"Nah. I have to check in with my dad anyway."

"Okay, text me later."

I walked outside. I needed to think. My phone beeped again. The same unnerving feeling swept over me as I glanced at the screen, expecting to see Unknown again. But it was only Asad checking on me. Everyone was always checking on me!

Pacing the school's front yard, I weighed the possibilities. Lucas seemed like such an unlikely suspect.

I got another text. It was probably Mackenzie this time, or Lucas trying to apologize. I'm sure B went straight to the table to report back. She loved to be mediator.

It was Unknown.

What did you do? Bad girl.

I tried to breathe through the rush of emotion. The game had gotten old fast. Whoever was doing this had more than my attention. They had my wrath.

I texted back. *Who the fuck is this?*

Seems you're upset. What are you going to do now?

I had no chance to reply before the next one came in.

How badly do you want your bag back, little girl?

I don't know what you're talking about or who you are, but leave me alone. My dad's a cop.

Oh, I know ;)

I wanted to scream. Rip my hair out. Stab someone. I didn't respond. I would not be played with. I needed to enlist some help. I needed Eric.

Chapter
FORTY-ONE

"Pick up, pick up." It rang about six times before Eric answered. "Finally!"

"Hello to you too," Eric whispered.

"I know you're on shift, but I need you."

"What happened? Are you all right?" he asked, sounding genuinely concerned.

"I'm not sure. I've gotten a few...harassing text messages from an unknown number. Is there any way it can be traced?" I knew there was, but I wanted him to feel like a hero. Maybe he'd be more inclined to help me.

"Of course. What did your dad say?"

I huffed into the phone. "We're not going to tell him. He's got enough on his plate. It's not that big a deal."

"It's a big enough deal that you're calling me."

"Well, you said you were my friend. I thought you'd want to help me."

"What can I do?"

"Can you find out who the phone belongs to?"

He stayed quiet for a minute, which seemed to be his pattern. I'd ask for something. He'd pause thoughtfully, then give me what I wanted. Of course, he didn't want me to think he was going to give in. He wanted to make me sweat a bit first, make it seem like he was doing me a big favor.

"We have a tech department for that."

"Well, is there any way you could have them look into it?" I put a little extra something in my voice. I could hear him clear his throat. I knew he liked me a little more than he should've, and I was going to play my hand.

"I can't bring anything in without a production order, which means you'd have to file a report or complaint so that I have grounds to run your phone. But you can call the phone company and find out what the number is."

"They won't give that info to me if it's in my dad's name. And if they did, he'd find out about it."

"It's not that easy, Ryann. Half the time we're too busy to even look into this kind of stuff. Bullying and unwanted contact happens all the time. We have actual cases to investigate, which don't include running interference for teens texting crap back and forth. You could just block the number."

"No. I need to find out who's threatening me."

"What kind of threats?" His voice became soft and quiet again.

"The kind that make me nervous. I'm not sure if it's serious or a prank, but I won't stop looking over my shoulder until I figure out which. Come on, Eric. There's got to be a loophole—some way you can do this for me." Perhaps seduction would work. "I'll make it worth your time."

He made the throat-clearing sound again. "A guy in tech owes me one. I'll see if he'll run it for me. But only because you sound so desperate. Besides, you have had contact with two previous murder victims. I couldn't live with myself if this creep was targeting you next and I did nothing to help."

"Thanks, Eric. Oh, and one more thing: it has to be anonymous."

"No can do. As soon as he runs your phone, you—or whoever the phone is registered to—will come up. It's not something I can keep secure."

"Then can you make sure he doesn't blab to anyone else? I really need help. I could be in serious trouble, and you're all I have." The whole damsel in distress thing seemed to work on him. Maybe that was why he'd become a cop in the first place.

"So you keep saying. What aren't you telling me, Ryann? I can protect you." He sounded almost panicked. I had to hand it to him. He was sweet. If I'd had more of a mushy side, I might've swooned.

"We can talk about that when I see you. When

can we do this?" My hand was practically strangling my cell. "Sooner is better."

"Okay. What about after school? Meet me at our regular spot. You shouldn't be seen at the station."

"How long will it take? When I don't answer my phone, my parents freak and track me down."

"Maybe an hour. Your dad's working a new file anyway. I don't think he'll be calling."

My curiosity got the better of me. I knew I shouldn't have, but... "What kind of file? Not the guy who got his throat slashed?"

"Yes, that one, actually. How do you know about that already?"

"A friend at school told me. Why?"

"I didn't think it'd been released yet."

"I checked it out online. There's a story about it on the front page."

"Vultures. The reporters in this town are relentless. They've been patrolling the airwaves with illegal police scanners and lurking everywhere, just waiting for the next thing to happen."

I don't know why, but his annoyance amused me. He really was a do-gooder. "Look, I've got to go. Meet you there at three fifteen, okay?"

"Okay."

The end of school couldn't come fast enough. I'd managed to avoid my friends the rest of the day, which wasn't an easy feat. I still had all my books with me because as I was heading back to my locker, I spotted Lucas camped out there. He must have

been waiting for me, but I had no time for his apologies. I needed to be at the park in fifteen minutes. I
turned back down the hall and left out the rear door.
It was shady of me, but until I knew for sure that
Lucas had no part in the intimidation, I had to be
extra cautious.

As I waited for Eric, I erased all the texts that
were incriminating and left only one he could use to
trace the number.

Eric's outstretched hand snapped up my cell. "I'll
have it back to you in less than an hour."

"Your friend's sworn to secrecy, right?"

"Yes. Now tell me what this is about."

I crossed my arms and avoided eye contact. "I
can handle it."

"Right. That's why you called me in a panic. You
can tell me, or I'll look myself." He crossed his arms.

"I received a few texts. I lost my bag and it had a
few personal items in it. The creep is threatening...I
dunno...to blackmail me. They haven't exactly
named their terms yet."

His eyebrows raised and he straightened. "What
kind of personal things?"

"It's not important. I just need to know who's
sending the messages, and then I'll know how to
deal with it."

He stepped closer, putting a hand on my arm.
Strange. I didn't mind when he touched me. "Fine,
I'll let it go for now, but you call me if you need
help. Don't let this get out of control. I know you

think you can handle yourself, but there's at least one psycho on the loose. You need to be careful. I'll meet you back here in an hour and fifteen minutes with your phone. Stay visible. Public places are safer, but I'm sure you already know that."

I nodded. "Please hurry."

I almost felt bad worrying Eric like that, but I needed to set a fire under his ass to get my results.

Since I had no cell and all my schoolbooks, I figured I'd squeeze in some homework. What else was I going to do? Sweet, perfect Ryann had to keep her straight-A streak going. I pulled out *The Catcher in the Rye*. Holden Caulfield could suck it. He didn't know what real problems were. I nestled into an unoccupied picnic table and began to read. I was halfway through and tempted to see if there was a movie version instead.

"What are you doing here?" A shadow moved over me.

"Better question is, what are you doing here, Lucas?"

He smiled wide and sat beside me.

"Did you follow me here?" I asked, indignant.

His smile quickly faded. "Don't say it like it's creepy. I saw you a few streets back so I followed you, but only to apologize for earlier. By the way, was that uniform you were chatting up the dude from outside Yvonne's?"

I detected a hint of jealousy in his usual cool voice. "He's helping me with something." I watched to see if he'd so much as twinge, but he stared straight ahead. I gave him credit.

"I bet."

"What's that supposed to mean?" I huffed.

His stone face lit up with laughter and he pushed me playfully. "I was only kidding. You're so serious lately. Sorry about my less-than-tasteful comments earlier. Bao-yu explained that I was an insensitive ass."

As much as I wanted to ascribe a weird, new eeriness to Luc, I couldn't find much of anything. Here he was, staring at me with the same stupid smile he had for years.

Although…it was kind of odd that he'd followed me here. Lucas was the kind of guy who didn't sweat the little things, and if he pissed you off, he'd wait till you cooled down then act like nothing happened. He wasn't the type to sincerely apologize. Ugh. I was going round in mentally exhausting circles.

"So what did supercop want? A date? Did he offer to play cops and robbers with you?" He laughed with abandon and elbowed me in the ribs. It was usually contagious, but I wasn't in the right headspace.

"No."

Lucas's eyes searched mine and I didn't appreciate it. "You always do your homework in the park?"

"Nope, but it's nice out and I wanted some alone time…so…" I motioned to the space around me, but he didn't catch on. He wasn't exactly Mensa material—another reason he probably wasn't Unknown.

"If you don't mind, I'd like to get back to this." I held my book up.

"I guess that's my cue." He stood and took a few steps back, shading me again. "Be careful, Ryann." He patted me on the head and jogged off.

What did he mean, be careful? Was that a warning? A threat? I didn't know whether to be freaked out or pissed off.

I spent the remainder of the hour trying to read but succeeded only in people watching and getting a mild sunburn.

Finally, Eric came trudging over.

"Well?" I asked straightaway.

"Uh, hello to you too. Are you always so abrupt?"

"I'm sorry. Hello. How are you? Now, did you find out who the number belongs to?"

He returned to his spot next to me on the bench. I couldn't help but notice the mixture of soap and sweet sweat radiating from him. The uniform looked warm. All polyester. "He's working on it. I didn't wait for the results. He got whatever info he needed off your phone and I rushed it back to you ASAP as per your demands." He raised an eyebrow at me.

"Okay. Thanks for the speedy service."

He pointed to the screen on my cell. "And not a minute too soon. Looks like someone's trying quite hard to get a hold of you."

I could feel my eyebrows scrunch together. Was it Unknown? I put in my password and saw that I'd missed three texts and one call: two texts from Luc apologizing followed by one call and one text from B. Thank God that was it.

"Yeah, I kind of freaked out on my friends earlier. They're making sure I'm okay."

Eric moved in closer and gazed into my eyes. "Are you going to tell me what's in the bag? I can't really help you if I don't have all the details."

"I appreciate that, but you're doing enough. None of this is your problem, and I've involved you too much already. Besides, I'd rather not talk about it." I bit my lip lightly. When was this guy going to make his move? I was adorable. The more smitten he was, the more I could get from him.

I watched his Adam's apple bounce as he swallowed hard and looked away. I needed to move things up a notch. Reaching out, I lightly traced the tops of his fingers with mine. I'd expected him to back away, but he allowed my touch.

"I really should go. I'll call you as soon as I find out anything." He got up from the bench and smoothed out the thighs of his pants, as if he'd been full of crumbs.

I stood too, keeping my proximity close. "Are you sure you have to go?"

"Why? Is there something else you need?" His eyes widened, as though he'd jump higher if I asked him to.

"Just your company, but if you're too busy..."

"I'm still working. Besides, we both know that would be a bad idea."

My chest grazed his shoulder as I whispered in his ear. "You're a really nice guy, Eric, It's a shame." I took a single step back to catch his eye, smiled, and walked away, leaving him standing there, agape.

It was fun to play with toys. Especially pretty ones.

Chapter
FORTY-TWO

I attempted to distract myself over the weekend with my favorite crime shows. Perhaps watching those guys get caught would dampen my itch to hunt and make me focus on self-preservation instead. Stupid priorities.

It had been three days, and I still hadn't heard anything back from Eric about the trace. He'd never ignored me like this before. My inability to control the situation made me crazy.

The constant chatter about murder and killers had diminished at school, probably because we were in exams and everyone was stressed, but there was still talk. People stayed in groups and made sure the locks were on their doors. I was quite impressed with myself—studying, acing my exams, and managing my new hobby.

B was back to drooling secretly over Asad, while Asad continued to play junior detective on the open homicide cases in town. Katie and Mackenzie were as flighty and carefree as ever, shopping, getting drunk and gossiping about who cheated on who. And Lucas was his effervescent, smart-ass self. All was right in my world—which meant one thing: I was bored.

I'd tried to message Unknown a few times with no response, which only inflamed me more.

The newspaper and online media hubs were all over the Dungrave murders.

It had spread to all the major networks: CNN, Fox News, ABC, NBC, you name it.

Our sleepy little town was on the map now.

It was a summer sensation, much like when David Berkowitz, the Son of Sam, killed six and attacked another seven victims in New York City in 1976.

Reporters and camera crews had become permanent fixtures around town. Mom had even become chummy with a few on-air anchors who liked to 'work on their pieces' at the diner, pounding back greasy plates of fries and countless cups of bitter coffee. She was so cute, coming home from work excited because Suzy or Bobby asked her opinion on something or other. Little did they know, she had the most exclusive inside scoop.

She was even in a great mood one day because Marvin was no longer a regular and she'd been getting great tips from the media people.

I wondered what people's reactions would be if they'd known it was me. Would Bri finally notice me? Would my parents blame themselves or disown me? Would my neighbors give the typical interviews? She was so sweet—a quiet girl, good manners, honor roll. We never saw any signs.

It didn't matter, because no one would ever know. The thought nestled itself heavily inside my chest. No. One. Would. Ever. Know. I'd have no legacy.

I needed a drink.

My favorite TV station was on. It was a twenty-four-hour channel dedicated to all things murder and mayhem. There were documentaries on killers, kidnappers, and stalkers, as well as the psychiatrists, investigators, and detectives that tried to hunt them down and figure out what made them monsters. My top pick was *Most Evil*. This shrink designed a twenty-two-level scale to rate the evilness of serial killers. The show went through a killer's crimes, their childhood, and their psychology. Sometimes it even featured interviews with them from prison. Really cool.

The doctor on *Most Evil* believed that one cause of psychopathy was head trauma in childhood. He argued that head injuries seem benign at the time, but can actually cause damage to the anterior insular cortex, where empathy and the ability to bond and develop attachments to others is located. It's like a switch is flicked, and from that point on, the person doesn't process things in the same way. I'd fallen out of a tree when I was four, smacked my head on the ground, and received five stitches. Maybe that did it. Or maybe I'd been born that way. Regardless, I wouldn't have changed it. I liked who I was. I liked what I was capable of. It made me different. Special. Skilled at doing what other people only fantasized about.

As the smooth voice of the narrator talked about dismemberment in the background, I took a little stroll through cyberspace.

I searched the local paper's site. About five pages in, while I was guzzling my Diet Coke, something caught my attention. It was a picture, a black-and-white sketch of a girl. The fizzy liquid caught in my throat. I coughed and it sprayed, drenching my laptop with sticky brown fluid. I grabbed a T-shirt from the top of the laundry pile next to me and wiped down my screen.

I needed to see her face again.

Light hair. Light eyes. Dark hoodie. Hood up.

Fuck.

It was me.

There was an article beneath the sketch. I tried to slow my breathing enough to actually understand the words on the screen.

Mr. Henry Murphy, father of the late Omar Murphy, who died of a drug overdose on June 16, is asking for help in identifying a young girl who he believes was in his son's room the day of his death. He would like

to ask her some questions, and pleads with this girl, or anyone who knows her, to come forward.

My eyes darted back to *my face* on the screen. I knew he'd probably seen me, but why would he want to meet with me? Who puts out a public ad? It was like a wanted poster from the Wild West.

Unless he suspects me of something.

My head pulsated rhythmically, making my eyes bulge.

The drawing wasn't spot-on, but if I could see the resemblance, someone else might too. Like my dad.

Estevez would be all over this.

Chapter
FORTY-THREE

I banged on B's door. It wasn't like her to not answer my calls or texts. I knew she was home. She never did anything on school nights. After I hammered it a second time, she came, wearing a headset.

Pushing the screen open, she motioned for me to come inside, but didn't really make eye contact. I followed her downstairs, where she had three computer screens set up with games going on all of them.

"What are you doing, Razor? Get your head out of your ass, will ya?" B shouted.

She waved me toward a chair so she could get back to her conversation with another supergeek gamer through her microphone.

I made a face at her.

She rolled her eyes and nodded. "Valinhall, Subzero, Half-Star, and Daddyfatsax, I've got to go. Company. Check me back in thirty. AFK."

I burst out laughing. "Daddyfatsax? Who are these losers you associate with?"

She stared at me, blank-faced. "They're my people."

"AFK?"

"Duh. *Away from keyboard.*"

This made me crack up even more.

"What's up that you would dare interrupt me during peak war hours? This better be an emergency." A smile crept along the edges of her mouth.

"Can't I visit my best friend? We've hardly had any time together lately."

"Since when are you sentimental?" B asked.

Truthfully, I was here for a small taste of normalcy within the chaos that was quickly becoming my life. "I guess since our town became a scary, murderous circus."

She nodded, satisfied. "Want anything to drink?"

"Coffee? Iced if you got it?"

"Of course I got it." She smiled again. "Be back in five." She sprinted up the stairs, leaving me alone in her sweet nerd lair. I walked around, snooping just a bit into a few of her drawers and shelves. It was best to know as much about those around me as possible. You couldn't really trust anyone, no matter how well you thought you knew them.

Magazines and newspapers were stacked on her

desk. I picked up the top few. *Game World, Hacker,* some anime comic, and a newspaper. I pulled out the paper. A chunk of it was dog-eared. My curiosity got the better of me and I flipped to what B had marked. It was the very same pencil sketch of the girl in the hoodie—me—circled in red pen.

What the hell? Why would Bao-yu have circled it? Gooseflesh ran up my spine. *She'd recognized me.* Why else would she have marked it? My head swam.

I heard her on the stairs and quickly closed the paper, plopped it back on the desk, and replaced the stack of magazines just as I'd found them.

"One iced coffee coming up." B handed me a glass and kept one for herself.

I took it, smiling.

And now I couldn't help but watch her every movement—from the muscles in her face to the way her hair fell across her eye—for any hint that she was onto me. I took a small sip. "Mm, it's good. Thanks."

"No prob. So what's up?" She positioned herself on a chair directly in front of me. Was she making sure I was in her direct sightline? I considered bringing up the sketch. If I did, she'd be sure to give me some inkling of her suspicions, and I could tell her how wrong she was. I could easily explain it away. Guilty people don't call attention to themselves, so I thought perhaps I *should* bring it up.

"Thanks for talking to Luc the other day. I forgot to tell you. He came and found me later and apologized—because of you, I'm sure."

"No biggie. You know Luc. He always runs his mouth before his brain can catch up. He didn't mean anything by it."

"I know. But don't you think he's been acting kind of weird since all of this stuff has been happening? I know it's normal to be curious, and we all have of a morbid sense of humor, but...do you think Luc's taking it a bit far? He doesn't seem affected at all. It's almost as if he's getting some sick satisfaction from hearing all the disturbing details."

B seemed to consider what I'd said. "I don't know. He's a teenage guy. Doesn't that automatically make him weirder? Look at Asad. It's like he's making a real-life game of *Clue* out of the murders. Who did it? In what room? With the candlestick?"

"I suppose you're right. Nothing like this has happened before, and people react differently. It's not like I'm handling it as well as I could be." I hoped she'd ask me about the sketch. It would be easier then trying to bring it up.

B cleared her throat. "How are you doing now? I know it's been rough for you, being so close to the murders and investigations." I swear I could feel her eyeballs on me.

"All right."

"I wanted to ask you a question." B looked funeral serious now. She placed her cup on the table, folded her hands in her lap, and glared. "Did you go to the hospital to see Omar?" She didn't even blink.

She was steady. And there it was, the question I'm sure we'd both been waiting for.

"No. Why do you ask?" I was steady too.

"You were pretty upset about him. I figured maybe you went to visit him or something. No big deal." She reached for her coffee again. One of B's flaws was acting nonchalant when she was actually really bothered.

I ran my hands through my hair and made a show of exhaling dramatically, like I was about to confide the deepest of secrets. She leaned toward me. "Fine, yes. I went. But only because I was afraid. Everyone around me keeps dying. When I heard he was on life support I wanted to see him—to see for myself that he was going to be all right."

She tilted her head. "But why keep it a secret?"

"Is this about the sketch in the paper?" I softened my gaze and smiled faintly.

"Well, now that you mention it…is it you?"

"Probably, but I can't say for sure. I went to see Omar, but I didn't know what to say to his parents. So when his dad stepped away, I tried to sneak by his door. He caught me. I didn't feel like having a drawn-out conversation about why I was there, so I ran."

B pushed her glasses back up the bridge of her nose. "I'm guessing that seemed pretty suspicious to him. Still, why would he release a sketch of you? Maybe he thinks you know something about Omar's death."

She was too close. I shrugged. "I guess, but I don't know anything—except what I saw at the dance along with a hundred other people."

Looking thoughtful, B said, "You should talk to him and tell him that. It will probably help him."

"No, B. Don't say anything. Just leave well enough alone. I don't want to be any more involved than I am. Can you keep this between us? Please?" I tried to sound sincere, but this bullshit was grating on me.

"Of course. But what if someone else recognizes you? The drawing isn't great, but I see the resemblance."

"Well, the picture's only been out for two days. Hopefully no one else notices it and I can move on. Going to the hospital was more about me than Omar, but explaining that to people would make me look bad."

B stretched forward and rested her hand on my arm. "I get it. Hopefully no one else will put it together."

I smiled and took another sip of my coffee. "I'd better go, so you can get back to your online loser horde."

"I'll send them your love."

❖   ❖   ❖   ❖

After I got home I decided to watch a movie online when there was a knock on my door.

"Come in," I shouted.

I was met with a shy, unsure smile.

"What's up, Dad?"

"Did you go to the hospital to see that Omar boy?" He stepped closer. "I didn't think you knew him well." He stared. Didn't even blink. It was unnerving.

I pulled myself to a sitting position and placed my laptop on the bed next to me. "Why do you ask?" It was all I could muster.

He closed my bedroom door. "Ryann, there's a picture—a sketch—of a girl that looks…well, looks a whole lot like you. Estevez told me that Omar's father made a report that he saw the girl in the sketch leaving his son's room. He wants to talk to her. He seems pretty convinced it's you. When he showed it to me, well, I couldn't argue."

"What does Mr. Murphy want?" I crossed my arms tightly around my knees.

My father shifted his weight from one foot to the other. "I'm guessing that's an admission. I don't get it. Why would you keep it a secret? You went to visit a schoolmate—why not introduce yourself to his parents instead of running away?"

I let out a sigh and covered my face with my hands. Show time. Pulling my hands down, I gave him my saddest eyes. "Yeah, I went to see him, but only because I was so upset about everything that's been happening. I was right there when he collapsed. I know he wasn't like the others because he overdosed, but still, I couldn't bear the thought of another person I knew dying. But yeah, we weren't friends, so I didn't want to stick around and explain it to his father, who was grieving. It was like…I just needed to see for myself that he was okay. I needed him to be okay." I don't know where it came from, but I blinked one rolling tear down my cheek. Perfection.

As if on cue, my father swooped in and held me in his arms. Maybe he wasn't as suspicious as I'd feared. "It's okay, honey. I understand." He pulled back to face me. "But why not talk to Mr. Murphy? It would put his mind at ease. He's grieving, and I think it would give him peace of mind to know you were only there to check on Omar."

"As opposed to what?" I snapped.

He stroked my hair gently. "Nothing sordid. But as a father, I'd want to speak to one of my kid's friends. Talk to him. Say a few kind words, explain that you were worried, and it'll be done." He grinned and pinched my cheek as if I were a five-year-old bargaining for an extra piece of candy.

"I don't have anything to say. Like I told you, I didn't really know Omar." I pulled away and kept my gaze ahead.

"Ry, come on. It's the right thing to do. You put yourself there, now you have to deal with the consequence of that action, just like we always talked about. I'll arrange for him to come down to the station after school tomorrow."

He walked out of my room before I could argue any more.

Chapter
FORTY-FOUR

$\mathcal{I}$ counted the minutes until school was over. I just wanted get to the police station and convince Mr. Murphy that I'd been thoughtfully checking on his dying son and not pumping a fatal air bubble into him.

But more important than meeting Mr. Murphy, discerning Lucas's weirdness, or ducking Estevez's subtle accusations was finding Unknown and the missing backpack. Eric was ignoring me, and I'd had enough.

Pulling out my cell, and careful not to let Mr. Rydell see, I texted him. *Why aren't you answering? I'll be at the station in a few hours. Need to see you.*

Can't talk there. Too many ppl + your dad.

Then meet me before. This can't wait any longer.

Nothing to tell you. Texts came from unregistered

prepaid phone. Disposable kind. No way to track who's messaging you. Sorry.

Incensed was not the word. I was furious. Raging. *Why couldn't you tell me that days ago instead of making me wait!? I've been freaking out!*

Sorry. Was busy, besides there was nothing I could do.

This isn't over. We need to talk about this. I'll see you soon.

I received no further messages from Eric. If he thought he could freeze me out…well, he had another thing coming.

The text messages from Unknown had stopped over the past few days. After Eric gave me my phone back, I received three more threats, playful as they were, about exposing what a wicked girl I'd been. I hoped that Eric and his IT buddy had no further access to my messages. Let's just say they were a tad more specific then the earlier ones.

I particularly enjoyed the one that said, *Tsk, tsk. What would Daddy think of his little girl now?*

This prick was a pro at getting under my skin. I had to discover—and eliminate—Unknown before it was too late.

When I walked out of school after last period, my dad was waiting for me in his cruiser.

"How was school today, kiddo?" he asked, before pulling away.

"Same as every day."

"Mr. Murphy should be there by the time we arrive. A quick chat with him and you'll be done. Look at it as your good deed for the day."

"Yeah, sure," I muttered.

"Mom's gone in for a double. One of the girls is sick. Bri can make you something for dinner if you want."

I grunted then laughed. "Um, no thanks. She'd probably try to poison me. I'll fend for myself. And thanks for picking me up. I could've walked."

"I'd rather you didn't until we catch whatever psycho or psychos are around here. Besides, I've got some follow-up stuff I can do."

My insides began to glow. "Follow-up on what?" I asked, trying to make my interest sound mundane. I was just a thoughtful daughter politely checking in.

"That older man who was murdered in his home. Detective Marcus and I are handling some of the interviewing. We're kind of swamped." At least if I was questioned about Marvin it would be by Detective Marcus, since my own father couldn't do it. But I was sure Estevez would worm his way in. I couldn't figure out why he had it out for me. Why would he think that I had any hand in the murders? No one else was suspicious. If he didn't cool his interest in me, he'd earn himself a visit of his own.

"Lucas told me about that one. Sounds disgusting."

"Yeah, it hasn't been a pleasant month."

"Has Estevez asked any more about me? He shouldn't have talked to you in the first place. Isn't that like, a conflict of interest or something?"

"It's also a professional courtesy that he didn't owe me. He's not a bad guy. He needed to follow up. He had your bike at the scene and a description that fit you—"

"—and hundreds of other kids in this town."

He grunted. We pulled into the station parking lot. He followed close behind as I entered the front doors.

"You can hang out at my desk while I see if Mr. Murphy is here."

I nodded and parked in his spot. The seat was hard and uncomfortable. It was a wonder any of them could sit there, doing hours of paperwork while wearing twenty-pound belts, and not get a herniated disk.

He had nothing interesting pulled up on his computer, but I did see a stack of files that looked promising. There were too many people around for me to start leisurely reading any of them. So I looked for Eric, that asshole who thought he could dismiss me.

So far, no sign of him. His desk was only two down from my dad's. I got up and took a little stroll over to see what he'd been up to.

"Can I help you with anything?"

I recognized his voice and the musk of his cologne. "Now that you mention it, yes." I turned, hand on my hip. He was closer than I'd anticipated.

"I told you that talking here was not a good idea." He practically pushed me aside to get to his seat, immediately typing away at the computer like I wasn't standing there.

I placed my hand over his screen. "We need to talk. And I'm sorry, but since when did you think that you called all the shots?"

"Since we both realized that it wasn't a good idea for me to keep seeing you." He tried to look as busy as possible, but he couldn't ignore me. I wouldn't allow it. "Go away, Ryann. We've been seen together way too much. People around here are going to start asking questions, if they haven't already, and the last thing I need is your father asking what I could possibly have to say to his daughter."

I moved a few inches closer to him and saw him stiffen. "I'll only leave if you agree to meet me in an hour. Just behind the station. At the top of the wooded lot."

"Not a good idea. Please, leave, Ry—"

"You'll be there because I need you to be," I said softly, before pulling my hand away and sitting back at my dad's desk. Just in time too, because he was heading back over.

"Okay, honey, we're all set up."

I stood and followed him toward the interrogation rooms, and I couldn't help but notice Estevez's eyes burning into my flesh the whole way. Was he trying to intimidate me, or communicate that he knew something about me? The truth was, I wasn't sure that he didn't.

I could see Mr. Murphy sitting at the same stupid table that I'd sat at with Estevez, and I wondered if I was going to be attacked again.

"Mr. Murphy, this is my daughter, Ryann. She'll be happy to answer any questions you may have about your son." He stood by the door and waved me over to the seat opposite Omar's father. I took it begrudgingly. This was all too familiar.

"Thank you for agreeing to speak with me. You can call me Henry if you like." Was he trying to disarm me with a buddy-buddy ploy? Cute. "If you don't mind me asking, were you friends with my son? I'm afraid he never mentioned you."

"No…not really. I'm a cheerleader, so we spoke a few times, but we didn't socialize, if that's what you mean."

He smiled and nodded absently. "Then why come and see him at the hospital? I looked up and you were rushing out of his room. You didn't stop when I called you. Were you afraid? Is that why you were trying to hide behind your hood?" He leaned in across the table, his hand extended, almost as if he wanted to hold mine.

Everything felt like it was in slow motion. It was best to go right into my spiel about my proximity to the victims and how helpless I'd felt. Blah, blah. "I thought my being there wouldn't make sense to you. It's not like we were friends, but I had to see him…"

I sniffled and grabbed a tissue from the box on the table.

He reached across the table and held my free hand in his. "You're a kind and sweet girl. My son was lucky to have you, even if he didn't know it at the time."

I smiled weakly, like it was all too much for my fragile psyche.

"Did you see anything at the dance? Anyone who could have given him the drugs he took? It wasn't like my boy to do something like that." He was shaking now. Holding back sobs and tears. "He was a good boy."

Yeah, so good that he was already wasted of his own accord by 7:30 p.m. "No, I'm sorry. I didn't. When I saw him he'd already collapsed. I'm really sorry that I can't be more help. I do know that Omar was very nice and popular, and that he seemed like a really great guy."

He wiped a tear away with the back of his hand. "Thank you."

I stood. It seemed the sensible time to depart.

"Wait. There's one other thing," he said. "My Omar died only a few hours after you left." I squared my shoulders and steadied my stare. Unwavering. "He didn't wake up when you were with him, did he? I know it sounds crazy, but I need to know." He looked at me, grief-stricken.

"No. He was asleep the whole time. Sorry for your loss, Mr. Murphy." Again I tried to move, but ol' Henry just kept chatting away.

"I thought he was going to make it. Pull through. The doctors said he had a chance, and then all of a sudden..." He wiped his runny nose on the sleeve of his shirt. "I thought we had so much time. I know we don't know each other, Ryann, but don't waste the time you have. Did you know that my boy was gonna go pro? A few colleges were looking at him for football. He was on his way. Make something of your life, the way my son would've."

I managed a pained smile and nod before I rushed out the door.

There went thirty minutes I'd never get back.

Standing there, waiting for my dad to 'excuse' me, only made my blood pressure rise further. I made my way a few rooms down and saw that one of the doors was cracked enough for me to see inside. My dad appeared to be having a heated discussion with someone. Then, stomping into view, was Estevez's smug face. I resisted the urge to run in and wrap my hands around his throat for what he was trying to do to me. Instead, I leaned against the wall with my ear as close to the crack as possible without being seen.

"You can't be fucking serious, Rob! You really think my daughter—who you've known since she was a kid—is running around town killing people? You're out of your goddamn mind!"

"Calm down and hear me out. All I'm saying is, there's a common thread through the murders. Ryann has some connection to all of the victims. Her bike was found at a crime scene, we have an eyewitness that can put her at Hastings's house, and then she's spotted at the hospital where the Murphy kid dies hours later. She used to babysit Olivia, and Yvonne was her ex-boyfriend's girlfriend. Come on, Dave."

"You have an eyewitness who *claims* to have seen a teenage girl. It's a small town. We're all connected in some way. There is no proof Ryann had anything to do with any of—"

"Are you that confident? If Ryann was in a lineup, would you be so sure that she wouldn't be picked out?"

I heard a loud thud, possibly a hand coming down on a table, and then my dad's voice. "That's enough. I get that you think you're doing your job here, but my daughter can't be the killer. Think about it. You know her; she's kind and sweet, not a criminal mastermind. Are you trying to convince me that she is fitting in elaborately planned murders between school, cheerleading, games, homework, her friends, and all the time Liz and I see her at home? I know where my kid is and what she's doing. And more than that, I know who she is. She's not smart enough, organized enough, underhanded enough, or bat-shit crazy enough to be responsible for anything other than studying for finals and giggling with her friends. Now, why don't you stop wasting the county's time and money and find the real killer?"

Despite the twist in my gut, that was my cue. The last place I wanted to be found was outside the room, eavesdropping on a conversation about whether or not I was the murderer they were after. I bolted down the hall and grabbed a chair near the desks.

Two seconds later, my dad stormed out and walked toward me. His eyes were narrowed, but he forced a small smile when our gazes met. He stopped in front of me. I tensed, unsure of what he would say.

"I know it's hard with everything you've been going through, but why go to the hospital? It doesn't make sense to me. You didn't know Omar, and going there wasn't going to solve anything, especially when you snuck in and out. Why didn't you go up to Mr. Murphy and simply ask to see him? And the pseudo-disguise?" He pinched the bridge of his nose. "Was it because you didn't want to be seen? I can't imagine why that would matter." He fixed me with a look that rivaled suspicion, and my body numbed. Was Estevez getting inside his head?

"I already explained it. Sorry if my actions seem strange, but you're comparing me to who—you? Someone who has a lifetime of experience dealing with the craziness of murders and death? I haven't had that luxury." We were face to face, and I refused to back down. "Don't look for problems where there aren't any, Dad. Just be grateful our family is okay. There are a lot of people in this town who can't say the same."

I knew he would try to drive me home, but I convinced him that walking the short distance in the bright of day was as safe as it was going to get. We both needed the space. I was released with a promise of a prompt phone call as soon as I walked into the house, alarm on.

My mind raced with all the things that Estevez had put together. I thought I'd been so careful. But thinking back…why the fuck had I picked people I knew? It was serial killer 101—don't choose people you know. Shit! My throat burned as I chocked back tears. But it wasn't too late. Estevez needed proof, and like my dad said, there wasn't any.

I hadn't, however, forgotten my meeting with Eric, and I headed around the station to our designated spot. He'd better be there, I thought grimly. I was not in the mood to deal with more bullshit.

Chapter
FORTY-FIVE

I wrapped my arms around myself as I slogged across the field behind the station, toward the woods. It was a small lot, but good for light hikes and taking your dog off-leash.

As I got closer, I could see a tall figure leaning against one of the trees. Good boy. He was waiting for me as instructed.

His arms were crossed and he didn't look amused. But dealing with whatever tizzy he was in was not high on my list of priorities. I closed in, stopping about two feet away, and stared him down. "I'd say you have some major explaining to do," I barked, crossing my own arms.

He huffed and snickered. "Oh really? Like what?"

"Like why, when you knew how freaked out I was, you didn't bother to tell me what you came up with. Not even a quick text. Dick move."

His gaze narrowed. I'd gotten his attention. "First of all, there was nothing to report because the phone was a throwaway. And second, I never should have agreed to help you in the first place." His face was flushed; his hands balled at his sides.

I got in his face. "And what? Thirdly? Just say it alre—"

"Thirdly, the best thing—the only thing—I can do is stay far away from you!" He ran his hands roughly through his hair.

"So you keep saying, yet here we are together, *again*. Why is it a big deal to you? Because of who my father is? Because you think I'm just a kid—" Before I knew what was happening, Eric's mouth was pressed hard against mine. His fingers cupped my cheeks as he sunk deeper into me, his chest heaving. I could feel the quickening of his breath, the pumping of his heart, and the urgency in his kiss. And for a moment I lost myself.

He pulled away, jutting his arms between us. "I'm sorry." He was shaking. "I don't know what came over me. I only met with you to say good-bye. We can't see each other anymore." He turned his face away.

I would not lose this game. Defiantly, I took another step closer and touched his cheek. It was slightly rough, the day's growth coming in already. "I thought you liked me." I pulled him close.

Wind tickled my face as he backed away a second

time. "It's wrong, not to mention illegal. I could go to prison."

"Not unless someone finds out. I'm certainly not going to say anything."

He grabbed my wrists as I tried to hold on to him. "Stop it. As much as I like you, I can't do this."

"You didn't have that problem a second ago— you kissed me, not the other way around. Why start something you have no intention of finishing? You must think it's fun to play with my feelings." I wanted him to hear anger in my voice and see the sourness on my face. I wasn't a doll he could play with.

"I'm sorry. It wasn't my intention when I came out here."

"Well, maybe it should've been." I grabbed his arm and pulled him a few feet farther into the brush.

"What are you doing, Ryann? I've got to go."

I stood square in front of him and undid the buttons on my shirt. The air was cool on my stomach, but not for long. Eric's body moved in. He wrapped me in his arms. His lips traced my neck, warm on my skin. Picking me up in one motion, he pressed my back into the tree behind me and his mouth found mine again.

❖ ❖ ❖ ❖

We lay on the ground together, spent.

Eric jumped up, pale-faced, like the realization of what he'd done had sucker punched him. "I really have to go. People are probably looking for me."

I began re-buttoning my shirt. "You have a radio and a phone. They would've called if you were missed."

He tucked his shirt back into the top of his uniformed pants. "And if anyone asks, where am I supposed to say I was for the last half hour?"

"Don't get pissed at me. I didn't force you."

Eric stopped, and his gaze softened slightly. "I know. I'm sorry. This is all really confusing for me. I'm the adult. I know better."

"Give me some credit. I knew exactly what I was doing. I'm not a victim, or a child, so you can save your guilt. It doesn't look good on you." I was up and put back together. As much as I'd enjoyed our little tryst, I was happier now that I had something on him.

"I really have to get back in. I care about you, and I'm sorry I didn't tell you about the phone trace. There wasn't any evidence, and I knew I needed to stay away from you. It was safer to avoid contact… for this exact reason. If you need more help, well, it can't come from me." He kissed me on the cheek and I watched him walk away.

I wasted no time wiping away the invisible kiss mark. Then I reached into my pocket and hit the stop button. The whole encounter, from the moment I walked up to the wooded lot, had been recorded on my phone.

You never knew when you would need certain provisions, and I was nothing if not a decent planner.

Chapter
FORTY-SIX

"What are you doing in the woods, Ryann?" Estevez whispered to himself. He did that some-times—speak aloud. Hearing the words, even if they were his own, helped him think.

He watched her hurry behind the station and into the wooded lot. She had no clue that he'd been charting every step she took within the confines of the station—including her conversation with Knox. They'd been pretty chatty lately. What could he want from Ryann, except the obvious? Knox knew better, especially after the misconduct report at his last station. It wasn't just that she was underage. She was the daughter of one of his commanding officers... and maybe a calculated murderer.

He cracked his knuckles.

And why the fuck was Knox waiting for Ryann

in the woods? He'd seen the two of them huddled secretively by Knox's desk. Then Ryann had gone to meet with Mr. Murphy and Knox had gone back to his computer, shut everything down, and practically snuck out the rear door. Estevez had hurried to the back window, curious, as Knox's large frame strode into the trees.

He'd turned his attention back to Ryann, who'd left the interview room only to slip out the same back door and up the same path as Knox.

Was this some sort of rendezvous?

His mouth went dry. His eyes burned. He'd barely slept the past few days. It was getting harder to compartmentalize this case. He'd been sure that Ryann had a hand in the murders, and had been more than relieved when Amelia had come to him with similar suspicions. They'd agreed to keep it hushed for Dave's sake, and Estevez felt like utter shit about their earlier exchange. He'd promised Amelia they wouldn't let on to Dave until they had solid evidence. Everything was circumstantial so far.

Ryann claimed that her bike had been stolen. He had nothing to tie her to Yvonne or Olivia's homes, and everyone else at the station liked the Cook kid for Yvonne's murder. Cook had been charged, and without hard evidence in another direction, there wasn't a damn thing Estevez could do to save him. He had Ryann sneaking in and out of Omar Murphy's hospital room. His research confirmed that the two weren't friends. They'd barely spoken to each other—

but she visited him in the hospital after an overdose? And the latest vic, Marvin Dodson, was last seen at the diner where Liz Wilkanson worked. She'd identified a snapshot of him and even put Ryann at the diner with her in the days leading up to his murder, completely unaware, that she could be incriminating her own kid. Liz told him that she knew what night he'd been in because it was the same night Ryann had surprised her at work.

It had been tricky to get the info without tipping his hand.

And now his partner was livid with him. What if he warned Ryann? The last thing Estevez wanted was for her to become more cautious.

His stomach churned. Maybe he could bum a few Tums off Dave—if they were still speaking.

All he knew for sure was that he didn't trust a word out of that girl's mouth.

His eyes hadn't moved from his vantage point at the window. Neither Knox nor Ryann had come out yet. It had been nearly half an hour. He had to fight the overwhelming urge to march in there and demand to know what the hell was going on. He even wanted to make sure that Knox was okay—despite the fact that he was up to no good with an underage girl. She wasn't just any girl. If his suspicions were right, she could more than handle herself.

He pulled out his phone and dialed Knox, since he was still on duty. It rang five times until the voicemail kicked in. He'd give it two more minutes. Then he was going back there.

He'd made it to the rear door when Knox emerged from behind a huge fir tree. Estevez tried to make out his face or discern something in his body language, but he was more than a hundred yards away.

As Knox closed in, however, Estevez was sure he saw a smile.

Chapter
FORTY-SEVEN

$\mathcal{I}$ wasn't ten minutes out of the woods when my phone went off. I checked the screen and came instantly to a halt.

Be careful who you associate with. Wouldn't want your cop buddy to find out who you really are.

My veins were on fire. Was Unknown watching me? How dare that asshole taunt me? If I only knew who the coward was, I'd cut their eyes out.

My fingers moved instinctually across the keyboard. *Wait till I find out who you really are…*

I'm counting the days. I think you'll need a bigger knife :)

I raised my phone in the air to smash it, but instead I inhaled, nice and slow. There was no use in replying and egging on the freak. Clearly they had other plans than turning me in to the cops. Was it like that when I hunted and played? Was I their version of Yvonne or Omar?

At least it gave me more time.

If Unknown admired my work—if that was why they hadn't turned me in—then why wouldn't they tell me? Perhaps we could swap stories before I terminated them. I was not a fan of competition or weak copycats. Not in my playground. If you want to kill—great. Just don't do it in my hood. Especially not when you have evidence that one particular asshole cop would trade his left arm for.

I had all this pent-up energy and nothing to do. Maybe looking into Lucas again wouldn't be a bad idea. I needed to cross him off the list as soon as possible.

It was unusual to call him instead of texting, but I needed to hear his voice. There's only so much one can tell from words on a screen. I wanted to see if there was a tell in his voice, in the rhythm and cadence of his speech.

"Hey, Luc. What you up to?"

"Just shooting some hoops with Asad and Katie. What's up?"

"Bored. Wanted to see what you were doing."

"So I guess you're not still pissed at me for being an insensitive jerk?" He laughed.

"That all depends on if you keep being an insensitive jerk." I laughed back; he needed to think things were normal between us.

"Cool. You want to come down here?"

"And get sweaty? No thanks, but you guys have fun. Message me after you leave if you wanna meet up." I could hear the basketball drumming off the pavement and Asad's distinctive laugh in the background.

"What did you have in mind?" he asked, sounding intrigued. I didn't often invite Luc out just the two of us.

"Grab a coffee or burger. Whatever."

"Give me a half hour. The diner?" he asked.

"Only since my mom's not working right now. See you soon." I hung up. That was easy. Luc was willing to ditch Asad and Katie to hang out with me? He didn't even ask if he should bring them. Either my paranoia was at a new high, or there was a reason he wanted us to be alone.

I picked the booth in the back. It was my go-to because it was tucked away, quiet, and out of most people's field of vision. Maybe Luc would give something to indicate the recent change I'd noticed in his behavior. I didn't have to wait long before I heard the diner's bell ring and saw him waltzing through the front door.

I waved him over.

"Hey, sorry if I'm a bit ripe. No time to shower, but I sprayed on some of Asad's cologne, so now I smell like a mix of sweat and one of those gross magazine inserts with the sinus-melting scent. Just the way the ladies like it." He smirked and slid into the bench across from me.

I plugged my nose and made a face. "Thanks for trying to spare me, but you may have just made it worse."

I'd analyzed him from the moment he came in. The way he walked, stood, sat. The way he coughed and moved his hands. Even the tone of his voice.

He laughed. "So how are you? Heard you went to see Omar at the hospital. That's nice of you, but kinda weird." His smile was gone now. Talk about getting right to it.

My fist balled under the table. I took a long sip of my Diet Coke to center myself. "Let me guess. B? Man, she has a big mouth."

He gave a confused grimace. "No, actually. Asad, who heard from Tyra, who, well…somehow knows everything."

"Oh." At least I had one loyal friend. B hadn't let me down after all. "So what?" I opened the menu and pretended to check out my options.

Luc reached his arm across the table, dropping his big meat hook onto the middle of my menu. "Hey, I was reading that," I grumbled.

"You have it memorized. Now tell me why you went to the hospital to see a guy you barely knew." His face was resolute. He wasn't going to let me blow this off.

"Like I told my dad, B, *and* Omar's father, I was feeling pretty messed up with everything that's been going on. I saw Omar collapse at the dance. It freaked me out, so I went to see if he was okay." I let my eyes linger on his a minute longer, in the hope that he'd take it as a sign of honesty.

He pulled his outstretched arm back. "Or you gave him the packet I gave you, and felt guilty that he OD'd, and went to see him. It didn't occur to me at the dance, but then it dawned on me. You might have smoked a little weed here and there, but never anything heavy. He paused for a second before placing his warm, moist hand on mine. "It's okay, Ry. Mistakes happen."

I smiled before slowly and methodically peeling his disgusting hand off me, finger by finger. "That is partially true. I did feel bad, which is why I went to see him, but I never gave him the drugs, because I lost them. I went to the bathroom about fifteen minutes after you left me to try some, but the packet was gone. I checked all my pockets, and nada. So I can understand your theory, but it's not what happened. Maybe Omar or one of his friends found it, or maybe they had their own stash. Either way, Omar did this to himself. I feel awful that he's dead, but he made a sucky decision that cost him his life. Seeing what happened to him and knowing it could've been me freaked me out. I was about to use that night."

His head lolled and his eyebrows collapsed with pity. "I'm sorry, Ryann. Is there anything I can do?"

I allowed myself to put my hand over his for a millisecond. "Just be a supportive friend."

"I guess I kind of shit the bed on that earlier."

"Nah. It's okay. You can make it up to me by telling me if you've heard anything more about Hayden."

He crossed his arms behind his head, leaned back, and made a face. "Not. Good."

I leaned in closer and whispered, "What? Why?"

"He has a hearing coming up to set the trial date. Can you believe he almost got away with murder?" He laughed in disbelief.

There it was again. His apparent glee at 'horrible' things. I grabbed his wrists and held them. "Wait a second. We don't know that. Hayden deserves a fair trial. Innocent until proven guilty and all that."

Luc pulled his hands free and waved them out in front of me. "Whoa, whoa. Sorry. Maybe you have more of a lingering affection for him then you'd like to admit?"

"It's not like that. He could go to prison for life. He must be terrified."

"Think about it. Most victims are killed by someone they know. Someone close to them. Jealousy is an ugly thing." He nodded, pleased with his simplistic deduction.

"Or someone else could have snuck into her room—or could have already been waiting for her inside." I tried to hide my curiosity. His face would tell me if he knew more about my extracurricular activities then he'd let on.

But his face remained unchanged. "Possibly. I mean, if we do have a serial killer, Hayden isn't exactly our target suspect. I can't see what would tie them all together." I thought he was going to finally rest his case. "But that doesn't mean Hayden *isn't* still guilty of murdering Yvonne."

"I just don't see it." I didn't want to give Hayden too much of the credit that rightly belonged to me. "Poor Hayden. A trial?" I asked.

"Yeah, he's in custody until it begins."

"Which is when?"

"Not for at least six months."

"That's bullshit!"

Lucas pursed his lips. "Our legal system is slow, but it's faster than in big cities. If this happened in New York or Chicago, it would take years."

"I'm not sure Hayden feels very lucky."

Chapter
FORTY-EIGHT

$\mathcal{T}$he next morning, I had been in front of the school for only minutes when the police cruiser pulled up, lights on but no sirens: official business. It wasn't my dad's car, and I couldn't quite tell who was driving. I prayed it wasn't Estevez coming to enlighten me with more of his theories. He usually drove a black Crown. Unmarked, but still completely distinguishable.

I let out an audible sigh of relief when I saw Detective Marcus step out of the vehicle. She looked up straightaway, like she had a tracker on me or something. I waved and smiled at her, but she only nodded, hand on her utility belt, with a serious-as-hell expression as she walked toward me. It did not look like a friendly visit.

She reached me in five long, purposeful strides.

"Hello, Ryann. How you doing today?" She stared at me from head to toe.

"F-f-fine. Why?" No time for small talk. "Is something wrong?" I asked, intentionally doe-eyed. It probably wasn't going to work on her, but I had to give it a shot.

"You could say that."

"Does my dad know you're here?" I asked defensively.

She put a hand up. "No, and he doesn't have to. I only want to ask you a few questions."

My shoulders squared. Chin up. "Is this on the record? Has Estevez been whispering in your ear about me?"

She bit her lip. "This is a delicate situation. You're the daughter of one of our own, so I'm trying to protect you."

I laughed.

She shifted her weight from one leg to the other without taking her hand off her belt. Her fingers lingered near her service pistol in a stance she'd probably memorized from her training days. Always be ready, even when you're talking to a sweet, fifteen-year-old high school girl. "Estevez does have some theories with respect to your possible involvement in Hastings's death. I want to help you, Ryann. I really do, but you've got to help me. Answer a few questions so I can prove him wrong." She was the one giving me the doe-eyed look now, and I wondered if she really wanted to help me. The woman bluffed for a living.

"I'm not sure my dad would approve, Detective. I know you're his colleague, but he wouldn't like us talking behind his back."

"He can't be involved. It's unethical and inappropriate, which is why...as your friend, I'm here now. So what do you say? Want to go for a drive and grab a coffee or something?"

"It have my final two exams today." I pointed to the building behind me and shrugged. "I can't skip." The excuse played perfectly into my good-girl, neurotic, A-student image.

She let out a sigh. "Okay, well can you answer me one thing before you go?"

I nodded curiously.

"Did you give Omar Murphy the drugs that killed him?"

The air left my body in one swift motion. I had to hold up a finger while I choked out a cough. Of all the things I was prepared to be asked, that was not it. "What?"

The Detective's gaze narrowed further. "I have a witness that claims to have seen you and Omar walking through the football field together shortly before his collapse. You denied knowing Omar well—certainly not well enough to be having alone time together. In fact, you claimed that you'd never said more than a few words to one another." She scrubbed a hand over her face before her eyes pierced mine again. "Tell me the truth, and not your truncated version. Were you with Omar Murphy the night of the dance, before he overdosed?" She didn't even blink as she waited for my answer. If I evaded her, I would only look guiltier.

"Yes, but please, don't tell anyone," I pleaded.

Her face turned unexpectedly hard. "You're going to need to give me one helluva damn good reason why."

"I was out there, alone at first. I was feeling anxious with the crowds and noise. Sometimes I get anxious in busy surroundings, and I thought I'd get some air. I went out to the bleachers—alone— and then Omar showed up. He was already pretty messed up."

She stared down her nose at me. "Keep going."

I swallowed. "He started hitting on me. He wouldn't back off. Kept trying to kiss me...putting his hands all over me. I pushed him hard and he stumbled back a bit. He seemed really dazed and was only getting worse, so I helped him to his feet and across the field back to the school. I didn't tell anyone because of what happened. How would I look if I smeared his reputation like that? The guy was in a coma. He died! What was I supposed to say? Everyone's shining hero was a creep who wouldn't take no for an answer. That wasn't going to do him, or me, any good. So I chose to keep it to myself." I felt righteous yet again as I stared her down.

Her lips formed a thin line. I watched her pupils move around my face as she analyzed me. "That's interesting."

"Why?" I was in no mood for cryptic games.

"My witness places you on the football field with Omar, yes, but on the way *to* the bleachers." Her narrowed focus didn't waver.

A fiery burn engulfed my insides, choking the air in my lungs.

I stifled a cough with every ounce of willpower I had left and forced my stomach to keep a hold on its contents. "Then your witness must be mistaken."

She remained silent a moment longer. "I hope you're right."

❖   ❖   ❖   ❖

I bolted to the bathroom. Things were unraveling faster than I could manage to fix them. I tried to steady myself. I didn't need to attract any more attention by hyperventilating or passing out in front of everyone.

People were putting things together. I'd been so sure I'd been careful. Suddenly the realization hit me: maybe Unknown had been following me back then and had seen me. The flowers had to have been from him. He was likely waiting for the perfect time to slowly and methodically unweave my lies. This new eyewitness could be part of his game.

I didn't know what was real or fantasy anymore. Who was on my side, and who was a suspect? B had circled my face in the paper, Luc was acting strange, my dad was questioning me like I was a criminal, and Estevez and now Detective Marcus were interrogating me. My lungs were on fire; they felt tight, like ropes were tied around them, squeezing and choking me. I couldn't breathe. Staring at myself in the mirror, I tried to calm down. I ran the cold water and splashed my face.

A few juniors came in, looked at me, nudged each other, and snickered. I sucked in a mouthful of air. Then another. And another. I grasped the edges of the sink with my hands, knuckles white, and breathed. The girls gaped at me. Normally I would have snapped at them, but I couldn't find my voice. Thankfully, they turned around and left.

I dried my face with a handful of scratchy paper towels. I only had to make it a little longer. I couldn't skip my exams. If I missed school, my parents would get a phone call home, and I couldn't handle any more scrutiny. My perfect routine, grades, and attendance were all part of my cover, and I couldn't risk throwing those into question.

I inhaled slowly. My pulse began to even out. I had control. I was in charge. No one was going to turn me into a sniveling coward.

Things were slipping, but I would keep them from crashing completely. I had to, or all of it would have been for nothing.

Chapter
FORTY-NINE

hank God I'd paid attention in my classes before all this started, because I remembered just enough to pass with decent marks. I managed to keep under the radar for the rest of the day. Just a little longer, I told myself. Things would settle down. They had to.

By now, Detective Marcus could have gone to my father, or worse, to Estevez, with her information. God only knows what other 'inconsistencies' she had. I'm sure Estevez had been hissing in my dad's ear every five minutes about me. How long could a father deny evidence, however circumstantial, when that father was a cop—and a very good one? I wasn't sure he'd protect me; it was just as likely that he'd help Estevez put me away. I wanted to believe that he'd look the other way, perhaps even cover for me, but he was too honest for me to be certain. Why couldn't I have had a crooked cop for a father?

Staring at the classroom door, I envisioned the scene playing out. The door busting open, cops in uniform flooding inside, guns drawn, as they screamed for me to get down on the ground with my hands behind my head. The weight of a knee in my back and the cold metal of handcuffs biting into my wrists.

I didn't hear a single thing the teacher said and jumped in my seat when the bell finally rang.

"Easy on the caffeine, freak," Lainey said as she and Whitney laughed.

I chose to ignore them.

Zombie-like, I dragged myself through the hallway to my locker. I wanted to get out of here. I didn't know where.

An arm wrapped around my shoulder and I flinched to attention.

"Shit, Ryann, are you okay?" B asked. "You're so jittery lately. Are you sure you don't want to talk to someone? I'll listen if you want."

"I flinched because you scared me. That doesn't exactly qualify me for electroshock therapy and happy pills."

"It's not only today. You know you've been off for a while. And don't give me the same story about being stressed over the murders. I've known you most of my life, and something more is going on."

She put her hands on my shoulders and stopped me. We were face to face. I tried to walk around her but she only held onto me tighter. "Let me help you. Can we please go somewhere? It'll be like old times—just the two of us. Besides we can celebrate not having to come back to this hell hole for two more months. What do you say?"

I needed the distraction while I decided what to do. "Okay, but I get to pick where, since I'm allowing myself to be subjected to your version of therapy."

"Anywhere. Name it."

I smiled, placing my hands on hers. "The library, for old times' sake."

Wally wasn't in his usual seat to the right of the stairwell, and I was glad for it.

I led the way to the very back of the stacks, where two chairs and a reading table were positioned against the wall. I dropped my bag and slumped down into the chair, grateful for its familiar embrace.

B followed suit, sinking into the one opposite me. "See, isn't this nice?" she said and smiled.

"So what did you want to do now?" I had so much on my plate, and I hadn't counted on the interference of one-on-one time. But I had to keep B appeased, and if an hour in the library would do it, I was happy to oblige.

My thoughts were all over the place. Detective Marcus, Estevez, Dad, Unknown, and the little detail of my bag, chock-full of murderous evidence. You know...no biggie.

"Hello? Earth to Ryann."

B's voice broke into my consciousness. "Sorry. What were you saying?"

"You asked what we should do, remember? God!" She was growing impatient with me.

"I have my iPod. We could listen to music or grab some of the magazines downstairs." The library kept a well-stocked magazine area on the ground floor. Sometimes when we were younger, we'd go there and grab a stash of teenybopper rags with tear-out posters of whatever teen heartthrob was big at the time. We'd pore over every page and fantasize about being whisked away on romantic dates and marrying our current flavor of the month. Though my enthusiasm had been for show—I'd dreamed more about what their corpses would look like—it was still kind of fun.

"I'll run down and grab some."

"Want me to come with?" I asked.

"Nah, keep our spot safe." She smiled. There was nothing to keep safe, of course. No one came up here but the old man and the solitary fourth-floor librarian who stayed at the other end reading erotic romances with long-haired half-naked guys on the covers.

I smiled and winked. "Aye-aye, Captain."

B mock saluted me before walking down the aisle toward the main stairs.

"I thought she'd never leave," a voice said from behind me. Startled, I flung my head around to find

Eric grinning at me like a moron as he came around one of the bookcases.

"What are you doing here?" Instead of feeling excited to see him, I was annoyed.

"I wanted to surprise you." His grin straightened out and his eyes narrowed. "Aren't you happy to see me?"

I shifted my weight to face him. "I guess, but I'm more shocked, so mission accomplished. You made this big stink about not being able to see me again, and now you're sneaking up on me in a library." I noticed that he was in regular clothes, which was strange considering he was still supposed to be on duty. "Why aren't you in uniform?"

His face dropped in an instant. "I already told you. I'm here to see you. I thought we could spend some time together." He spoke in a grating tone I hadn't heard before. The look in his eyes—the shift from shiny to empty—startled me.

"So you left work?" I asked.

His smile returned and he nodded eagerly. "Yup. I told them I was sick, got changed, and came here."

"But…how did you find—" The fine hairs on my arms and neck stood on end, and I wondered if this was the same feeling I'd caused in my victims.

His eyes darkened under scrunched eyebrows. "You're not happy to see me, are you?"

I wanted to back up but held my ground. "Not right now. My friend will be back any minute. Besides, I thought you were all concerned that someone would see us together. And now you call in sick and show up out of the blue. How did you know I'd be here, anyway?"

His hand clamped down on my arm. "Because I know everything you do." His eyes were the color of steel, hard and icy, void of any of the tenderness I'd seen in the woods and at our meetings in the park.

I tried to yank my arm away but he squeezed harder. "Hey, you're hurting me."

He moved swiftly until his nose was practically touching mine. "Then don't make me. All I'm trying to do is surprise my girlfriend. Why are you being such a brat?" Angry spittle sprung from his lips—the lips I'd kissed not long ago. How was this freak the same guy who seemed so shy and sweet? If anyone knew about the art of wearing masks, it was me. I'd worn one my whole life. Had I miscalculated with Eric?

"You couldn't have followed me. I left school and you were at work." And then it hit me—smacked me in the face, to be more accurate. I pulled away from him as hard as I could and stood up. I thought of the bouquets and the anonymous notes. "Unless… you were following me long before that." My voice was raw. My mind raced. Did this mean that Eric was Unknown? If he'd tracked me down here, he could have also seen all the places I'd been. My legs turned to jelly. Had he been watching me this whole time? He had been at the sandbox that night! He'd dropped me back at home! Terror gripped me—and then rage.

Shit! I gave him my phone. He probably put a GPS in it to make stalking me easier. I needed to manage the situation. I calmed the edge in my voice and forced a smile through gritted teeth. "You were looking out for me, weren't you?"

His jaw and shoulders relaxed. "Yes, that's exactly what I was doing." He stepped closer to me and placed my hand between his. His skin was slimy and hot. It took everything in me to let him touch me and not knee him in the groin.

"Are you okay, Ryann?" Bao-yu was armed with a stack of magazines and a look of sheer confusion.

I pulled away and slowly wiped my slick palm on the side of my shorts. "You remember Eric, right? From outside Yvonne's house." I grinned, not wanting to alert her. This was far too convoluted already.

"Uh, yeah. Hi." B gave me a look that begged me to tell her if I needed help. We'd had unspoken signals since we were twelve for just such occasions. But what I *needed* was to get rid of her, before Eric the freak show blabbed about something.

"Hey, B, would you mind giving us a few more minutes to talk? I'd really appreciate it. There's some stuff going on with my dad, and Eric's filling me in. It's not something my dad would want out there." I tried to seem at ease, smiling again.

She seemed to relax. "Oh, okay. No problem. Just text me when you guys are done." She hefted her load onto the small table before sauntering off. In that moment, I was both relieved and disappointed that she was so easily maneuvered.

"She seems nice," Eric said, as though nothing weird was happening at all.

It was only then that I noticed the bag on the floor behind him. "What you got there?" I asked, peering around him to get a better look.

He stepped out of the way and I gasped. It was my bag. *The* bag. The one that housed the gory content that could put me away for life. "What... what are you doing with that?" My voice was quiet and controlled. I didn't want to alarm him further.

"It's your bag. I brought it for you." I could see him watching me, taking in every expression and movement. "You don't look very pleased. I thought coming here with your stuff would make you happy. You wanted it back." He hit himself in the head with an open palm. "Stupid." I grabbed his hand to stop him. "Are you mad at me?"

This guy was completely off the rails. Ignoring my gelatin legs and rolling stomach, I tried to ease him. "I don't want you to hurt yourself, Eric. Why don't you tell me what you're doing with this bag?"

He dropped his hands and nodded. "It's not any bag, it's your bag. The one you buried in the sandbox. Don't you recognize it?" He watched my face carefully.

I nodded. "But why do you have it?" I stroked his arm gently. I needed to know what I was dealing with. He'd clearly followed me that night, but whether it was to Marvin's or only to the playground I wasn't yet sure. He knew what I'd done...or at least part of it. Why hadn't he turned me in?

"You said you needed it back. I brought it to you."

"Okay, thank you. Did you—"

"Look inside?" He smiled wide. Almost proud.

I nodded again. My insides tangled into a mess of knots. I'd never felt so terrified before.

Though, I'd never been so close to getting caught.

"Of course I looked. I want to know everything I can about you." The corners of his mouth turned up. He bent down and retrieved the backpack. Unzipping it, he said, "It's all in there still. The knife, the goggles, the—"

I rushed to cover his lips with my palm. "Shh." I pulled my hand away, motioning around us.

"There's no one to hear us anyway." He raised his voice to prove his point. When there was no response, he said, "See? No one."

I had no idea what the hell to do. I hadn't come across a situation like this in any of my research. The Greats never had to deal with outside psychos. "Let's whisper just in case. What if Bao-yu comes back up? No one can know what's in the bag."

He nodded, looking at once like a little boy who'd been disciplined by his mommy. "I thought you'd be grateful. You don't seem happy."

"I am. Thank you." He didn't seem the slightest bit fazed about its contents. I didn't know whether to be relieved or even more alarmed. "How did you know where to find it?" I asked in a singsong voice. I motioned for him to give it to me and smiled.

Slowly, eyeing me all the while, he passed the pack over. I clutched it tightly to my chest.

"I watched you bury it."

I took a deep breath. That explained what he was doing there that night. I felt violated. "You knew I was looking for it. Why didn't you tell me you had it the whole time? You saw how frenzied I was." I tried to keep my voice steady. The guy was a lunatic.

"Don't be mad. I had to be sure."

"Sure of what?" I wanted to grab his face by my fingernails and scream as I squeezed him bloody.

He tried to reach out to me, but I backed away. "I wanted to confirm it was all you. That *you* were the one we were after. Yes, I texted those things. I was testing you to see if you'd panic and give yourself away. It was the only way to see how serious you were." He said this as though it were the only logical explanation.

"You're going to have to help me out a bit more than that."

"I liked you from the moment we met. I wanted to be around you. Your dad would sometimes talk about what you were up to, so I would go there and watch. You're so pretty." He gave me a stupid smile and touched a piece of my hair. "I wanted to get to know you better at first. I figured that if I could find out about you, I could see if we had anything in common, so I waited outside your house and school a few times. I was in an unmarked car so you wouldn't see me, and then I followed you. You have some interesting hobbies." He laughed, like I'd taken to playing badminton in my underwear and not slaughtering people.

"I saw you go to that old guy's house. At first I wasn't sure what you were doing, but then you rushed out. You had blood all over you. I was worried. I almost jumped out of the car and ran to you, but you took off the shirt and you were fine underneath. That's when I realized that it wasn't your blood. I was torn at first. Should I go to the house and see what had happened, or should I shadow you? I couldn't leave you alone. What if you were in trouble? So I followed you to the playground. You know the rest." He looked strangely calm.

"But if you knew, why didn't you tell me? Why did you torment me with those texts?" Anger seeped through my voice despite my best efforts.

"Don't you get it? I needed to know how committed you were. I suspected you had a hand in the others. Yvonne for sure, the kid, your math teacher, maybe even the guy from the dance. You forget that I'm a cop. I know the details of the cases. Your dad might be in denial, Ryann, but I'm not. And it's okay. I knew that if I tried to rattle you, you would show me who you really were, and you know what I found?" I was holding my breath, still trying to comprehend what was happening.

"That you were real. When push came to shove,

and it all almost came crumbling down, you never wavered. You stayed strong and focused—innovative. When you came to me with the idea of tracking the texts, I could have kissed you right then."

"Wait. You're okay with what I've done?" I asked, incredulous.

He placed both hands on my shoulders, staring me in the eyes with a big stupid smile on his face. "Of course I am. Don't you see? We were meant to be together." His low chuckle chilled me to the bone. "We're the same."

I considered the possibility that he was as good an actor as I was. No one at the station suspected him of doing anything peculiar—if they had, he wouldn't have had a job. And yet, I remembered my dad mentioning some rumors going around about him—something that made Eric leave his last precinct. I watched him, all twitchy and pathetic. No one worthy of being my partner would ever put me in danger by outing me in a public place with a bag of fucking evidence in their hands. "We're not the same, Eric. Not in the way you want us to be."

"What do you mean?" He stepped closer to me, but I stood my ground, refusing to back away.

How dare that amateur think he was anything like me? "What have you done? Have you ever pulled off anything like I have?" I squared my shoulders, still grasping the bag. I wouldn't let it slip out of my hands again.

"Maybe not as much as you, but I could. That's

what I'm trying to tell you. I understand who you are. The only difference is that you've actually done something about it." He was getting more excited. "Don't you see? From now on you don't have to be alone. I can come with you. We can do it together."

His hands rested on either side of my face, but this time, instead of wanting to melt into him, I wanted to choke him. He leaned in, ready to put his lips on mine. I yanked myself away. "Stop it," I snapped.

His eyes widened. "Isn't this what you've always wanted? Someone who understands you and shares your desires?"

I knew the answer, but thought I'd ask anyway. "Have you ever killed, Eric?"

He ran his hands roughly through his hair. "What does that matter?"

"Answer the question," I demanded. There wasn't an ounce of gentleness in my voice.

"Not exactly, but—"

I huffed. "So then we are *not* the same, because I act, and you think about it."

He looked shattered. "But I'm ready to act, that's what I'm telling you. I've had these thoughts and longings, but I was waiting for—"

"What? The courage? You either have it or you don't." The truth was, I didn't care if he 'had it' or not. I didn't want a partner, especially someone as broken and psychotic as this guy. He was a liability.

And liabilities have to be eliminated.

Chapter
FIFTY

*E*ric pouted. "You don't know that."

While he'd been pleading his case, I'd dug into the pack and pulled out the knife. Sure, it was dirty with Marvin's dried blood. I'd be mixing their DNA together, but I didn't really have a choice.

Eric's face reddened. His clenched jaw and pulsating neck veins made their reappearance with the added bonus of tightened fists, which he flexed at his sides. "Don't do this. Don't shut me out, or I'll be forced to turn you in. I have enough evidence to put you away forever. No one will save you. Especially not your daddy."

I laughed. "What? This bag?" I was calling his bluff and could tell, from the tiny flicker on his face, that I was right. "I have it now, thanks to you. If anything, I owe you a huge debt of gratitude. Not only did you return this to me, but you eased my conscience—no one out there is on to me after all. If you are Unknown, I'm in the clear."

"Not if you turn me away. Who do you think they'll believe? Some bratty kid literally holding a bag that connects her to a murder, or a respected officer of the law?" He smiled smugly.

I placed a finger against my chin as if I was considering his words. "So, you'll call my dad. And say what? I have proof that we slept together, Eric. There's a recording. I'm also a minor and a very respected officer's daughter. I can easily convince them that you made me help you kill Marvin— it's the only crime you have actual evidence for." His nostrils flared and I could hear his breathing quicken. "Young, sweet Ryann was forced into it by a depraved and sick man—"

He lunged at me, his hands pressing into my shoulders then making their way around my neck. The pressure of his grasp tightened. He squeezed. I began to gasp and choke from the pressure.

He set his gaze on mine, and I watched his expression change from rage to shock as my blade found its way into his stomach.

"Wha—"

I held it there as his fingers left my throat and fumbled instead around the soft, impaled tissue of his gut. I gulped in air. "You shouldn't have come here," I whispered in his ear. His fingers tried to slap my hand away from the knife's handle, but it only encouraged me to tighten my grip.

He let out a soft groan. "Why?"

I stepped back, pulling the blade out nice and slow. "Because you're a burden."

His face began to pale. The wound was deep, but I wasn't sure it was fatal. My study of anatomy was good, but imperfect. If I'd calculated correctly, I'd hit him somewhere in the intestines. Eric bent forward, clutching the hole in him as blood oozed through his shirt and between his fingers.

"It looks like you're a real bleeder."

He looked up at me with angry, crazed eyes. I had to finish him off once and for all. I raised the blade to strike again when I heard a distant muffle.

I froze, arms in mid-air.

Eric went to his knees. "I need help here! Somebody! I'm at the Dungrave Library with Ryann Wilkanson, please, I've been—"

I kicked Eric. He stumbled backward, and then I saw it. His cell was on the ground. It was connected. He'd somehow managed to dial the dispatch office at the police station. My heart raced. I landed another boot to his side and reached for the phone, pressing the end button before slamming it against the wall and shattering it.

"You idiot. What do you think you're trying to do?" I kept my voice controlled instead of shrieking at him the way I wanted. The feeling of my knife entering and leaving his body would be far more satisfying. "You really made a mess of things, Eric. We were both doing just fine, but you had to push me, and now…well, look at us. We had something nice until you went batshit crazy on me, and coming from me, that's saying something." I waved around the blood-covered blade as he lay at my feet. I'd have to finish him and somehow get rid of any evidence that I was ever there.

"Please, Ryann. You don't have to do this. I love you…" His eyes pleaded. His face was teary and red as sweat ran down his forehead. His arm was outstretched, as though he could somehow keep me at bay.

I sneered. "You love me? Is that why you called the station, because you love me so much?" I was practically spitting the words. "Well, you know who I love, Eric? Me." I was about to plunge my knife into him again when I heard a piercing scream.

I stiffened, my arm raised behind my head. I'd heard that scream during every scary movie, Halloween, and campfire story. I knew it definitively.

Bao-yu.

B backed away, her unblinking eyes fixed on me, her mouth gaping, her body trembling. She must have come to check on me. I felt bad for her. This wasn't anything I'd ever wanted her to see.

"B…it's not what you're thinking. He attacked me!" The timbre of my voice quivered. Still holding the knife, I put both hands out in front of me as though I was about to surrender. She studied my face. I could tell she wanted desperately to believe me.

She took another step back, her chest heaving with each breath. "But I heard you..."

"Please help me! She's going to kill me," Eric pleaded, a heap on the floor. Fresh blood pooled beneath him. If I was lucky he'd still bleed out, but that didn't solve all my problems. He'd called the station, and I wasn't sure how much they'd heard. But it didn't matter. Any call from an officer would be tracked by their GPS, especially if danger was suspected.

And now there was the added problem of B.

I turned my attention to my horrified friend and in my most convincing voice said, "B, you need to believe me. Eric's the one who's been killing all those people. He confessed. Said he wanted me to join him, kill with him. When I said no, he tried to attack me. I got the knife from him before he could hurt me. I was only protecting myself. You have to trust me."

Eric coughed, and bloody saliva bubbled from his lips. He was growing paler. It wouldn't be much longer. Disappointment and anger flooded through me. I wasn't going to get to finish him after all! B had ruined it, but all was not lost. She could still come through for me if I could get her to believe.

"B, we've been friends our whole lives. You know me! You know I'm not capable of attacking anyone.

Please..." I whimpered.

B's eyes darted from me to Eric and back. "I...I don't...you said..." She shook her head and looked ready to run.

I couldn't have that.

Chapter
FIFTY-ONE

$\mathscr{A}$s B turned on her heels to make a break for it, I lunged forward, hand out, ready to grasp onto anything I could. My fingers found their way into her thick nest of hair. I entwined my fingers and squeezed before yanking her as hard as I could, all the while keeping a grip on the knife with my other hand. She thudded backward. I tried to get out of the way, but the inertia of her body hit me and took me down with her. She struggled to get up, frantic. My hands kept their grasp on her as she pulled and thrashed.

"Stop moving, B. I'm not going to hurt you, but you need to calm down," I said, as steadily as I could.

She kept wriggling, her arms flailing and legs kicking, but my knuckles were practically buried in her scalp. I could hear her crying and begging through her hysterics. "No, Ryann, no," was all I could make out.

"Shh. You don't need to be afraid of me. I only need you to quiet down, then I'll let you go and explain everything. I only grabbed you because I was worried you were going to tell someone I'd done something bad. But it's not me, B, it's him." I looked over at Eric, who seemed to be unconscious. I loosened my grip on her a fraction. "Just take a deep breath."

B stopped moving and inhaled shallowly.

"Good girl. One more," I said soothingly. She did as she was told. "Okay, I'm going to let go of you now, but you have to promise me that you're not going to scream or run. I need my best friend. Do you promise?" Her head nodded below my fist, and I was about to let go when I heard the sound of a door opening. Grip tightening again, I looked to the stairwell behind Eric's body. Estevez was staring back at me, his gun drawn. The look in his eyes told me he was not fucking around.

"Let go of her, Ryann," Estevez said in his calm cop voice. I knew that tone well. I was raised by it. Did every cop have it? Was it taught at the Academy or something?

"This isn't what you think it is," I said. He kicked the door open wider and stepped forward. "Eric attacked me—"

Estevez's brown eyes stayed trained on mine. "Just let the girl go, and you can tell me everything later." His hands were steady, and the barrel was pointed directly at my head.

"B, we're going to stand up now." I started to move slowly, not easing up on her an inch. We moved to our feet in unison, B sobbing all the way. My mind was racing. I had to come up with a story that could explain everything—including the bag at my feet, full of evidence. There was no chance Estevez would ignore that.

"I'm not kidding around, Ryann. Let her go." Estevez took another few careful steps toward me and I pulled B a few steps back. Keeping the pistol trained on me with one hand, he knelt down and put two fingers on Eric's neck to check for a pulse. "He's breathing, which means that it's not a murder charge yet. So why don't you put the knife down and you can tell me what happened here."

I laughed loudly, putting the knife close to B's throat. I felt her stiffen and snivel. I was sorry we were in such a situation, but she was my only way out of there. Not that I knew where I was going. "Yeah, right. Like you'd believe anything I have to say. You've had it out for me this whole time. You blamed me for Mr. Hastings's murder. You interrogated me like I was a common criminal. You'd never believe anything I had to say. Eric's a cop. I know what assaulting an officer means, Sergeant, but he attacked me first."

"So why are you holding your best friend hostage?" He kept his gaze steady, studying me. I wanted to wipe his arrogance straight off his face with my knife.

"Because she doesn't understand what happened. I only wanted her to see what Eric did to me, but she panicked. She's scared. You need to back off and let us go."

"I'm afraid I can't do that."

I let out a frustrated huff. "Why not? I already told you I was only defending myself. I need to leave."

"I know what you've done. All of it. And don't tell me those killings were accidents too. You thought you were smart, and you were, but you made mistakes, kid. You slipped up. Don't make another. Let the girl go. We can get you help."

"Listen to him, honey."

A chill seized my insides. A figure stood to my right, but I didn't need to look to know it was my dad. *How could this be happening?*

Estevez could think what he wanted, but my dad would believe me. "Dad," I called out, my eyes never straying from Estevez.

"Yeah, baby."

"It's not what he's saying! He hates me! He's been out to get me since you let him interrogate me. I didn't do those horrible things, Daddy. You've got to believe me." I let the tears fall freely, trying to look as scared and confused—and innocent—as possible. "Don't let him take me," I whimpered.

"You've got to let Bao-yu go, sweetheart. She's

your best friend. Look what you're doing to her." He slowly moved into my line of vision.

"I don't want to hurt her, but he's going to make me, because he won't let me go," I cried. The tip of the knife was pressed into the underside of B's jaw. One move and she'd be dead. Estevez needed to know who was in charge. "Tell him to leave, and I'll let go of B."

My dad stared at me for what felt like forever and then nodded. "Okay. Estevez, I can handle this. I need you to turn around and head back down that stairwell." His face was drawn. Serious. And I wondered if it would work. I hoped it would.

"You know I can't do that. I get that she's your daughter, but I can't leave. She's dangerous, Dave. She's killed a lot of people. I gotta take her in." His gun remained trained on me, steady as ever.

I was growing impatient. "Listen to my dad and back the fuck off!" My lungs burned.

"Not gonna happen, Ryann. Let the girl go. When you're safely in cuffs, you can talk to your dad, but I'm not going anywhere before then." He squared his shoulders and stabilized his stance. I had a feeling this guy could hold out for the long haul, and I was getting tired.

"Rob, I'm not going to let you do this. She's *my* daughter. You have to let me deal with this." He turned his attention back to me. I'd never seen him look so shattered before, and I knew I should have felt something more about it than I did. "Just leave us. I'll bring her in, I promise. Come on—"

I would never let him bring me in, but he could say anything he wanted if it would get the big ape off my back.

"Help me, Mr. Wilkanson. Please..." B was shaking as she sobbed. My arm was around her neck, blade at the ready.

"Shut up, B. Don't make me hurt you, 'cause I really don't want to," I said. "Dad, who are you going to believe? You know your little girl. You know I could never do those things that bastard is saying. I love you." I smiled at him, taking in his deep, kind eyes and his smile. I watched his lips form the words.

He loved me.

It was going to be okay.

This was my last chance. If I was going to be arrested, I was determined to go out with one last victory. It was sad that it had to be B, but also fitting, somehow. For years, we'd done almost everything together. Thick as thieves. And we would do one final thing. I raised the knife and let my hand swing toward B's neck.

A burning pain tore through my shoulder.

Chapter
FIFTY-TWO

*L*etting go of the knife and B, I dropped to my knees, trying desperately to catch my breath.

I looked at Estevez. I expected to see a look of utter satisfaction on his cocky face but was met with an expression of disbelief. My attention turned to my dad. He was still pointing his gun.

My hand went instinctively to my wound. I pulled it away and saw red-coated fingers. I felt the familiar, sticky texture of the fluid, just like with Veronica in the woods those years ago.

I was bent over, coughing in pain, when my dad rushed to my side. His arm went around me. I could see Estevez rush in and usher B out of the way.

"Call an EMT," my dad screamed. Then to me he said, "It's going to be okay. We're going to get you to the hospital, and then we're going to get you help. I'm not leaving you."

I let myself lean into him. I was tired and shaking now, like B.

"You shot me," I said, staring up at the man who had eased my nightmares, helped me ride my first bike, and taken me for fast rides with loud sirens. My protector.

I didn't know my father had it in him.

And I couldn't help but think we were a lot more alike than I'd ever hoped.

My hand fumbled to his face and I held my gaze, staring into my father's eyes. "I know you wanted something different for me, but I was happy. Estevez was right." I choked out a laugh and forced a weak smile through the hot pain that radiated down my chest and arm. "I did it all, and I almost got away with it."

Chapter
FIFTY-THREE

Three days later

*E*stevez finished typing the file and still couldn't believe the events of the last few days. In all his years on the job, with all the criminals and crimes and takedowns, he'd never expected to see his fellow officer shoot his very own child. The thought gave him the chills every time he pictured the scene: Dave holding Ryann in his arms, stroking her hair, crying. They'd worked hundreds of cases together, and he'd never seen Dave flinch, but in that moment he witnessed his partner and friend weeping, with his baby in his arms, for all he had lost. And it almost broke them both.

There was nothing he could do. No words he could say to make any of this better.

Ryann was in the hospital with guards posted

outside her room. She'd had surgery on her shoulder to repair the gunshot wound. Dave was on temporary leave, keeping vigil at her bedside with Liz.

Estevez had read Ryann her rights on the way to the hospital. It was both sad and satisfying.

Once she recovered, she'd be transported to Dungrave County Prison, where she'd be kept locked up until her trial. He knew in his gut that if she was given the chance, she'd manipulate her way into a juvenile detention center or a mental health facility. He could picture her in therapy, crying and blaming everyone else, all the while being incapable of remorse or sincere emotion of any kind.

The evidence and eyewitness accounts came pouring in after news of what had happened spread through Dungrave. Everyone claimed to have seen Ryann someplace or other. Some of it was valid, but most of the witnesses were just bored losers who wanted some part of the action.

Officer Knox died of his injuries, which was a blessing, since a search of his house proved he was just as depraved and soulless as Ryann. After his death, the specifics of his history came out. He'd been asked to leave his last precinct because he'd stalked a fellow officer, proclaiming his love for her. He'd denied it, and she'd agreed not to press charges if he left the station and never contacted her again. Pictures of her at the grocery store or having dinner with a girlfriend were found in a hefty file in Knox's apartment, along with some pictures of Ryann. He'd clearly been tracking her too.

Knox had also constructed elaborate plans to kidnap and torture victims, plotting out various scenarios in a diary. The last five or six had included Ryann as his prospective partner.

Dave had a hard time believing that his daughter was guilty of all the murders, but photographs of Ryann from surveillance cameras around some of the crime scenes were shown to him.

It was tougher for Dave to deny once they had the wire cutters, found in Yvonne Borgdon's bedroom, tested for prints. Hayden's weren't on them, but Ryann's were. When her laptop had been accessed, it was discovered that Stanley Hastings's home address had been searched. And then there were the eyewitnesses that Ryann had so confidently disregarded. Both had picked her face out when shown the images of ten blonde teenage girls.

Estevez knew that as a father, Dave would be blaming himself: How could he not have seen the signs? Would his wife and oldest daughter understand? Was there a way to have stopped it all? To have saved her from herself?

But he also saw that such questions were best unasked, because there were no definitive answers.

Estevez didn't know if some people were simply born evil, or if something in their lives—some trauma or circumstance—made them that way. It didn't matter, he supposed. What's done is done.

He'd just printed out the last section of his report when a cup of steaming hot coffee appeared on his desk in front of him.

"Thought you could use this," Amelia said.

"Hm. Thanks. What I really need is a do-over." He reclined in his chair, letting Amelia perch on the edge of his desk. Her arms were crossed, and she wore a sympathetic smile.

"There wasn't anything you could have done to stop her sooner. We didn't have the evidence. Sure, we had a few leads, but nothing conclusive. You can't beat yourself up over this. It's tragic. I knew Ryann too. I liked her. No one could have seen this coming. The girl was smart. She played us. She knew the system." Amelia took a sip of her own coffee and waited for him to respond.

What could he say?

"I know what you're trying to do and I appreciate it, but you...you weren't there. How do you—" He stopped to compose himself. "How do you shoot your own kid?"

"Dave is a cop. He saves people, and that little girl would have died if he hadn't stepped up. His daughter killed six people, Rob. Six, and she was only fifteen. Can you imagine if you hadn't figured it out? If Knox hadn't managed to call in? Can you conceive how many more victims there'd be? Ryann had no empathy. No remorse. How does a little girl grow up to be like that?" Amelia asked, a dumbfounded gaze on her face.

"I don't know." He exhaled, releasing a little of the pent-up tension, but only a little. "Have you spoken to Liz…or Dave?"

She gave a weak smile. "No. I know I should call, but what do you say?"

He reached past her to collect the papers in the print tray and secured them in a file. "I've got to get these upstairs. Check in with you later."

She nodded.

He took the stairs. He didn't want be stuck in the elevator with anyone. Too many awkward stares and questions. If there was one thing cops lacked, it was tact. It went with the territory. Desensitized and all that.

Estevez wasn't sure if or when Dave would come back. He'd been sleeping and eating every night under the same roof with a serial killer, and he didn't notice anything. His colleagues would try not to judge Dave for all the things he didn't do and didn't see, but there would come a time when the town's anger would build and drown his friend.

He just couldn't accept that somewhere deep inside, Dave hadn't seen something. His cop instincts were sharp. His paternal instincts should've been sharper.

Of course, Estevez felt for him, but he couldn't blame the town for its rage and demand for justice.

Besides the preliminary file, Estevez's work was only beginning. He had a shitload of interviews to do, starting with Ryann's circle of friends. Someone

KELLY CHARRON405

had likely known something, even if they hadn't realized it at the time. He had to make certain that no one had helped her along the way. He couldn't let anything more happen in this town. And he sure as shit had to make sure Ryann would never see the light of day again. He'd go to his grave making sure she stayed locked up tight, where she couldn't hurt anyone.

He knocked on the commissioner's door, and she called out for him to come in.

He entered and waved the file in his hand. "Got this for you. Just about to begin with the interviews downstairs."

Commissioner Lillian Parker looked up from her computer screen and slid her bifocals down the bridge of her nose. "Thank you. Who's assisting on them?"

"Marcus, Schmidt, McLeod, and Shook."

She nodded and resumed typing.

Estevez closed the door behind him. He sprinted down the stairs, stopping by his desk to grab his coffee. This was his favorite part. He loved the nerves—loved the way witnesses and suspects alike shifted in their seats and went pale. He wasn't mean, per se, but he knew that most people, even the sweetest and most unassuming, had a story to tell. Everyone has a secret, and he wouldn't stop until he found them all. It could make the difference between a stalemate and breaking a case wide open.

He walked toward the interrogation room, unbuttoned his sport coat, smoothed his shirt, took a sip of his coffee, and opened the door.

"Hello, Lucas. I'm Sergeant Estevez. Tell me a story."

The End

About the Author

Kelly Charron is the author of YA and adult horror, psychological thrillers and urban fantasy novels. All with gritty, murderous inclinations and some moderate amounts of humor. She spends far too much time consuming true crime television (and chocolate) while trying to decide if yes, it was the husband, with the wrench, in the library. She lives with her husband and cat, Moo Moo, in Vancouver, British Columbia.

Acknowledgments

There are so many people I wish to thank for helping me along the way.

To my husband Jason for constantly pushing me and encouraging me to live my dream, and for spending countless hours talking through characters and plotlines. You are the best man.

To my parents for cheering me on and believing that I could pull this off (and for understanding that my writing about murder is no reflection on my amazing childhood). I'm so lucky to have you in my corner.

To my sister, Kristin, my brother-in-law, Steve, and the greatest nephew and niece, Braeden and Mckenna, for supporting me and being generally sweet and wonderful.

To Kevin and Pam for making my awesome website, being my tech call center, and generally giving me support—you are the best in-laws ever.

To my entire family for their love, support, and encouragement. Thank you for listening to me talk about writing for a decade and being patient that one day an actual book would exist.

To Eileen Cook for years of mentorship and friendship that I can never repay. Thank you for being a first reader and helping me navigate what it means to be a writer.

To an amazing group of friends that is always there to calm me down, give me advice, and point me in the right direction. Thank you Helen, Rachel, Owen, Deb K, Debbie B, Kathy, Adrianna, Johanna,

Nicholas, and Jessica.

To my critique (and life) partners: Deana, Bee, Tiana, Cara, Lindsay, Lisa, and Ashley. You guys have saved me more times than I can count in every way imaginable. Thank you for your wise advice, offerings of wine and chocolate, and friendship (oh, and for reading countless drafts). Special thanks to Helen, Deana, Bee, Cara, and Tiana for reading and poking at early drafts.

To Crystal, Amanda, Greg, and Constance for their incredible work on this book. You are an amazing and brilliant team. I can't wait to work with you again. You made this process so much easier. Thank you for calming my anxieties (of which there were a few).

To Kellie Dennis, of Book Cover by Design, for the gorgeous cover and images.

And finally, a giant thank-you to everyone else in my life who has supported and inspired me, been excited about this book, and helped me through this process.